The Reluctant Princess

Lee kissed and bit her belly and then licked and nibbled his way down towards her pussy, using his big rough hands to stroke her hips before inserting a finger to feel her wetness. And, baby, she was wet just like that.

His rough hands felt so good. He was a sexy, dirty dog with the body of a god.

'You will do exactly as I say,' he growled.

To reaffirm his point, he gave her left breast a firm slap. The sting made her gasp.

He slapped her other breast and then used his fingertips to twist the tight end of both her nipples. Ouch!

The nasty Warrior paused long enough to lick his fingers. Then he tweaked her nipples again. Sting. Ouch!

When she squealed a painful protest, he simply straddled her body and used his weight to hold her down. He would have his way, and there was nothing she could physically do about it.

The Reluctant Princess
Patty Glenn

BLACK LACE

To the Viking god.

Also, thanks for the help and advice to Shannon
Donnelly, Regency Writer and the smartest woman I've
ever met.

First published in 2003 by
Black Lace
Thames Wharf Studios
Rainville Road
London W6 9HA

Copyright © Patty Glenn, 2003

The right of Patty Glenn to be identified as the Author of
the Work has been asserted in accordance with the Copyright,
Designs and Patents Act 1988.

Design by Smith & Gilmour, London
Printed and bound by Mackays of Chatham PLC

ISBN 0 352 33809 1

Prologue
Once Upon a Time, There Was a Princess . . .

The Princess was lost. Vulnerable and doing that stupid Dante *Inferno* thing in the freakin' Valley. Crap. She hated the damn Valley. Totally to the max. Always had.

'This is hell!' Martha complained aloud to the unsympathetic summer night. The San Fernando Valley heat and the stink of the smog did nothing for her lousy mood and hangover. She felt absolutely horrendous, but worse than her physical agony and concern for Big Gus was the new financial crisis of her life.

For the first time in her whole pampered life Martha was absolutely penniless. No rich Daddy. No Big Gus. No lover. No friend. No money coming in to support her extravagant lifestyle. No one. She was alone and without plastic or even chump change, thanks to her sanctified sister who now held all the purse strings.

Stupid bitch. If puritan Mormon dogma wore a perfume, her sister Margaret would reek of it.

Closing her burning eyes, Martha rubbed her throbbing temples. She felt like shit and smelled like hell.

'I can survive this,' she whispered as a mantra.

Martha still held Big Gus's keys in her hand and that was the first step. She made her way through the parking lot of the St Joseph Hospital in beautiful downtown Burbank.

From directly across Buena Vista the big lights cast shadows from the powerful dwarfs of the Disney Studio across the hospital parking lot. Later the applauding thunder of the NBC *Tonight Show* crowd would echo from the block west across Bob Hope Drive. Martha stared at her own reflection in the windshield of the old Cadillac. This was not good. Trembling, she sat behind the wheel of the vintage classic until almost midnight. When she finally forced herself into taking some kind of physical action, she drove back to Gus's private investigation office in North Hollywood to spend a night in a safe place.

Hell, yes. In Gus's office, she'd pull herself together. No doubt she'd get lucky and come up with some kind of plan before the bimbo secretary threw her out in the morning.

What she needed was money for a bath, food, sleep, clothes, and a party to make her blissful again. She'd toss her stinking dirty clothes away and put on something feminine and frilly. Silk, that is what she needed – nice, cool, delicate silk fabric next to her burning skin. Oh yes. This Princess required silk and a party.

Martha didn't turn on the office lights. The street lights of Lankersheim Boulevard and the Television Arts and Science Academy across the street glowed through the huge darkened windows, filling the office suite with more light than she really wanted. Martha rushed to Gus's private bathroom and rested on the cool green tile floor. The Princess was a casualty suffering in the living hell commonly referred to as the San Fernando Valley.

Lying curled up in a ball of agony, hugging her knees tightly to her chest for hours on the remarkably cool tiled floor, Martha listened to the traffic and nightlife outside. North Hollywood could be a wild place on a Saturday night. Nightclubs, theatres, and sex shops cluttered the neighbourhood. Good sinful amusements outside.

Martha needed a little sinning right now.

Any number of sins were happening outside on the streets of No Ho. Sinning always made her happy. The only trouble was, Martha wasn't feeling up to tricking or picking the pocket cash necessary for purchasing a good transgression. One lucky pick would take her one underground ride to a pawnshop in Van Nuys. From experience, she knew a few guys who moved outlaw stuff. All right. She'd go buy a sin or two and some fresh clothes. Get a decent room.

'Fer shure. Fer shure.' Find a good Valley mojo experience. Sin was the kind of companion she understood.

Rising to her feet Martha now had a plan. Go forth, pick, pawn, and sin. Find some temporary relief from the dark abyss of her financial crisis and check out the local grit and grace in quest of weekend booty buddies. Go Princess. Go Princess.

Successful picking required effort and concentration. Lock and load. Pawning required travel. Head 'em up, move 'em out. And sinning? Bada Bing. She'd rather just skip to the sinning part. But a Princess's path is never easy.

Picking sounded like too much work tonight. So to make it easy the Princess would just pawn something. One step into a pawnshop could bring some big cash and a clean hotel suite. This was good. The Princess had a plan.

Of course Big Gus would have rescued her treasure. He always did. All she had to do was search the office and find it. The jewels were here somewhere.

But she couldn't do it.

Instead, she collapsed on the cushioned leather coach opposite Gus's big desk, where she sobbed violently until dawn. Breakdowns were always so horrible.

And she had a big one.

Crap. She was entitled. Her Daddy was dead. Big Gus lay struggling for his life in a damn ER. And Margaret – who'd inherited the entire family fortune – wasn't willing to share unless a massive lifestyle change occurred. But she'd get Margaret, the bitch. And her little dog too.

Up yours, Dorothy.

1 **The Big Tease**

The morning sunlight arrived, bringing a renewed hope; she heard the distant call of the bells. The big belly bells of St Charles's Catholic Borromeo Church down the street were then joined by the good Lutherans' tingling west at the Laurel Hall Chapel.

Martha loved the sound of religious bells; anybody's church bells. She wasn't fussy. The beauty and tradition of bells gave her the courage necessary to sit up. It was a good idea to breathe. She took a deep breath.

Shit!

Martha choked on her own stench.

Her throbbing head added to her general dizziness. Crawling towards the shower in the private bathroom, she stripped off her dirty white shirt and threw it in the trash. She didn't wait for the water to warm up; instead she flopped into the cold stream, and the force of it threw her back against the shower wall.

Oh, baby. Oh, baby. It was cold. It was good.

The coolness of the water quenched her intense body heat. Opening her mouth wide and closing her eyes tight, she breathed new life into herself. Oh yes!

It was fucking fine.

Misery sizzled and cooled.

She grew stronger. She could survive this shit.

Hell, she was nothing if not a true survivor. True, she was now officially broke, and the lonely thing was pure hell. But she could survive it.

'Bad luck to have lived long enough to be an aging

Princess with no sugar daddy,' she chastised herself aloud. 'Shitty, bad luck.'

But her assets did include one sister.

More bad luck because, regrettably, the powerful and respectable sister demanded terms for her assistance. Martha hated Margaret's terms. Besides, her reputable sister Margaret always filled her with guilt. Guilt was a mighty powerful demon to battle. Best for this bad girl to avoid the sanctified Margaret. Let the conservative and decent bitch rule the family empire.

It was painful, but Martha accepted she was no longer Daddy's little Princess, and acknowledged she could never be the respectable sister Margaret deserved. Martha did love her older sister. She always had. But Margaret wasn't an easy sister to love. It was difficult to love someone who was totally perfect. And unfortunately, Margaret suffered from perfection. Martha had found growing up in the shadow of a saintly sister abominable. She'd often joked with Gus, 'Margaret got all the virtue in the family and I got all the vice.'

However, sometimes Martha had wanted to do the right thing and be the perfect little Princess. But then internal and external demons always appeared. Besides, it was fun being bad and Martha had always lacked the needed courage, conviction, and strength to be good.

After their mother had died when Martha was nine, and through the years that followed, all the shrinks had told her Daddy that she was bad because she was incapable of feeling and emotion. That wasn't true.

Life was just easier and more fun when one buried all that demanding discipline necessary for a respectable life, shoved aside the nagging emotional crap, and worked at living just in the moment. Life in the

6

moment was all that counted. After all, what was life if not one cheap thrill ride?

Martha loved cheap thrills.

Using the bath soap Martha washed her designer jeans and her red lacy underwear while still on her body. She tossed her wet clean clothes into the bathroom sink while she scrubbed herself.

Her full breasts ached with a dull unrecognisable throb. Massaging the soap into the dark thin line of her bikini-waxed pubic hair Martha thought about pleasuring herself, assuming it would make her feel physically better. Sliding her fingers between her lower lips, she sought her pleasure point. But she didn't feel sexy. Shit, what if she couldn't come?

Nothing made Martha feel more worthless than when she couldn't find pleasure while masturbating. This morning she lacked the stimulation necessary for success and therefore stopped. She didn't need one more unfulfilling moment in her life right now.

After carefully wringing them dry, she hung her clothes in the warming sun now streaming in through the big window and searched around Gus's office for a fig leaf. Big Gus had a pair of clean blue and white striped boxers in the bottom drawer of his desk. She borrowed the male underwear but they slipped and barely clung to her narrow hips and full buttocks. Suddenly aware of how thin and weak her slender body truly was, Martha continued her quest for a costume by searching the bimbo secretary's office.

There, she found a deep-blue hair scarf in one of the desk drawers and tied it around her ample bosom. Not that it did a good job of covering her breasts; it didn't. Margaret may have gotten the great legs in the family, but Martha got the astounding full breasts and beautiful ass.

'Thanks for saving my partner's life yesterday.'

Startled by a deep rich tenor voice Martha looked up to see a tall man of colour with long black wavy hair, dressed like a biker, standing quietly in the office doorway. Immediately conscious of her own semi-nudity, she remained seated and continued to search the bimbo's desk.

'Who are you?' She almost snorted the question.

'Joaquin Xavier Lee. Name's on the door.'

Martha checked it out. Sure enough the name was on the door along with Big Gus and the other private dicks. He was one of the security Warrior types. Not good! Those types were always trouble. Warriors were by their very nature aggressive; not what she needed at this moment.

Flustered and a little frightened Martha licked her full lips and calmly gave him her best Mae West attitude. 'Got a cigarette, big boy?'

Quietly he locked the door behind him. 'You won't find one in Julie's desk. She doesn't smoke.'

Slamming shut the bottom desk drawer Martha considered moving to check on her clothes. No way they could be dry. But she'd worn wet underwear and jeans before. All her survival instincts warned her that she shouldn't be dressed only in Gus's boxers and the bimbo's scarf in the company of this particular man. She licked her lips again and established eye contact to appear more aggressive.

As if he read her mind he smiled in amusement and commented, 'Like your fashion statement.'

'Oh, aren't you a sweet talker, Chief.'

His laughter stopped as he dropped a dark canvas bag on the floor. 'How many Indians you ever met named Lee?' Stretching out on the reception area's leather couch, he gave a huge sigh of physical relief.

'Bet you're looking for the keys to the kingdom, Princess. That's what Gus calls you, isn't it? Princess?' He waved a large manila envelope in her direction.

Her fear subsided. Clearly the guy was physically exhausted and not about to tangle with her, so she took courage and got a little cute. 'Not unless that key can cure a hangover, get me high, or offer breakfast.'

'Gus had me fetch the trinkets of your treasure. I believe the contents belong to you.' Without hesitation he tossed the package at her and began unlacing his black combat boots.

So he was some kind of super Warrior saviour or Prince Charming noble or Elmer Gantry deliverer, huh? Returning the family jewels to her was that noble Warrior/servant thing to do. All right!

It was the bells.

Bells always brought her good luck.

Yup, right now a tested knight was removing his dusty heavy boots in front of her. Stripping down was good. Interesting. The morning was undoubtedly looking up.

The aggressive nature of Warrior types, male or female, almost always drove them into the gym to work out. Hence, they usually sported toned bodies. A true Princess always appreciates great abs.

Oh yes. Bells were ringing now. This Warrior might just be the stimulation needed to fulfil her lusty nature. *Boogie Nights*.

Even distracted by her sexual thoughts Martha managed to catch the flying gems without totally exposing her nipples, now firm beneath the thin fabric of the scarf. Now. Now. She had to quit mind-fucking every man she'd known less than sixty seconds.

Bad Princess.

Not good.

Why did being bad make her feel so good?

Placing both of her feet up on the desk and pulling both knees into her chest, the Princess checked out the treasure. Oh goody. The family heirlooms were once again safe in her hands. Looking up, the gracious Princess thanked the trusty Warrior.

'I appreciate the return.' She made sure her voice lacked any hint of the hostility growing from the guilt she suddenly felt for fantasising about him. 'But –' she paused for only a moment, unable to stop the mind-fuck '– hide them in a safe place for now. Tell Big Gus I owe him for retrieving them.'

All Princesses hate having flaws. Because flaws are eventually exposed, most often at unlucky times, Martha despised hers. She hated admitting she was weak. Why was it so damn hard for a Princess to admit that she couldn't be trusted with the family treasure?

If she'd had the jewels with her last night, they'd be gone forever, and she'd be high on Hollywood Boulevard somewhere. It was a big street, a big, wide, weaving road with lots of pitfalls, lot and lots of demons in the dark, and lots and lots of cheap thrills.

Hell. She had to escape the Valley before she ended up in the fucking Hollywood Hills or, even worse, the City of Lost Angels.

No.

This time she'd do the right thing and save the heirlooms for Margaret. Her good sister deserved the gems. If Martha was the bad little Princess, than Margaret was the reigning divine queen.

'Lock 'em up and my sister will pay for their return.'

With as much sass as she could muster, the bad little Princess stood and tossed the family jewels back to the trusty Warrior who sat relaxed and bootless now on the dark leather couch. Returning his stare, she studied him.

He was a great fantasy object, but would he really be any good?

His rich burnished skin tone was deepened by the sun, but he was clearly of mixed blood with some white man somewhere in his genetic code.

He was tall and brawny, and his thick dark locks contained natural curls. He appeared an odd racial mix with eyes shaped like an Asian, but hazel green in colour. Damn, he was hunky cute.

Wasn't anything Asian small about him. 'Lee, huh? Isn't that the most common name in China?'

The hunk smiled, displaying beautiful even white teeth. Hell, everyone who worked with Gus had great teeth. The agency must have a great dental plan.

All the better to bite you with, my dear.

She examined him again with heightened lusty interest.

But something wasn't quite right. His tenor tones and body language screamed sexy. But his words carried a nasty something she couldn't yet identify. 'Well, as a love child I developed all kinds of skills and talents at an early age in order to survive. Not all of us are lucky enough to have a rich daddy and family pedigree, Princess.'

Oh, so he was playing it humble? Cute. Poor love child. No culture. No problems. No shit. Bad luck. He was just another snake in the grass.

Martha hated snakes. Even if they were hunky.

But what really pissed her off the most about him was the way he called her Princess with that deep sexy voice of his. Somehow, he made it sound much nastier than bitch or slut or worse.

Oh, he was charming.

An anaconda kind of charming.

Tugging on the waistband of the oversized boxers, Martha gave him her Mae West/*Gilda* mix, batted her long lashes, and wiggled her hips sensually as she strolled past him back into Gus's office space. What an exit. Her acting coach would have swooned at her performance.

Hell in the Valley was heating up again, but unfortunately the fig leaves were still wet. She fondled the fabrics and calculated drying time in her head.

Damn it! More bad luck! She was trapped. Almost naked, she was trapped with this snake for at least another hour while her clothes dried. Feeling more uncomfortable and exposed than she wanted to admit, Martha rubbed her swollen eyes and headed towards the bathroom. OK. She could survive this.

'So tell me, love child, how's Gus doing this morning?' The Princess gave him her best James Brown pitch and moves before she turned the cold water on in the sink.

It was wasted on him. No soul brother here.

He sounded almost Latino but not quite. 'Looks like we'll be without the big guy for a while. They're doing some fancy surgery on his heart tomorrow. It doesn't look good.'

As his words sunk in, and she caught her own reflection in the mirror over the sink, Martha splashed water into her swollen light-blue eyes and gently massaged what remained of the grit from the corners. Damn it. Crying always made her look like hell.

Well, at least her bleached blonde short hair sported a decent cut and was clean from the earlier shower. She fluffed it with her fingers. Once the swelling in her face went down and the redness in her eyes disappeared, she could be gorgeous again. Martha enjoyed being physically gorgeous; it was an advantage in life. Pretty Princesses always received their hearts' desires and lived happily ever after.

But she wasn't living happily ever after right now. No. She was in the Valley, bordered only from the City of Lost Angels by the fucking Hollywood Hills. Gus always took her from the Valley. She didn't know how to leave it alone. She needed Big Gus.

Big Gus and she had established a pattern years ago when she first ran away from a New York boarding school with an outlaw biker from Jersey the week before her fourteenth birthday. What a party! Glory days.

Of course Daddy had lectured her, scolded her, and threatened her before shipping her off to the next school and then the next, always making another great plan for her future.

The wayward Princess and her Daddy and Big Gus had the whole rescue thing down to a routine. Big Gus would bring her home to Utah. Then Daddy would always set new goals for her and she, of course, would listen respectfully and agree to his new plan, promising to try her very best, behave properly and attend church regularly, without any intention of changing her wicked ways.

Depending on the new location he'd selected for her, sometimes Martha had actually made an effort. However, when she'd fucked or flunked out of six snobby schools, Daddy had gotten the grand idea that her higher education could be found outside the walls of respected academic institutions. Then Daddy had sent her to cooking schools, art schools, design schools, modelling schools, and a number of acting studios. In between he'd actually financed her three skiing winters at exclusive resorts where famous Olympic coaches had attempted to teach her the self-discipline necessary for a serious sporting life. Oh, what a giggle. Fat chance of success there!

Discipline wasn't in her vocabulary.

Not even in a companion volume.

Most often Martha enjoyed herself for a time and pretended to be a good little Princess until she'd fucked everyone with any appeal or grown totally bored with her surroundings. Then she'd hit the road, partying and scamming her way along until she pawned the family jewels. Then, like clockwork, Big Gus would show up and take her home to Daddy. Martha liked Big Gus. She could count on him. The memory of him suffering a heart attack in her arms last night returned. She shoved it aside.

Martha had to focus. Looking at her hands helped. It was while waiting for Big Gus to liberate her in Miami that she'd last had a manicure. Oh, she did enjoy the quick thrill ride provided by Latin-blooded gangster types partying for the first time in America.

Everything good in America.

Zorro OK in America.

Viva Zapata!

Admiring the long scarlet nails now, Martha wished she had lipstick to match. She felt too thin to be sexy. That happened when she did lots of cocaine; she lost her appetite. It was the biggest downfall of hanging out with those gangster types, the drug storms.

It had been snowing in Miami and she had tooted way past her limit, blowing off at least twenty pounds. Had she eaten the salad at the horse club with Margaret yesterday? She couldn't remember. If she had, it was the first solid meal she'd eaten in days.

'I'm hungry,' she announced loudly, but the Warrior didn't respond from the other room.

Out of drugs, out of money, and without a sugar daddy to rescue her, Martha now examined her thin body with a new concern. She looked like hell. This was not good. Not good at all.

She strolled back to the doorway of the office and leaned into it. 'I don't suppose you brought breakfast with you.'

Now sitting behind the desk, Lee had turned on the computer and was putting on a headset phone, shaking his head at her. 'Sorry, I don't feed the needy.' Then, with a lecherous eye, he visually examined her body. To her disappointment, he turned away, uninterested.

What the hell?

Surprised to discover that this virile Warrior didn't find her appealing, Martha ran her tongue over her teeth and considered her current predicament carefully. Men always found her sexually attractive; it was one of the constants of her life. Damn cocaine.

'Harvey, what you got for me?' He worked the keyboard of the computer while talking on the headset phone. 'Give me good news.'

Pausing, he listened to some guy named Harvey on the other end while Martha watched his facial expressions change with interest. This guy had some serious problems.

Oh, goody!

She smiled to herself. Things were looking up for the Princess. Maybe she and the Warrior could help each other.

'Did you manage to get into the house?' Stress echoed in his every word.

Warming up her little pussycat attitude, Martha

strolled closer to get a look at the computer screen over his big broad shoulders. He flashed her a bad-tempered glare and she retreated a little, turning her attention to the traffic outside the window.

No Ho was alive. The Starbucks across the street on the corner of Magnolia was crowded. Her stomach growled. Food. She needed something in her belly.

'That's not good! What about the short order restaurant? Any luck there?'

Following a short pause, his forceful 'NO!' made her smile. Oh yeah, the big brave Warrior was in some kind of serious trouble and the desperate frustration was rising to the surface quickly.

He was on the verge of losing control. Vulnerable. Good.

'Are the girls OK? Have you seen them?'

Cats stretch. Pussy cats stretch and purr. Sex kittens do it all with attitude.

Yawning, stretching her arms above her head and twisting her spine, Martha moved to the centre of the room, strutting her almost naked body in front of him.

Hi ho, Silver, away. This Princess was hitching a quick ride to the next castle with the new anaconda Warrior. He didn't know it yet, but she was his new camp follower.

No problem. She'd do this hurting hero. Thrill him. Ride him. All the way to the next castle. Her body might temporarily be seriously thin but she knew it was good. Besides, sexy was an attitude; she could do attitude. Hell, attitude was her life's work.

Turning on her most playful persona for him she reached high above her head, stretching her stiff body sensually into the morning sunlight. Then and only then did the Princess flash him her best come-hither smile. It worked. It always worked.

She purred good. Her little sex-kitten routine captured his visual attention as he listened to Harvey on the other end of the phone.

'OK, send my PO your paper. We web from now on. We're shutting down the North Hollywood office. At least until we can tell what's happening with Gus.' He listened, nodding to himself, before adding, 'Me too.'

Lee then ended the phone conversation and turned his full attention back to the computer. After a few moments he spoke to her in those rough tenor tones of his.

'Get dressed, Princess. We're moving the agency out of here. Julie will be here to pack up the files any minute.'

'I don't have a shirt.'

The corner of his mouth curled into a wicked small smile. 'I noticed. Go buy one.'

Oh, he did sport a nasty Warrior nature all right.

'I don't have any cash.'

'So pawn your dead mommy's diamonds and pearls. Isn't that your game, *Princess*?'

The Princess never lost her cool. She merely frowned at his attitude, placed her left leg seductively on his desk, bent over to touch her toes and, letting the large boxers slip enough to one side to flash him her pussy, she purred.

'Don't be an asshole. Give me fifty bucks.'

'No.'

Flabbergasted by his coolness, and with her pulse pounding, she forgot to play the cute sex kitten role. 'Why not?'

'I don't give money to women. It's against my personal code.'

'Then –' She paused and chewed on her lower lip.

Obviously playing demure with him wasn't the best choice. He probably had a happy camp follower stashed someplace, or she'd blow him for a little quick cash.

Instead, she detoured to another thrill ride.

'Give me a job.'

He burst out laughing.

Excuse me?

Nasty Warrior here.

The Princess flashed him her Shirley Temple smile. 'I need a job and you're short-handed with Gus in the hospital. We can help each other out, you and me.'

'I don't think so, Princess.' He laughed again, longer, and harder. It was truly nasty.

'Why not?' She followed up with her best pouting jail-bait lower lip routine. Keeping her leg on the desk, she bent her knee, and with her ample bosom leading, moved in towards him for the kill.

Oh yes. She had his full attention.

No man could resist her tits. She did have magnificent tits – large, full, and with pert little pink nipples that naturally pointed upwards.

'Why won't you give me a job?'

Oh, he admired her tits all right, but unfortunately his tenor tones echoed hard and distant. 'Because you're a total Princess without any job skills and there isn't a trustworthy bone in that body.'

'You like my body?' Coyly she placed her fingertips to her lips.

He smirked. 'It's got *ho* written all over it. I don't do ho, especially Wonder-bread ho.'

Playing her best little hungry-ho manner to the max, Martha forced herself to giggle her choice *Gilda* giggle. 'Every dick does ho, baby. Every dick.'

Wiggling her toes and noting with pleasure that the scarlet polish on her nails caught his eye, Martha sighed deeply, letting her gorgeous tits rise and fall with dramatic emphasis. Removing her leg and tits from his direct view, she did her finest sulky model spin-around, then hit him with her own cute bump-and-grind move. And for the grand finale, she turned her magnificent backside, covered only with the striped sagging boxer shorts, to him, before sensually sashaying her way over to the leather office couch.

She'd played this game before and was a pro.

Come to Mama, baby boy.

Oh yes, the money was in the bank.

Although he pretended to focus only on the computer screen, she knew she had his full attention before relaxing on the soft warm leather. Letting the crotch in the boxer shorts fall open, she sat cross-legged, exposing the thin line of her dark pubic hair. He continued to pretend not to notice, but from experience she knew different. Licking her fingertips with girlish glee, she casually slipped her index finger down between her lower lips, relaxed her head back, and sighed as she began to gently stroke herself.

'Listen to me, tough guy – ho or not, I need a regular job, a people job.'

'Take it to the streets.' His hard-ass attitude was annoying.

'You don't understand,' she purred. 'I really *need* you to help me.'

His narrow green eyes left the computer as he flashed his pearly whites at her and snickered. 'I don't know about that. You obviously know how to *help* yourself.'

This damn Warrior with his attitude and smart mouth was really beginning to piss her off royally. She didn't have time for this crap. The Princess was hungry and needed to find a party.

'Believe me, I've spent my entire life developing the job skills necessary to play private dick. Help me out here. I need you. I need a real job. Help me now and I'll make it *good* for you.' Arching her back slightly, she let her breathing become more wanton.

'Good for me?' He didn't laugh as hard this time. 'You got anything that might be good for me, Princess?' This time the way he said 'Princess' lacked the hostile undertones. 'Maybe you want to throw a little something in my direction, huh?'

Knowing full well that no one ever took anything from her that she didn't want to give, the Princess stroked her pleasure point more aggressively. 'My sister Margaret is going to give me a million dollars if I can hold down a job and arrange not to get arrested for twelve months. We could share, you and me.'

Of course. Money did the trick. No surprise. Sex and money, a combination no dick could refuse.

She saw the flash in his beady green eyes.

But like a jerk he made her work it more for him while thoughtfully turning off the computer before he responded. 'I heard something about Margaret's offer. That agreement has lots of clauses.'

Surprised, she pretended it didn't bother her that he might know the terms of her agreement with her sister. 'So, are you interested?' She gave a little gasp and threw her shoulders forwards, faking a little sensual delight.

Oh, he liked it.

And she liked him liking it.

Running his big hands through his shoulder-length dark hair, he flashed her a voracious grin as he watched her work it. 'Maybe.'

Come to Mama, bad boy. A bead of sweat appeared on his stern upper lip. Now he was obviously interested. Not daring to smile yet, the Princess sat silently and rubbed herself until moisture oozed forth in sufficient amount to dampen the boxer shorts. Her breath quickened. 'Help me,' she pleaded sweetly. 'Even a Princess ho needs a little help sometimes.'

He couldn't take his eyes off her pussy, but did finally manage to speak. 'Half.'

'Half? What?'

'I want half of your inheritance and I heard it's between eighty-seven and a hundred million.'

The greedy little bastard! Licking her lips, she didn't let her annoyance show. 'Sorry, too much. But listen, you give me a job and a little eating money now, and I'll give you a million dollars one year from today.'

At first he appeared to consider her offer seriously, but after only a moment he shook his head. 'I don't do risky women, and white-bread Princesses like yourself are nothing but trouble for a guy like me. Besides, you're a very bad girl. I've met too many of your former associates to be duped by your baby-blue eyes, pouting full lips, and magnificent tits, but the masturbation thing is a nice touch.'

Removing her damp fingers from her clit, she stroked them across her lips, tasting her own juices. 'You can keep the family jewels as security.'

'Didn't you just say they belonged to your sister?' Clearly unappreciative of her finer talents, he did manage a lewd smile.

'Not if I can stay clean for a year.' Now she gave him a regal smile while wiping her fingertips across the transparent blue fabric draped tightly across her chest. Her nipples were at full attention.

He was cute and she had now worked herself up into a prepared state. Her confidence returned.

Oh, baby. She could do him right now and really

enjoy it. His sexy broad shoulders would fit nicely between her legs when she shoved that smirky mouth into her hot wet pussy.

But unfortunately his attention had moved from her pussy to her money.

'But to prove you're drug-free, you have to pass a blood and urine test, don't you?'

Obviously he knew all the details of the agreement with Margaret. Muddled, and with her hunger growing, she managed not to lose it all and talk trash to the asshole only because she could tell he was seriously thinking over her proposal.

Leaning forwards, he pulled off his thick boot socks and rolled them into a little ball that he bounced in the direction of the bag on the floor. He was very sexy in a rough, base, low-life, and blue-collar kind of way.

Yum. Yum. The Princess would do him.

He responded by speaking to her in his deepest sexy voice, but in a manner someone might use with a stupid child.

'Listen, Princess, no offence, but we both know that you're a bad girl without any sense of ethics. I'll give you a shirt. Then, you take your fancy gems and get the hell out of my life.'

He was refusing?

No way.

'Please,' Martha pleaded in a whisper. 'It's true I've taken advantage of some seriously wicked people in the past, but why not? They'd do the same to me.' Pausing, she licked her lips again. 'But Gus makes this different. You can trust me because you're Gus's partner. Didn't I prove myself trustworthy when he needed me yesterday?'

Her words impressed him; it showed briefly on his face. But in the end words weren't enough. Shaking his head, he kept that deep, rich, comforting-a-child tone. 'I appreciate what you did for Gus. We all do. But the answer is no. Even if you were serious about giving it an honest go, we both know that you're too weak and too selfish to work a regular job. Besides, I can't waste an entire year of my life babysitting you.'

Regardless of what he was saying she felt him weakening, so she sweetened the pot. 'Not even for the jewellery and a million dollars and the great fucking?'

From his facial expression she thought she had him. But in the end, the strong-willed asshole only shook his head again. 'Nope.' He stood and stretched before moving to his bag, on the floor near the door. Unzipping it he found a clean black cotton shirt that he tossed to her. 'This is all there is, Princess. *Adios.*'

If Martha's stomach had had anything in it, she would have vomited. It didn't, so she dropped her sexual role-playing and headed into Gus's office to collect her clothes.

Damn cocaine. It made her too thin; ruined her edge. But what the hell! She didn't need him. She didn't need anybody . . . ever. She was a Princess.

Her lacy underwear was almost dry, so she stepped out of the boxers and slipped on her red panties without bothering to close the office door between the two of them. She felt his green eyes on her, but she didn't care. The bargaining game was over and she'd had it with this jerk. Let this low-life loser get an eyeful of what he was never going to have. Stripping off the thin blue scarf she exposed her exquisite full breasts and caressed each to tease him before putting on his shirt.

The cool damp jeans were a struggle to get into, but she managed. Then she located her designer red high heels with the open toes, stuffed her lacy bra into her pocket, and headed for the outer office door. She had nothing but what she stood in now. Nothing. She turned off everything inside her. She had to in order to survive.

The road to the next castle might get very rocky.

'You're forgetting something.' He held up the manila package containing the precious jewellery of generations of her maternal family.

No. No. No. A damn test.

Afraid she might let her emotions show or take the gems, Martha kept her eyes down as she shrugged, and unlocked the door. 'Hang on to those trinkets. They're worth more than your whole damn stupid business. If I'm not back in a year, send the family jewels to my sister. Gus knows the address.' She slipped on her dark glasses and left with full venomous attitude oozing from every pore.

2 **Hopping Along the Bunny Trail**

Pausing only a brief moment, the Princess hit the streets of No Ho. Hungry now beyond belief, she considered pressing up against some guy for coffee and a muffin in the Starbucks across the street but decided against it. She'd failed enough with men for one morning and didn't want to totally destroy her ego. So instead she headed slowly north towards Chandler and the underground train station, figuring she would either lift a wallet on the train or hit someone up for spare change.

As it turned out she ran into a chatty gay couple who graciously gave her a cigarette outside the old La Porta movie theatre on the next block. They offered her a free pass to a new film inside if she'd fill out an opinion card. With nothing but time to kill, she agreed, finished the smoke, and stepped into the air-conditioned theatre where she took deep long breaths.

The cool air felt great!

The moment was blessed. Martha loved movie theatres, particularly the old ones with balconies and Art Deco interiors. They were her favourite places to hide. Reality was such a royal pain. Make-believe was much better. Pretend was good. Counterfeit life was much better than real life. Pretend people were prettier, sexier, smarter, and more sympathetic than the authentic version. In fact, the best part of living was pretend. Flicks were the perfect escape.

While some guy put butter on his popcorn at the concession stand, she stole his drink and hot dog. Taking a seat near the back row she wolfed down the hot dog, which was unfortunately covered with too much mustard. But it was good to have something, anything in her stomach. Nursing what turned out to be an iced tea, Martha removed her dark glasses and spent some quality time alone with make-believe.

Forgetting the hell of her physical existence she escaped into the screen enchantment for the next two hours and was lost in the security provided. But when the credits rolled and the lights began to come up, the agony of reality reared its ugly head again. The magic dissolved and she felt sick.

Making a trip into the ladies' room saved her life. There she got real lucky and managed to lift and palm a prescription bottle full of Vicodin out of an open purse while the distracted owner washed her hands.

Waiting for the woman to leave, Martha looked in the mirror and fingered her bleached stylish hair. Oh, she was good. Life was looking up again. A hot dog, a few hours of good old-fashioned make-believe in the air-conditioned dark, and a bottle of pills made life liveable again. She was back in the game! Alive and well and working it.

As soon as her unsuspecting victim left, Martha stuck her mouth to the sink faucet and swallowed a couple of pills. There was a God and today his name was Vicodin! True, Vicodin was not her drug of choice, but today it worked its miracle magic. Viva las painkillers. And today, as always, painkillers were her best friends.

Knowing that relief was on the way, she'd hoped to blend in and slip back into the film again, maybe stealing some popcorn or something else to eat, but unfortunately the unkind ushers were watching. They forced Martha back out onto the street and into the stifling Valley heat. Hiding behind her dark glasses she continued her trek towards the train station that was now less than a block away. She tied a knot in the long tail of the cotton shirt, exposing her bare belly and her damp jeans to the sun and intense summer heat. The Vicodin rush started almost immediately.

'Hey, Princess. Did everybody live happily ever after?'

Oh, certainly, life was good with her new God. Attitude adjustment made all the difference. Recognizing his tenor voice the Princess smiled and kept on walking. The greedy bastard had rejected her, played hard to get. But he was back now. They always came back. It was the tits. Good tits and strong drugs were truly a gal's best friend.

Lee followed at a short distance before stepping forward to whisper into her ear. 'I want to talk to you.'

With her new no-pain attitude she stopped abruptly; he bumped into her, making her feel like maybe she had the upper hand temporarily.

She gave him her best Garbo. 'I vant to be alone.'

Unimpressed, he looked up and down the street as if looking for something or someone to appear. 'Let me buy you something to eat.'

But the Princess didn't need him, not any more. 'I ate already.'

'A hot dog is not a meal.' He chuckled and stuck his hands into his pants pockets, emphasizing the width of his broad shoulders. 'I saw you lift it. Very smooth, Princess. And you were going straight for a whole year?' He gave her a nasty little smirk.

'Correction. I'm not going to be arrested.' She looked into his almond-shaped eyes and gave him nasty attitude. 'Why are you following me? Spying on me? It's my marvellous tits, isn't it? Sorry you passed and I never offer twice.'

Grinning, he turned on his anaconda charm. 'Maybe it's your great ass.' Unimpressed, she started walking again. He grabbed her elbow. 'OK, so maybe it was the sticky finger routine. Whatever. You offered to pay for a legit job, right? I thought about it. Maybe we can work something out.'

Gracefully she removed her arm from his clutches. The drug god had smiled on her, and the numbing effects of his blessings made her bold. Seeing the jerk so eager to talk improved her mood. He'd given her bad-ass attitude earlier. Well, she was the master of attitude and goddess of bad-ass.

'That was this morning's offer. Now your crummy dick job is no longer worth a million.'

'You're high.' He announced his discovery with honest astonishment. 'When and where the hell did you get high?'

Flashing him her best junior-miss smile Martha did her little runway model turn, showed him her great ass, and kept on walking, working her backside for all it was worth. He grabbed her almost violently by the shoulders and she allowed him to guide her back towards Gus's office.

They didn't go inside the building. Instead, he opened the door of the black jeep parked in front and silently, with true Princess posture, she climbed in while he walked around. When he started the engine, she relaxed. All was good; the Princess was back on the road to the castle.

'I require a vodka Martini,' she announced. 'With two olives.' She gave him her best bored-with-the-lowly-cabaña-boy look.

Lee eyed her with an odd distant light in his green

eyes. 'Gus wants to thank you. He wants me to take you to the hospital for a little chat.'

'He wants to try to make me feel guilty and play Big Daddy,' Martha corrected him, knowing full well that what she wanted most now was to avoid ruining her high with a traumatic scene. 'My Daddy is dead and gone. So I'm not into playing any more of the good daughter scenes, especially today. Besides, you can feed me ... two olives or get lost.'

'You're a selfish bitch.'

'Duh!' It was her turn to laugh. 'Was *selfish bitch* your best shot? Oh, I'm so impressed.'

He kept his voice calm but his hands gripped the wheel hard enough to make his knuckles pale. 'Gus cares about you.'

'I know, and I care about him.' It must have been the drugs, because she told him the truth. Martha *never* told the truth.

They drove in silence down Lankersheim Boulevard and turned left on Riverside Drive. When they reached the hospital she held her breath. Hallelujah! He kept driving, taking her into beautiful downtown Burbank to a classy Chinese restaurant on San Fernando Boulevard. There he ordered her a Martini, a beer for himself, and more food than she could possibly eat.

The first Martini added to the glow of the pills, but unfortunately the second upset her stomach. Figuring she needed a third to make everything right, she waved at the waiter.

'Don't drink, eat.' He spoke down to her as if she were a child again. So she behaved like one.

'I need another Martini,' she whined loudly, and stuck out her lower lip in a true Princess pout. When he gave her a nasty glare she shovelled several mouthfuls of fried rice into her mouth and swallowed, then pleaded sweetly in her best Tennessee Williams Southern accent, 'Mr Lee, kind sir, *please* may I have another Martini?'

He frowned. 'Let's talk business.'

'Only if you fuck me.' It slipped out of her mouth. Actually she was more surprised than he was, and he was damn flabbergasted. Oh, what a rush! Life was good again. The Princess realised she wasn't bored.

'Why would I want to do that?' His voice was harsh.

'You might enjoy it,' she answered. 'I'm very good.'

He frowned. 'I don't do desperate women.'

'Why not?'

He sighed. 'Because I'm proud and know that I can do a lot better than desperate ... or you.'

'What if I demand it as part of our employment agreement?' She almost giggled. But he frowned. Insulted more than she wanted to admit, Martha silently watched him pay the check. It wasn't that she was all that attracted to the jerk. He was nobody, a working stiff who probably had a small cock and preferred the missionary position.

She told herself that she was just lonely and wanted someone to hold her, touch her, and make her feel alive. He wasn't all that great; he was just handy. It didn't mean anything that he wasn't interested. It was the damn cocaine. She'd temporarily lost her edge. But it would come back. It always did.

'Excuse me.' Martha went to the restroom, where she examined her reflection in the mirror. She didn't like what she saw. The expensive hair and nails couldn't hide her poor health or make up for her bloodshot eyes and puffy face. It was a nice shirt, but clearly didn't fit or belong to her. What she needed more than a good fuck was a lifestyle adjustment. Unwillingly, she thought about her sister Margaret.

'You're a selfish bitch,' she said aloud, quoting Lee. Then she added, 'You're a tramp who broke her Daddy's heart and has done nothing but embarrass her family.'

Feeling depression sneaking up on her, she pulled the bottle of painkillers from her pants pocket. Maybe with a bottle of liquor it would be enough to help her make it through the night. She didn't really want to commit a slow suicide on drugs and booze but she sure didn't want to be Princess Martha any more. Didn't want to hurt inside any more. Didn't want to disgrace her respectable family any more.

Swallowing three pills, she tossed the bottle in the trash, wrapped the handful of what remained in some white toilet paper, and slapped them into her pocket before rejoining Lee.

'We're out of here.' He spoke to her politely, respectfully. He didn't have to do that. She was desperate and he was smart enough to see it. She was a tramp and a slut and a con artist and he knew that too. They both knew that he didn't need to treat her with respect, but nevertheless he did. It upset her. For some reason it really pissed her off.

Outside the street was crowded with slow-moving cars, each packed with teenage boys who were shouting at each other while playing loud, thumping electronic music. It would be light for several more hours but the heat was beginning to dissipate. Martha wanted to find somewhere cool and lie down.

Continuing to play the gentleman, Lee opened the jeep door for her. 'We're going to Vegas. The job starts there. Then on to Utah. Anyone you want to call first? Anything you need to do? Anyone you want to see?'

'Nope. I'm all yours.'

He touched her shoulder softly.

Refusing to look up into his eyes, Martha climbed

into the jeep. To her surprise he didn't close the door immediately but instead leaned in to talk to her. 'About Gus –'

Martha didn't want to hear it and quickly cut him off. 'Listen, dude, it's a long hot road to Vegas. I'll require a bottle of vodka and a carton of cigarettes, Marlboro Reds, in boxes.'

Annoyed, he slammed the door shut. Suddenly she could picture her father's face clearly. Losing control, she burst into tears. By the time Lee was behind the wheel she was sobbing. She loved her Daddy and now he was gone. Before she could clean up her act and make him proud of her, he'd died. Martha remembered the stressed look on Margaret's face at the lunch table yesterday, and Gus in the parking lot almost dying in her arms. Martha covered her face with her arms and sobbed. She wanted to die; instead she had a total emotional meltdown.

To his credit, Lee said nothing. He let her cry all the way to Baker, California. While he filled the gas tank, Martha slipped into the restroom and swallowed another pill. When they were on the road again he handed her an ice-pack and a box of tissues from a brown paper bag.

'You'll be OK, Princess. You're with me now. You can trust me.' He spoke softly and with more kindness than she deserved.

'Fuck off.' She tried to give him tough attitude but wasn't strong enough to pull it off.

Sighing deeply, he kept his eyes on the road ahead. Martha watched the headlights of the passing cars and emptied her mind. She was asleep before they pulled into the old motel off the Las Vegas strip and sat in the jeep while he got them a room.

3 The Shark Has Such Teeth, Babe

The two-storey motel, with its small pool surrounded by a chain-link fence in the front parking area, must have been fashionable once – about fifty or sixty years ago. Now the quiet place lay in the shadow of a gaudy castle and a glass pyramid. True, it would be a quiet sleep – but shit. Martha had hoped for something more: a five-star, spacious, modern casino/hotel with excellent room service, a beauty spa to pamper herself, fashionable shops where she could begin a whole new wardrobe and, of course, a celebrity-studded nightlife. She should have known that a cheap private dick would take her to an out-of-the-way, classless dump.

But at that moment, she was just too exhausted and numb to care where they stayed, as long as the air-conditioning worked, the bathroom was clean, and the bed didn't have bugs. Lee got them one room with two queen-size beds in the corner of the second floor at the back of the dump, away from the street noise.

Once in their room, there was absolutely no end to his benevolence. Thoughtfully he offered to go for food, but she had no appetite. Then later, without her requesting it, he provided her with ice and three mini-bottles of vodka. Hell, he even let her use the bathroom first and didn't complain when she took forever.

Life was kind. And Martha took advantage of the opportunity to strip down, take a quick cool shower, and rinse out her underwear. With the bathroom door carefully locked she removed the Vicodin from her pocket and the placed what was left of the pills in a clean crumpled toilet tissue before dumping them in the small trash basket where she hoped he wouldn't discover them. She wasn't into sharing.

Martha hated the place. The whole beige bedroom with its monotone striped wallpaper carried a hidden musty odour overlayered by a strong disinfectant smell that rose from the brown shag carpet. Wrapped only in a big white towel, Martha paraded past Lee, who sat on one of the two beds with his cellphone to his ear. Hanging her red lace underwear on the back of a chair that she positioned to receive the direct air from the powerful air-conditioner, Martha acted like she wasn't listening to his conversation. But of course, he knew she was.

'I'm not guaranteeing anything, and watch what you say in front of her. She's a flake but even if it only works out for a few days, we'll be ahead in the game. Stan is faxing the agreement. We'll meet at noon. The usual place.'

Taking a moment, Martha hung up her jeans and the shirt he'd given her in the open closet before pulling down the covers of the other bed. While he watched she turned off all the lights except the small lamp above his bed before tossing the towel aside. His green eyes never left her naked body as she slipped between the clean white sheets, sighed, and curled her toes in contentment. She loved clean sheets.

Lee continued his boring business telephone conversation. 'Be careful. Norm says she's got someone following me.' He listened to a long statement from the other end of the phone.

Exhausted, Martha closed her eyes and was immediately sorry that she hadn't taken the opportunity when in the privacy of the bathroom to pop the last of her pills. She wanted immediate slumber, a deep, numb, dreamless kind of slumber that only extreme medication could provide for her. Oh well.

Martha yawned, curled up, and was out before he was off the phone.

It was a heavy sleep but not necessarily entirely without dreams. At first Martha thought someone was yelling at her. Confused, she fought to open her eyes but found herself in total darkness. After a moment she realised where she was and that the yells came from Lee in the bathroom, on his cellphone. The door was shut, but it was as if his booming voice were right next to her.

'Please. Please. Don't do this, Emily. Don't.' He seemed really pissed off with some babe named Emily.

Behind the hot-tempered words, she recognised a deep emotional pain. Interested and a little concerned, she sat up in bed and listened. Who was Emily? And what was happening?

This Lee guy had better not have some jealous babe stashed someplace. Martha was not into being torn apart by some furious wife or lover. No. No. No. Not a Princess scene.

'I'm working.' Pause. 'Wait! Don't. Give me three days, OK?' Another pause followed. 'You know I can't. I won't.' Pause. 'Bite me!'

Boy, was he pissed! Martha smiled. It sounded like Emily (whoever the hell she was) was really working it while dumping old Lee. His little heart was breaking. Poor baby. Couldn't happen to a bigger jerk.

Martha missed the last words of his conversation but it was clear that it had ended very badly. He was *not* a happy man. Good. Smiling, she relaxed again in the clean bed. Revenge was sweet. The stupid bastard deserved to be tortured for giving her attitude earlier.

Martha pretended to be asleep when the poor wounded guy finally opened the bathroom door, moved to the window, and pulled back the blackout drapes to peer out. Wearing only his white boxers, he stood silhouetted against the bright flashy lights of the strip beyond.

Woo. Hunky meat here.

The dude did have a great body; huge shoulders with powerful arms and next to no ass. Just the kind Martha liked best.

'Don't play childish games. I know you're awake.' He spoke harshly to her.

Trying not to smile, she sat up holding the clean sheet to her naked breasts in false modesty. 'Hey, I was asleep. You were very loud,' she defended herself.

'Sorry.'

She shrugged. 'No problem.' He continued to stand with his back to her. 'So Emily is your wife?'

'No.' He didn't attempt to hide the anguish in his deep voice. It impressed her. Obviously he had really cared about this Emily babe.

'You want to talk about it?'

'No.'

Sighing, Martha pulled back the covers and patted the mattress beside her. 'Come here, big boy, and let me hold you.'

He didn't respond.

She used her sweetest compassionate voice. 'Hey, big guy, you let me bawl from LA to Vegas. It'll be good for my karma if you let me return the favour. Come to Mama. I'll let you rest your head against my big tits while you cry.'

Still he hesitated.

For some strange reason Martha tried one last time to be nice to the poor jerk. 'OK, but in my vast experience with such matters, it's somehow always the most agonizing at night. An empty bed can be a dreadful place in the dark. But the sun always rises. This sort of misery is allergic to the sunlight. Tomorrow you'll be that cold-blooded, brawny *hombre* again who can take care of whatever macho crap needs to be done. The trick is to make it through the night. Trust me – been there, felt it, done that. Survivor.'

Martha patted the mattress again and this time he responded quickly. The drapes swung back into place, throwing the room into total darkness again. He crawled into bed next to her naked body. His flesh felt extremely cool as they wrapped their arms around each other. She pulled his head towards her and he nuzzled his nose against her breast as they rested in each other's arms.

This was much better. Clean sheets were nice, but clean sheets with an almost naked hunky dude between them worked much better for her.

Letting her fingers stroke the back of his head, Martha enjoyed his firm muscular body against hers. His masculine scent somehow comforted her probably more than she comforted him. It was great. His big, needy hands clutched at her back muscles, making her smile in the dark.

They lay in silence in the darkness, holding each other, each lost in their own thoughts. It took a long time, but in the end he relaxed first. Sensitive to his breathing pattern, she knew exactly when he'd finally drifted off to sleep. But only after listening to his light snoring for a while did Martha finally allow herself to soften her guard.

Tonight had turned out OK after all. Hugging and

squeezing this stranger softly while running her fingers through the thick curly locks on the back of his head and then stroking his broad shoulders made Martha feel good. Safe. Sexy men always made her feel good. But for some reason Joaquin Xavier Lee, with his almond-shaped green eyes and glorious tenor voice, felt extremely good tonight. Smiling, and with his warm breath on her bare skin, Martha finally drifted into sleep.

He stirred first. His gentle touch on her face coaxed her from her heavy sleep. She wiggled her nakedness against him but refused to open her eyes.

'Princess?'

Aaaaah! She adored the way his tenor tones purred in her ear. This was good. His teeth nibbled on her ear lobe and she moaned in approval.

All right! Work it, baby boy.

The calluses on the palm of his hand sent warm ripples shivering across her shoulder and down her arm. Now this was the way for a Princess to awaken.

When she dug her nails into his shoulder, his cock reacted, growing rigid against her thigh. He too was naked. Wondering what had happened to the white boxers, she closed her fingers around his erection, and while her eyes remained closed, her lips slightly open, Martha stroked him. He grew larger and harder.

Goody.

He had a huge, long, *thick* dick. Just the kind she liked best.

Woo. Baby boy.

'Hey, Princess,' his sensual whisper coaxed her softly. 'How about a pity fuck for your new bossman?'

Smiling, she released his cock and let her fingernails scratch a light trail down along his muscular thigh, then back up to his massive hairless chest and shoulders. She wanted him to touch her all over.

He jerked and turned abruptly, almost rolling over on top of her, then with barely restrained savagery bit into her neck. 'Take pity and fuck me, Princess.'

This was more like it. She loved it a little rough, particularly first thing in the morning. She started to pant in short little gasps. Pity sex, huh? The big bad bossman wants a little pity sex from the Princess?

Arching his back, he rubbed his immense erection against the thin line of her pubic hair in an imitation of sex. Pressing his lips against her ear, he made small thrusts with his tongue, in and out, matching his tongue's rhythm to that of his cock pumping against her sensitive skin. She liked it. A lot.

With a squeal of delight she dug her long, red nails into the smooth roundness of his tight little butt. God, did she love a guy with a big dick and a little butt. This job thing was really working out all right.

His tongue withdrew from her ear as he growled and grasped her head between his powerful hands. Covering her mouth with his, he plunged his tongue forcefully in and out, matching the pace of his hips to his exploration of her mouth. He was good at it, very good. Oh yes! He tasted fine.

This felt too good for her not to watch, and her eyes fluttered open. In the dim dawn light from the bath-room window which spilled into the dark bedroom, the skin on his broad shoulders appeared the colour of rich honey. Slowly at first, and then with more enthusiasm, she pressed her hips up to meet his. Oh, she was going to enjoy fucking the hell out of this guy. And she was going to love how it would change their boss/employee relationship.

His mouth released hers and his tongue moved

sensuously around her lips, across her cheek, down to her throat and then traced a path to her ample breast. He tasted her with his tongue, bit at her playfully with his teeth and sucked whatever he liked best. Martha couldn't help smiling when he pulled his head back to admire her nipples. Great tits. A Princess did need great tits.

Cupping a rose-tipped nipple in his hand, he tossed his head slightly to remove his long hair from his eyes and squeezed hard before he licked, then nibbled, and then bit until the peak grew painfully hard. God, yes. He knew how to treat a good tit.

Only when she moaned with deep pleasure did he suckle, slurp, and suck harder, swallowing as much of her boob as he could into his mouth, his tongue circling her nipple before he bit down, released, and bit again. All right! The Warrior was aggressive.

It was working for her. Martha loved a hungry guy who knew how to use his teeth. She was wet and working up for the big one.

Her breath came in short jagged gasps. All right, he was working it good now. Oh yeah.

The tip of his cock worked its way around her moist pussy, sliding into her ever-increasing wetness as he continued to pump in mock penetration. The intense pressure of his mouth on her nipple released and while she glowed and panted, he sucked, nibbled, licked, and kissed his way downwards to her navel, moving his rough hands to her inner thighs and forcefully jerking her legs far apart.

Oh yes! Oh, baby. She was ready.

Continuing to lower his head as his thumbs massaged both sides of her clit, he grunted at her muted little squeals of enjoyment. God damn! Those big rough fingers of his sure did stroke it fine. Moisture oozed forth uncontrollably and she tingled all over. Martha was definitely appreciating his careful attention to details.

Oh yes! Stroke this, baby boy.

Opening her thighs even wider with blatant encouragement, and bending her knees so her heels could dig in, she raised her hips higher while matching his pulsing rhythm, roughly kneaded her boobs and tugged on her tight nipples. God, she did love to fuck first thing in the morning.

Using his thumbs he pulled hard and held her cunt lips open, exposing her full pussy to him. His facial expressions went rigid with concentration as he took a moment to admire the view. Then he attacked with brutal force, his mouth pressing hotly against her open sex, driving his tongue in then out, using his teeth to gnaw, unleashing the beast within her.

Oh, baby. Oh, baby.

Fully aroused, her entire being jingling with wanton anticipation, Martha whined out in eagerness. Arching her back and undulating with him, her demand for climactic release escalated. He licked at her, sucked at her, gnawed at her, lapping up the juices of her passion as he worked her closer to the edge. God, she needed to let it loose. She was almost there. Her body tensed on the edge. She gritted her teeth.

'Not yet, Princess,' he growled as he tore away from her.

'What the fuck?' Martha screamed at him in lust-filled rage. Furious with him, she locked her fingers in his thick dark hair, and attempted to shove his mouth back to her throbbing pussy. 'No! Finish it!' she bellowed.

But he only laughed at her and tumbled away just out of reach on the bed, leaving her panting with sexual urgency. With wicked glee in his eyes, he watched her.

'Finish it!' she commanded.

'Beg me,' he whispered in response. 'Beg me to fuck you. Beg for it, you little white-bread ho.'

Oh crap!

Beg? *Right*. She'd never beg. His attitude unleashed a frenzy within her. So he was into games? She'd show him power games.

Without warning, she slammed his shoulders flat on the mattress. Pinning him down, she threw her leg over his hips and attempted to mount his erect, pulsing cock. This asshole had better deliver or he was going to be so fucking sorry.

But he was stronger than her, more powerful. He easily grasped her buttocks, digging his fingers into her flesh, and fiercely held her hips just above his, with only the very tip of his cock touching her warm, wet, throbbing pussy. His physical strength and power both surprised and unnerved her.

'Beg me to fuck you, Princess.'

He wasn't kidding. He expected her to beg.

Shaking with both wrath and passion, Martha gritted her teeth together and said nothing. If he didn't make her come right now, she didn't know if she could survive. She hadn't expected him to play hard-ass, dominant games with her, and she was not amused.

Instead of begging she struggled to get her panting under control while giving him her best I-don't-need-this-shit glare. Didn't this asshole know how to treat a Princess? She was a Princess, after all, and he was nothing, a low-life, working-class worm. How dare he play power games with her?

Her glare only seemed to amuse him. Digging his fingers in deeper and holding her tighter, he playfully thrust his big dick at her pussy, but didn't enter. Her hot juices rolled down his cock and she held her head high in defiance. She'd never begged for anything in her entire life, let alone a good climax. She was a Princess, not some lowly, submissive life-form. This Princess wasn't going to beg this asshole for anything, no matter how badly she needed release. Hell, she was almost there. She could finish it herself and make him watch.

With her proud Princess head held high she pulled away. Enough was enough.

But he wasn't having any of it. He was so strong! In one quick, powerful move, he jerked her pussy back into position right over his cock and then added one short violent movement that shook her hard enough to make her head snap. Both thrilled and frightened by his brutal strength, Martha could only pant as she studied his commanding expression.

'Beg, Princess,' he growled.

'I don't think so!' Martha unleashed her indignant fury, slapping him hard across the face. The sound reverberated around the room.

Surprised, he smiled at her, slowly revealing his perfect white teeth. God, he was sweaty and gorgeous. Martha hated him, and his amused reaction to her fury only ignited her passion more. She slapped him harder, again and again, while struggling to lower herself down onto his hard cock.

What physical strength! His upper body curled slightly towards her, his bulging stomach and arm muscles holding her with only the head of his cock inside her as his eyes narrowed and his face grew dark. She'd never been more startled by the power of any man before, or more aroused.

She couldn't stand it any more.

'OK. Fuck me.' She said it casually, as if bored with the game.

The light in his eyes changed. 'Say please.'

'Please.'

He smiled. 'Say it again. Louder.'

An inner, unfamiliar ferocity continued to shake her. It made her feel different, elated, excited, almost ... reborn. It brought a whole new dimension to her sex life. No man had ever dared to treat her like this. She hated him, and she loved the hate. The raw fury. The violent emotion. The passion.

Oh, baby. The rush.

Stinging with the new arousal, she dug her nails into the iron-like muscles of his shoulders. He was incredibly, mind-blowingly strong.

'Please fuck me,' she begged, but with hostile undertones.

'Joaquin.' Amused, he undulated slightly, his cock sliding deeper into her. 'Say, *please* fuck, Joaquin. Make it sound sweet, Princess. Make me believe you want me.'

Feeling needy and uncertain, totally desperate to reach a climax now, Martha surrendered. OK, she'd play along this time. She wanted it that bad. She wanted him inside her bad enough to let him believe he had control of her.

'*Please, Joaquin*, fuck me. Please. Please. Joaquin. Fuck me,' she begged sweetly.

He smiled.

'Fuck me. Fuck me,' she begged again and again. After all, it was only a game.

Slowly, ever so slowly, he relaxed his vice-like grip on her, flexed his hips, and pierced his cock cleanly into her warm, wet pussy. The pleasure almost choked her.

He filled her, pounding into her, thrusting again and

again, until she was lost in his animalistic supremacy. His big, thick cock crushed and pounded and beat inside her with vicious intensity. She totally lost it.

A guttural scream tore from her.

Throwing back her head and shoulders, Martha let him dominate her very essence. Lights flashed before her closed eyes and her body exploded, rolling with hot, overwhelming sensations.

'Joaquin!' She couldn't help screaming his name between the throaty shrieks.

Oh yes! Oh, Mama's baby boy!

It had *never* felt this good.

Again and again she shouted out his name. Again and again her body shook with pleasure.

It was glorious. It was wonderful. It was the best goddamn fuck she'd ever experienced.

But he didn't come.

When she was moaning with satisfaction, he simply rolled her over and rested on top of her with his hard cock still in her convulsing pussy. Struggling to breathe, Martha ran her fingers through his long locks and studied his rigid face.

'You know what's even better than a good pity fuck, Princess?' he teased.

Martha grinned and shook her head. 'Tell me.'

He raised one eyebrow slightly and gave her a little smirk. 'A revenge fuck.'

If this was revenge, she was ready to embrace it.

Martha couldn't help but giggle softly as her hands explored his muscular sweaty body. He smelled macho. Not like some wimpy pretty boy or a society flop or wannabe gangster or tough outlaw or power-hungry politician. This guy didn't need to pretend power or fake strength. He was the real thing.

Deep within her his cock, stiff and strong, began to

slide slowly back and forth, back and forth, in and out, in and out, urging her back to passion. He concentrated on breathing deeply and maintaining control.

Their gazes met, held, and locked.

Her pale skin contrasted against his darkness, his cock deep within her. She kissed him. She really kissed him. It wasn't some come-fuck-me-in-the-heat-of-passion kiss either. It was the real thing. But he seemed suddenly to have lost interest.

'Julie and Norm will be here soon with the paper-work and a new spy toy, all for you.' Unlike his now tender touch, his voice carried a note of cold professionalism.

Ignoring his businesslike tone, Martha concentrated on the way his powerful hands felt as they caressed her naked shoulder softly, before he shifted his weight up onto his elbow and withdrew from her.

'I'll be back within the hour.'

'No.' Martha tightened her arms around him and squeezed. 'No. Don't go. We aren't finished here,' she demanded in childish confusion. 'It was good for me. Stay. I *want* to make it good for you.'

'Later, Princess.' His flat hand lay softly along the side of her face, cradling her chin along the palm. She couldn't believe it. He was stopping when his cock was still standing strong? What the hell kind of fucking game was this asshole playing with her? His finger stroked her eyebrow.

What a jerk! This wasn't good. This wasn't right.

'Martha.' It was the first time he'd ever called her anything but Princess. His rich voice lost its authority. She smiled and purred softly in his ear. She had him back where she wanted him.

'*Gracias* for the kindness,' he whispered warmly in her ear. Then he pulled quickly away.

She couldn't believe it.

'No,' she protested, as his strong arms and warm body left her alone in the bed. She groaned loudly in objection. This was not right!

He laughed lightly.

'You're a bullying, sadistic freak,' she moaned, and curled up, pulling the clean sheet snugly around her. 'Sure, make me beg. Make me come like a freight train one time and then leave me cold and alone when we're not finished here.'

His only answer was a low sexy chuckle.

Taking slow, deep breaths Martha listened to him move around the motel room dressing, and when at last he left the room she drifted back to sleep. Only now her sleep was light and the dream visuals strong. In her mind's eye she saw the rugged mountains of home clearly, the rocky peaks towering majestically against the sky. The tips were covered with snow, reflecting the pink of a sunset against the blue sky. It was so real.

The knocking on the door jerked her wide awake. Assuming it would be Lee back to finish the fuck game, Martha opened the door, still naked. Standing there looking startled were Gus's bimbo secretary, Julie, and a butch-looking, large black woman.

Disappointed, Martha left the door open and climbed back between the sheets, stretching and yawning.

'He isn't here.'

The two women entered and quietly closed the motel door behind them. With vicious delight Martha noted that they both looked at the other bed, still neatly made, and then at each other with a concerned, knowing look. They didn't like what they assumed had happened here last night. Good. Martha relished their disapproval. For the most part, Martha hated other women.

'This is the Princess.' The blonde, overweight Julie nodded her head at Martha as she spoke to her companion. 'Martha, this is Norm, short for Norma Jean, as in Marilyn Monroe.' Julie dumped her packages at the foot of Martha's bed and moved directly towards the bathroom. 'How long has Joaquin been gone?'

Without waiting for a reply Julie closed the door, and Martha heard her lower the toilet seat. Turning her attention to Norm, Martha smiled. 'Joaquin who?'

Norm smiled at her, displaying a huge mouth of white even teeth. Starlet smile. Jeez, everybody who worked with Big Gus had great teeth.

'You know, Joaquin Xavier Lee, the guy you fucked all night. Look, honey, in my experience it's usually not necessary to catch their name, unless you're going to work for them. No judgment here. Just a tip for the future.' Norm laughed and threw a big canvas duffle bag onto the other bed.

It was a good laugh and Martha winked at her. 'I'll remember that, for future reference that is.' Curious about Julie's companion, Martha sat up and reached for her clean panties. 'You work with Gus too?'

'I'm the agency's Q.' Norm unzipped the big bag and began pulling out boxes of electronic equipment. 'Joaquin had me make this for you. Try not to break it. Our budget is blown and this stuff isn't coming down in price.'

'Oh, Q, huh?' Interested and amused, Martha slipped on her red panties.

'Yeah, Q like the character in the James Bond films who works in the lab creating those gadgets for him. You're not what I expected.' Norm sat cross-legged on the other bed and began fooling around with wires.

'Well, what's life without surprises?' Martha teased sweetly.

Norm laughed. 'Touché. Got to admire your guts on this one. Those paranoid religious freaks are hard to fool. We've been trying to learn the location of these fugitive females for almost a year now. Be careful. Your job is just to supply the information by wearing the camera. So no brave heroics. Make no mistake, these religious nuts are the killing kind.'

Martha had run enough cons in her life to know when and how to keep her mouth shut. Not wanting to appear totally stupid in front of Norm, Martha nodded in agreement. Of course, Lee had told her absolutely nothing about any fugitives, and she was clueless – although with her family background she was no stranger to religious nuts. She'd grown up with them. 'I'm no hero.'

'OK, Joaquin paid for a replica of your grandmother's locket to encase the camera. Adding the antique engraving was a bitch.' In Norm's big hands lay Martha's grandmother's treasured locket.

'This is a copy?' Martha examined it closely. At first she didn't believe it. In the end it was the added weight and thickness that finally tipped her off. The damn thing was a copy. Impressive.

'Beautiful heirloom. My compliments. By the way, beautiful tits, Princess.'

Wearing only red lacy panties, Martha slowly flashed her a Liz Taylor smile. Norm was a dyke; an appreciative dyke who was obviously admiring Martha's marvellous tits with lecherous interest. Good. The Princess liked dykes, particularly when she could only find guys with small cocks.

Never one to turn from a lusty eye or compliment, Martha smiled coyly at the butch woman with interest.

'Thanks.' It never hurt to let any admirer, male or female, feel that their lust wasn't appreciated.

The dyke lifted an eyebrow in warm response. Mind-fucking was happening.

How exciting. Mind-fucking and spy toys! Opening the locket, Martha discovered a miniature photograph inside. 'What's this?'

'Oh, Joaquin's personal touch. Your infamous ancestor. I'm counting on his image to distract the eye from any close examination of the workings. Don't want anyone to spot the camera lens. They'll have copies of the photograph, so it helps your pedigree entry. Not to worry. You're exactly who you're telling them you are. That's the true beauty of why this may work. Relax. You'll be entirely safe.

'Our computer will record everything. If you're in trouble, we'll know as it happens, and Joaquin will ride in on the white horse wearing armour. I can see by the sleeping arrangements that he has already taken your safety seriously, sticking very close for safety's sake and everything. Good to see the guy's earning his buck.'

Norm was making a joke, testing the waters with her. Martha gave her a serious nod. 'I think we're learning to communicate.'

Norm laughed. They looked at each other, a deep flirtation going on. Norm had the hots for Martha and Martha liked it. A lot. Besides, Martha figured it wouldn't hurt to encourage another member of the agency. Actually, it would give her a fallback fuck in case Joaquin tried to play his power games with her outside the bed.

The flushing toilet announced the bimbo Julie's return to the room. Immediately Norm was all business again. She held up a pair of fine pliers. 'I'm locking you into it. Someone with the access code will watch twenty-four seven.'

With a surprised nervousness Martha allowed Norm to lock the fake heirloom around her neck. Big Brother moment.

'Remember,' Norm breathed sensually into her ear, 'someone will be watching your every fuck, every move.'

'Watching is good. But in truth, I'm more the participant type,' Martha whispered as Norm's warm breath tickled her breasts. Still hating to appear clueless about the job assignment, Martha attempted a little humour. 'So now I'm hot, huh?'

Norm let one corner of her lip smile. 'Baby, from what I can see, you be a burning witch.' The back of her fingers lightly brushed across Martha's nipples. A witch? No. No. No. A Princess. Her tits peaked in response.

Martha was likin' this working thing after all. But when Julie cleared her throat and frowned, Norm stepped back reluctantly.

As Martha wondered about the new spy game she was about to play, the motel door opened and Lee walked in wearing a light summer suit and carrying a manila folding file.

'Hey, ladies, pleased to see you're playing nice with the Princess. Norm, you got about another ten minutes before you're missed.' Norm responded immediately and without a word left the room. Lee continued to issue orders. 'Julie, you get Martha's signature fast. Go home. File everything and don't forget to check the paper trail for holes. Remember, Gus expects information in the hospital. Tell him only what he needs to know.'

'I understand,' Julie commented as she took the manila file from Lee and pulled back the chair at the small motel desk. 'Over here, Princess. Sign.'

As Lee began rummaging through the black bag Norm had left on the bed, Martha allowed Julie to shove a pen in her hand. 'What's this?' Martha sat and examined the first document.

'You've never seen a W-2 form? You've never held a job before so it's probably a foreign concept to you, but us working stiffs have to fill this out for the payroll office in order to pay taxes and collect pay checks. Just sign and date. I'll fill in the rest.'

Feeling a little foolish, Martha signed.

The bimbo frowned. 'This is for the bank. We'll deposit your check and it will be waiting for you. Joaquin will give you operating cash and cover expenses.'

Martha signed on the line where the bimbo pointed.

'This is a confidential agreement. Once this job is over, unless subpoenaed, you don't talk about what you did for the agency. You never drop names, not ours, not the client's. We are a *private* investigation company.'

It was Martha's turn to frown as she signed. 'Don't trust me, huh?'

'We all signed it,' Lee explained.

Julie suddenly turned and gave Lee a nasty look. 'I don't understand this.' She held up the next paper. 'What's Gus going to say?'

Lee shook his head and kept his eyes down. 'Say? Nothing. He'll give me a big bonus for pulling off a damn near impossible job without him while keeping his darling Princess close. Have her sign it.'

'I don't like it,' the blonde bimbo commented again

as she placed the document in front of Martha. 'This is a pre-nuptial agreement.'

Stunned, Martha looked at Lee as she spoke to the bimbo. 'I know you're in a big hurry and everything but just out of curiosity what does it say? Skip to the big points.'

It was Lee who answered, in a serious tone. 'It says that if you stay married to me for one year and collect your inheritance, which means you have to stay clean and work as my partner, then I get half. If not, I keep the family jewels and you don't get alimony.'

'How about child support?' Martha kept her tone sarcastic.

Julie snickered.

Looking up, he gave a nasty glare. 'Sign it. These freaks survive because they're smart and double-check everything. We'll marry on the way out of town. You'll play the poor white Princess who the man of colour seduced into marriage in order to get his hands on the family fortune. Hopefully these cult people will try to help you. After all, you are family.'

'I don't like it,' the bimbo repeated. She wasn't kidding. She really was upset.

Lee shook his head. 'You know how they check every detail. Our only hope of pulling this off without anyone getting killed is to get someone in close enough to confirm. The Princess can waltz through this. Trust me, she's perfect. I can pull it off.'

'Does Gus know you're doing this?' The bimbo wasn't giving up.

Annoyed, Lee delivered his answer in firm, no-nonsense tones. 'Gus is fighting for his life. The Princess is my new partner and I'm running the agency.'

The bimbo scowled and pulled the document away

from Martha. 'That means you didn't tell him or Emily. Neither of them are going to like this.'

Martha grabbed back the legal paper and without hesitation signed it. So she was going to be Mrs Joaquin Xavier Lee for a while. She'd never had a husband before. How exciting! Head rush. Cheap thrill happening!

Handing the document back to the bimbo, she said sweetly, 'Lucky me, now I have a job and a husband to complain about. I'll fit right in with all the other girls at the coffee clutch.' She batted her eyelashes but no one was amused. Tough audience.

Obviously unhappy, the bimbo secretary collected the paperwork. 'What do I tell Emily when she calls?'

'Tell her the truth. Tell her I eloped with a white Princess in order to get rich.' Lee kept his voice cool and level. However, both the bimbo and Martha knew that he was disturbed.

The bimbo left. Lee walked her out, returning shortly afterwards jiggling some keys. 'We got new wheels. Here. I got this at a pawn shop, what do you think?' He tossed her a black velvet ring box. 'Want to marry a guy who only wants to fuck you for your money?'

Martha opened the box. Inside lay an exquisite diamond engagement ring with matching platinum band. The more she studied it, the more surprised and pleased she was. It was tasteful, with stones big enough to say big money without being crude.

Good stone clarity. Great colour.

'Can I keep it?' The question slipped out before she could stop it. Lee looked at her, very surprised by her sincerity. 'When our partnership is all over and there is no more Mrs Joaquin Xavier Lee, can I keep it?'

'Looking for a souvenir, Princess?'

Martha sighed and flopped onto the bed, the box in

her hand. 'You may not believe this, or maybe you will, but you're the first man who ever wanted to marry me for any reason. Silly, isn't it? I mean with all the men I've known and with all Daddy's wealth, no one ever proposed. You'd have thought some gigolo would have suggested it.'

'You're not exactly the marrying kind.'

Again Martha sighed in disappointed agreement. 'No. I'm not the kind that men want to take home to meet their mothers or make the mother of their children. Too crazy. Thank God! I'm not much good for anything but a quick good time. Not even for all that money.'

Lee stopped what he was doing, paused, and looked at her. She thought he was about to say something, but he didn't. To cover her nervous embarrassment she attempted to put him on the defensive. 'Whatever will I say to Emily?' She laughed.

In a serious tone he answered, 'Tell her the truth. Tell her we're partners until death.'

'OK.' Flustered, Martha sat up and looked at the black box. 'So, do I get to keep the ring?'

'Only if we consummate the marriage.'

'Does that mean we get to finish this morning's business?'

'That's as close to a romantic proposal as you're getting out of me.'

'Then I accept.'

'Good. Get dressed. Let's go get married.' Pause. 'Partner.'

4 Treat Me Like a Fool
Treat Me Mean and Cruel
But . . .

Their actual whole ridiculous wedding ceremony took all of seven minutes. But to Martha's surprise, Lee paid for two full sets of fancy wedding photographs. The posing took much longer than the ritual.

The wedding chapel had been a riot of colourful flash. The preacher was an Elvis impersonator who, in full wig and sequined jumpsuit, sang a melody of the King's love tunes as part of the nuptial dialogue and vows. He'd been a pretty damn good King too. The Princess had popped the last of her pills, slurped three bottles of champagne, and enjoyed the hell out of the whole glitzy game.

'I do.' She'd actually said it without puking and everything. What a rush!

The wedding had been an entertaining cheap thrill, but the following photography game had turned nasty. Luckily Lee had continued to buy her champagne cocktails, or she'd never have been able to maintain the illusion that she was a happy bride.

Being married seemed to have changed Lee's personality. Immediately following the vows he turned into a total jerk, forcing her to pose in outlandishly humiliating ways and then smile for the camera. The guy was

an absolute beast. The Warrior simply didn't understand the word *no*.

What was that all about? Who and what didn't
understand *no*? Martha knew dogs smarter and better
trained than this mutt.

It wasn't like she hadn't forcefully told him to piss
off; he simply didn't hear it! He shoved her around.
Gripping her upper arm, he physically forced her to do
what he wanted. He was without a doubt the most
controlling freak she'd ever met.

She simply had no free will around him. He was in
absolute physical control of her body. He was a tyrant.
A dictator. Macho didn't begin to explain his DNA. He
was a beast. It was horrible. It was dangerous. It was
way too primal. A smart Princess would run.

Unfortunately this Princess was temporarily without
running funds, or the creep would've been history. And
she had been committed to playing along with him
and the job partnership thing until she got her money
from Margaret. Fat chance.

She'd find another way. It only took Elvis leaving
the building for her to understand that the whole new
controlling job/husband thing was not working for
her.

Bad luck too, because this guy was seriously
dangerous.

It was scary. It was fun. It was sexy. And she was
wet from the power rush.

It wasn't like she was fooling herself. The Princess
understood that his machismo was actually perilous.
In reality getting away from Lee might be tricky. Her
escape would be all in the timing. Hell, Martha was a
timing bitch, a pro, a regular damn stopwatch.

No problem. This Princess could give this macho
freak the slip. However, it was going to be a good

game. A challenge. Yup! A cheap thrill that made her wet just thinking about it.

'Eat!' the bastard commanded with that booming tenor voice of his.

Oh, baby. Oh, baby. He did have a sexy voice.

'Eat, I said.' He shoved a chilled plate of fresh fruits, berries, and cheese back in front of her while he buttered her a Hawaiian soft roll.

'I don't want that crap,' she whined. 'Buy me a Martini, please.' Shoving out her lower lip, she gave him her best Princess pout.

'I don't care what you want,' he replied. 'Eat.' It was a command.

The Princess had lived on the road long enough to understand that people controlled other people through diet. Everyone did it. Mothers controlled the behaviour of their babies with food. Throughout history Warriors and whole armies moved on their stomachs. Empires could change hands. Whoever controls the food supply controls the people and their quality of life. Unfortunately Princesses often suffer from eating disorders.

This one did.

'I ate some of the apple. Now leave me alone.'

He frowned. 'Open,' he commanded, and when she ignored him his large callused hand went under her white cotton skirt and pinched her left knee, hard.

'Ouch! That hurts.' It really did, and Martha wasn't interested in eating or making a scene in a casino coffee shop, but rather in escaping into a dimly lit bar to maintain the weak buzz she'd acquired off the cheap champagne.

'Hurt? Oh, Princess, don't tell me you don't like it rough. We both know better.' His hand slipped further up her inner thigh towards her pussy, with very clear intentions.

Not that she cared about him feeling her up in public – hell, when buzzed enough she liked having sex in public places. It was often thrilling. Cheap, but thrilling.

However, there was nothing exciting about sex in a brightly lit coffee shop filled with runny-nosed teenagers and middle-class tourists. Not her audience of preference.

Squeezing her thighs together, Martha gave him her best bored Tudor Rose glare. 'Stop. Don't.'

A smirk appeared on his upper lip. 'Don't? Now, Princess, you are about to be ridden hard and long and without mercy, so eat while you've got the chance.'

Martha really hated food, and Lee was the most aggressive food-pusher she'd ever encountered. She felt like all he ever did was shove food in her face. She hated it. It was the worst part of his power trip.

Now the guy was insisting she eat. Eat, not nibble. Eat. As in clean the plate or you can't get up from the table. It was horrible. He had her trapped in a red corner booth with no way to escape, while he made continual calls on his cellphone. It wasn't as if Martha didn't realise she needed to gain back the twenty pounds, but not all at once.

Conflict happening.

The Warrior had his own ideas. He wouldn't forcefully feel her up under the table unless she stopped chewing or swallowing. But, oh Lord, if she stopped to take a long breath before the plate was clean, the guy turned into a sexual beast.

'If you want to fuck me, take that damn cellphone out of your ear and get us a room. I'm not into being the sideshow for the kiddies.' Nodding over to a table full of loud teenagers, Martha tried to act like she was interested in fucking him. 'Let them learn about fucking from cable like everybody else. Do I look like HBO?'

But in truth, all she wanted was to break out of the ugly booth and find more drugs to calm the rising panic in her. Then, when she was good and tweaked, she was going to fuck Lee until those gorgeous green eyes of his rolled back into his head.

His response to her was simply to unzip his white linen trousers. 'Now listen to me, Princess, you can either fill your mouth with food or with my dick. Your choice. But you aren't getting up from this table until that plate is clean. Understand?'

When Martha refused to allow the jerk to shove the thickly buttered bread into her mouth, he slammed her hand into the table hard and then forced it under the table and pushed her fingers into his open zipper. He wasn't going to let her refuse. The asshole didn't understand *no*.

But the Princess wasn't having it and fought back by digging her long sharp red nails into his soft balls. Unfortunately, he liked it.

A nasty gleam appeared in his startled green eyes. Smirking, he stuck out his tongue and wiggled it at her. The old ladies at the table across the narrow aisle giggled, making the waitress turn to look and then frown in disapproval.

Holy hell! Las Vegas had turned into a damn kiddie-town run by respectable corporations. In the Rat Pack days of yore a couple having rough sex in a corner coffee shop booth in the middle of the day wouldn't have even turned heads. But now? Hell, they were on security cameras and would surely be arrested if he pulled his cock out of his pants.

Damn it! Getting arrested for crude sexual behaviour in a public place was not what this Princess had in mind, thank you very much.

Not good. Not good at all!

'Let go of me,' she whispered threateningly. It only made his dick harden.

'Eat me or eat the food. Your choice, Princess.'

'Fuck you.'

'Your choice.'

He was so damn quick and strong. Before she knew what was happening, he'd released her hand, grabbed her neck, and shoved her face down into his lap. The smell of his arousal assaulted her nostrils.

Warriors do battle. Constantly. It was dangerous. It was exciting.

Regrettably, it made her wet.

But shit, not in a damn coffee shop booth with little kids watching. The whole menacing Mrs Joaquin Xavier Lee role was hardly fulfilling the fantasy of an ideal Princess.

'Eat me,' the bastard commanded, loud enough to turn every head in the damn place.

Damn. She was just pissed enough that if they hadn't been on security cameras, she would have.

'I will, but not here. Not now!'

'Then you're going to be a good girl and eat your lunch?' It wasn't really a question. 'All of it?'

His rock-hard cock was pressed hard against her cheek.

Oh, baby. Oh, baby.

She did want to suck him off.

So she surrendered. 'Yes.'

For the Princess, the Warrior was proving to be an exciting new cheap thrill, but good only for a short run. Yes, she'd eloped with a mixed-blood dick that she'd met yesterday morning and was more than ready to fuck all night. He sported a great cock and was a controlling asshole. This made him dangerous. What else did she need to know about him? Only that she could survive him.

A great big, hard, powerful cock was all Martha ever needed from a man. A nice, thick, long, throbbing, pulsing cock. It was all any Princess really required to live happily in the moment. Living in the moment was a good thing. It was thrilling.

It was her life.

With a brave face Martha forced down the strawberries, raspberries, melons, and a little of the cheese. But that wasn't good enough for him. No. He refused to zip his pants back up until she ate two buttered rolls and a small bowl of vanilla ice-cream.

Barf reflex happening. She hadn't eaten that much at one sitting in years. At first she felt sick, but when they stood and were finally walking around, the nausea left, along with her champagne buzz.

Fortunately, they didn't return to the dumpy motel, but instead checked into one of the new European-style hotel/casinos with all the glitzy lights and tourist trimmings on the far end of the strip. This move made the well-fed Princess very happy and certainly improved the Warrior's disposition and manners. Their new casino junction shone with rich gaudiness and smelled like *whale* territory.

Not many of the big-time professional gamblers actually came to Vegas much any more, not since the whole lousy town had turned into one massive middle-class Disneyland. The kids running everywhere had destroyed the serious guys and dolls scene made popular by genuine gangsters before and during the Rat

Pack and Elvis eras. But if *whales* were in town, they'd be in a joint like this. A Princess could smell the money through the sea-water glitter.

Their honeymoon suite was high enough up to provide them with an outstanding view of the whole glittering city and the rugged desert and mountains beyond. The tinted floor-to-ceiling windows filtered out the intense heat of the afternoon sun. The suite smelled of fresh roses, and Martha was pleased to discover that the rooms were decorated with some class, not that tourist crap. Las Vegas was not a city famous for class, only for the gambling carnival and gaudy entertainment.

The thick pearl-coloured carpet was brand new. Although the suite's walls were white and trimmed with light oak, the rest of the furnishings were a pleasant eggshell and a gentle gold, creating a lush pampered quality. Martha hated plain white walls; they reminded her of her childhood home. But the Princess found that the gold-gilded mirrors and modern erotic prints broke up the white walls enough that she was actually pleased. She kicked off her two-inch red heels while Lee tipped the bellhop.

The Princess was back in a palace.

The jerk was playing the gentleman again. Gone was the food-pushing asshole from the coffee shop. It was the night and day of his personality. That damn Jekyll and Hyde thing.

Weird. Strange. Freaky.

Talk about excellent con skills.

Now he was playing the perfect-mannered gentleman. He'd dressed to play the part. Her new husband's simple but expensive light linen suit accented his broad shoulders and powerful physique. His dark lush curls framed his strong, freshly shaved face and he stood tall, proud and sexy in an all-male, commanding sort of way. In truth, she found the look very exciting.

Yup. It worked for her.

But Martha knew the truth about what lay just underneath that façade. He was low-life come from low-life. But she had to hand it to the guy. He could hide it well enough from someone who might not be looking.

But she was a Princess. The real article. It was in her blood and breeding. Him? He would never be anything but a fake.

But she studied him with renewed curiosity. He was charming, absolutely charming. His facial features and skin were bronzed by the wind and sun, and his hands were callused like a labourer's, but still he somehow managed to play the gentleman. As a con artist she appreciated his skilful front and was totally dazzled by his anaconda manners. Her acting teachers would have been impressed.

But it was his body that impressed the lusty Princess most. She admired his beautiful profile and decided he was indeed handsome in a passionate, authoritarian, asshole, mixed-blood kind of way.

Clit twitch happening.

She wanted to get him naked fast and go straight to the fucking and sucking part of their relationship.

The Princess still wore her wedding gown, a simple white cotton sundress with spaghetti straps that Norm and the bimbo had delivered earlier to the dumpy motel room. The long full skirt, tapered waistline, and provocative neckline accented Martha's better features, making her feel semi-beautiful again.

Oh yes. The Princess was back.

Roll cameras.

She was ready for her close-up.

Her dress was all she wore because the new gal-pals from the agency had dared to deliver some white all-cotton granny panties for her; she'd never wear them. A true Princess never wore any undergarments unless they were silk. After all, a gal had to uphold her standards.

Better to be naked than in ugly cotton.

When the bellboy left, the Princess and the Warrior were left standing, gazing at each other like strangers. He removed his jacket and flung it over the back of a chair. Holding his gaze with unwavering control, she watched as he unbuttoned his shirt, displaying his hairless muscular chest.

Her Warrior had done his time in the gym and sported the muscles to prove it.

With his hard gorgeous chest and his naked stomach muscles he walked straight towards her with that gleam in his slanted green eyes; he too was interested in getting right to the fucking without any meaning-less conversation first. Good. Just the way the Princess liked it.

Fast. Rough. And exciting.

Discarding his shirt, he reached over her shoulders, gently pulling her body into full contact with his. Just looking at his abs and shoulders made her wet. Macho oozed from his every pore and intoxicated her.

Her arms met his, embracing him, rubbing up against him, feeling him all along the full length of her body. He felt good. She nuzzled her soft full tits against his hard chest and thrust her pubic bone against his hardening cock.

This was good.

Damn good.

It was working for her.

The Princess teased him a little, warming up his cock for the sexual festivities ahead.

'You were a total asshole in the coffee shop,' she cooed. 'Turned me on.'

Smirking, he bent over as if to kiss her, but didn't. Instead, he spoke without emotion or passion.

'We're partners, but you'll do as I say. Princess, our marriage is a business partnership and I'm the boss. Relax. I'll take real *good* care of you. You can trust me. We're partners.'

With one aggressive sweep, he took her entire mouth in his. Warrior types were always forceful when they knew what they wanted. And right now, this one wanted her. She could smell it on his skin.

Oh joy. He had it bad for her.

Goody, goody.

He kissed her, slowly and gently at first. This tenderness crap made her a trifle uncomfortable. No, no, no. This tenderness crap was all wrong for her today.

The Princess wanted and deserved much more. Hot, hard passion. She needed to heat things up. Tease him. Piss him off a little like in the coffee shop. Make his blood boil.

All right. Bring on the forceful bad boy.

The Princess pulled back slightly, giving him one of her best Princess smiles, and with demure sweetness asked, 'So, tell me the truth, big guy. It's more than the money. You want me, huh? I told you I was a great fuck.'

He didn't like her words. Thank God, the gentleness had only been some kind of controlling ruse. That hot threat of violence simmered just below the surface and was rising.

Good. Rough was better between them. She understood rough.

Using his powerful arms and hands, he jerked her back into his chest. There was no escape, not yet. But she struggled a little, just to keep his blood warm before surrendering. It worked for her.

Unfortunately it didn't work the same for him.

Amused by her little surrender, he rested his tongue at the entrance of her open mouth, moving it only when she playfully enveloped it with her own.

Damn. He was into playful.

What the hell?

First tender. Now playful?

Not good.

The Princess hated it; she didn't want playful tongues and tender kisses. She wanted serious, hard fucking.

As if he read her thoughts, he jolted into aggressive action. Without warning he attacked, vigorously sucking her lips and tongue into his mouth, and then releasing them over and over again violently.

Ouch.

She almost squealed.

Opening his mouth wide enough to contain hers, he paused and rested his tongue on hers, his lips on hers. Briefly she continued to resist his little mouth game; this seemed to make his day. He was so fucking physically strong.

It was thrilling.

Their tongues darted around each other until the Princess quickly grew totally bored. She couldn't bear it. Enough of the silly tasting games; the Princess demanded much more. Using both her hands and arms against him she pulled back, panting.

Give me a hard cock, bad boy.

She gave him that look, the hungry jungle, beat me, whip me, make me write bad cheques look. She wanted it hard and nasty and right now. He understood the message behind her expression and his muscles immediately tensed. A different essence oozed from his skin.

Oh yeah, primal macho. He was powerful.

Power oozed from every pore, every muscle. Like most women, Martha appreciated that there's always a hint of danger attached to sexual intimacy with any alpha male. Particularly when the Warrior possesses a body of incredible strength! All right. This hunk was strong. He could hurt her good. Oh yes. Please.

Oh my. Ouch. Ouch. Ouch. Please.

Unfortunately her readiness only made him sneer. And then, to her surprise, he released her. Something close to disgust overwhelmed his posture.

Stepping back, the big bad Warrior stroked his bare chest and studied the hungry Martha with those mysterious green eyes of his before his deep rich voice spoke to her in a matter-of-fact fashion.

'What's the matter, Princess? Disappointed in our marriage so soon?'

Fuck! He wanted to talk? She tingled all over with sexual energy and he wanted to waste fucking time in verbal combat? Damn it. He felt her frustration.

With a curling upper lip he sneered and kept talking. 'Emily spent the last six years trying to trap me into marrying her.'

Emily again, huh? Puking reflex. Panting and wet, the last thing she wanted to do at that moment was waste sexy playtime listening to him unload about his ex. No. No. No. Boring. He didn't care. He obviously didn't get it. Shit, no wonder this Emily dumped him; he evidently didn't understand a damn thing about satisfying women.

Enough all ready! Maybe it was her full stomach,

because suddenly the whole scene made her physically sick. This job/marriage straightening-up-her-life thing with this Warrior partner just wasn't working for her. The Princess was taking it back to the streets. Her eyes searched for her discarded red heels as her lips flashed him a sweet smile. She was ready to be gone.

But the Warrior either misread her sweet smile or understood her thinking because he swiftly reacted. Grasping her with brutal force, squeezing her shoulders hard, he lowered his lips to hers. He sucked and bit at her lips before opening his mouth to kiss hers. Then as abruptly as he'd attacked, he stopped.

'Don't be getting any ideas about scamming me, Princess. Remember, I know all your dirty little tricks.'

Something in his deep voice sent a chill up her spine. Problem! He knew that she was thinking about dumping him, right here, right now. He knew, and his knowing threw her temporarily off balance. Woo. This incredible strong guy had that ugly predator controlling side along with instincts to match her own. This was not good.

'You need to fuck; we'll fuck,' he growled.

Gripping her firmly by the wrist, he forced her to follow behind him into the bedroom. His grip was merciless. Martha felt panic rising in her gut. This was not good. Not good at all. The Princess might be in some serious trouble.

With one massive arm stroke, he removed the top layers of bedding, tossing the bedlinen aside, so only the clean white bottom sheet and a few of the huge pillows remained behind. With incredibly swift strength he lifted her off the floor and then threw her down hard on the mattress. She actually bounced.

OK. Strongman at the circus.

The Princess was a little unnerved by his intensity.

Rough sex was good; it was what she often wanted. But this hinted at more than rough; it smelled of something else.

Surrendering, she lay on her back, gazing up at him, searching his face and eyes for hints as how best to proceed. Her breath was coming short and shallow. Damn. He wanted what he wanted, and was capable of taking it by sheer brute force if necessary.

'Take off the dress, Princess.' It was an order.

Unfortunately this Princess didn't take orders well, never had. But she did know how to handle difficult men in sexual situations. After all, she was a pro.

She'd play him.

Not prepared to take Lee's commands seriously, Martha took several long, deep breaths, allowing her tits to rise and fall in mock passion while considering her next move carefully. Maybe the gorgeous tits would work their magic.

But he didn't react.

Sighing erotically, she reached forwards with both hands to tease his erection through his linen trousers. Both delighted and a little alarmed by the fierce hardness of his cock, she hesitated only a moment before unbuckling his fine supple leather belt and unzipping his fly. With absolute confidence that she could tame this arrogant power freak, the Princes only pretended to be submissive. It was only part of the game.

A game she intended to win.

Oh yes.

Victory was hers.

'I'm going to be *good* at one thing in my new life,' the good little Princess whispered sincerely.

Unfortunately he wasn't fooled by that sincerity. His rough hands met hers, gripping them forcefully. Then he pressed her fingers up against his cock, still covered by the linen pants, and let yet another ugly smirk cross his lips.

'*Good*, Princess?'

Swallowing, and slipping only her fingertips beneath the linen fabric, Martha studied his huge solid erection. A few drops of pre-ejaculation wetness moistened her fingertips.

Her eyes met his.

Neither of them blinked.

Without hesitation she flashed him her sweetest little Princess smile, the one she used to reserve for only Big Gus and her Daddy, before returning to caress his cock. But for some reason, her sweetest little Princess act didn't work for him. It only made his chest muscles ripple with tension, threatening brutality.

He was not happy.

Knocking her hands away, he literally ripped the fabric of her dress, exposing her beautiful full tits. A startled gasp escaped her lips.

Ah. This was not good.

Control. Control. She had to maintain control.

Brushing her erect pink nipples with the knuckles of his dark, rough hands, he studied her intently. She could see his brain working, but had no clue what was happening. Nope, this was not good.

'Answer me, Princess,' he commanded with a hint of pleasure. 'What's that *one* thing you're planning on being so *good* at?'

Hell, she could do this. She could play him and win. Moaning and licking her lips slightly, she pushed his hands aside and cooed sensually, softly, 'Being Mrs Joaquin Xavier Lee.'

Wow. It worked. The light in his eyes blinked, softening in surprise or affection or tenderness or something. She smiled with new confidence. Now was the time to lay down a few ground rules. Martha was a Princess and expected to be treated like one. Even the most vicious and aggressive dogs could be trained. So could her new partner.

But her confidence must have shown in her face, because he reacted sadistically, ripping and tearing the rest of her dress from her body. The violation of the delicate cotton echoed loudly through the suite as she struggled back on the bed away from his fierce assault.

Oh no. This was not good.

His green eyes savoured her naked body. Danger. Not good at all.

He wouldn't seriously hurt her, would he?

Usually her survival instincts were very good about this kind of thing. This time Martha wasn't sure.

Lee removed the black belt from his sagging linen pants before shedding them. Standing before her entirely naked, his god-like body alive with menace, the frightened Princess could only answer with a glare. His huge erection forced her to lick her lips.

Yum, yum.

He pounced, taking both of her wrists in one hand while he looped the belt around and bound her tightly to the headboard. Her intuition told her he expected her to struggle, wanted her to fight back; she didn't.

Instead, her knee slowly and playfully rubbed his hard cock lightly back and forth. She'd played bondage games before; she could handle this jerk. Just because she was bound didn't mean she wasn't in charge.

Keeping her voice calm, Martha whispered, 'So, is this how it's going to be between us? Mercenary-style?'

'Mercenary?' He smiled slightly. 'You think I treat you bad, Princess. Mean. Cruel.'

Shoving her knee away from his cock, he ran his coarse fingertips over her immobilized torso, his erection quivering slightly; a delightful hint of a little awkwardness showed in his green eyes.

Embarrassment, perhaps? Oh hell, he wasn't all that tough. He wasn't despicable. Anyway, not yet.

The Princess had control of the battlefield.

Moving her body slowly, sensually, she spread her legs and flashed him her pussy. Success! His green eyes said it all. The Princess had the power!

Hot damn.

After all, the Warrior was only a big bad child playing a hard-hitting, ugly supremacy game. One she would ultimately win. She always won power games. She was a Princess.

'You don't need to be rough with me. Baby, I'll do whatever you want. Treat me nice. Untie my hands and I'll do you right. Promise.'

The Warrior almost laughed. 'Treat you nice? You'll do me right? Baby?'

Straddling her body, he placed both of his hands firmly on the brass headboard and thrust his cock towards her face.

'How many men believed those words from your lying lips, Princess? How many men have you treated right, *my* sweet little wife?'

Annoyed with his sudden possessive attitude more than physically frightened by his behaviour, she adjusted her position slightly so her mouth could reach his cock.

It was her turn to sneer.

'Enough to know a good cock from a bad one. Enough to know a real man from a wannabe on a power trip. Enough to suck you, fuck you and forget you.'

So the little tough Warrior wanted to play power games?

OK, she'd show him mastery.

Sucking both his balls into her mouth at once made her slightly dizzy with his smell. He immediately moaned with pleasure, moving his hips gently back and forth, setting a rhythm for her sucking and biting, which had not yet reached his cock.

With a rising sense of her own power and domination the Princess nipped at the tiny textured folds of the skin on his balls. Alternating the top and underside of her tongue she then nipped, licked, and caressed with her lips.

Oh yes. She was good.

His entire body shuddered as he moaned, 'Oh, Princess. Treat me right.'

She was working it good. The Princess might be bound, but the Princess ruled as long as his balls were between her teeth.

Oh my. Yes, yes.

And right now, the Princess held all the power and knew how to make him submissive. Suck 'em and fuck 'em and leave 'em. It was the motto of her life.

Releasing his balls, she slurped her tongue around and around the tip of his massive cock. His juices ran down her chin. Taking only the very tip between her lips, she made playful shallow thrusting motions with her mouth and tongue.

The idiot went crazy with enthusiasm.

His fierce hands encircled her head and held it tightly as he moaned again and again, 'Oh, Princess, do me right.'

Encouraged by his appreciative moans and increasing juices, the Princess sucked him harder and harder, concerning her attention on the back of his cock as she pumped his enormous erection in and out of her mouth. He wanted to play power games; she'd show him omnipotence.

Oh yes, the Princess would be queen. Sweeping her tongue around the head of his cock one final time, she went in for the kill. Sucking and swallowing the full length of him deeply into her mouth, she moved her tongue around its pulsing power and length, and then swallowed.

When his large solid cock reached all the way down into the curve of her throat and she could feel the heat of him, his powerful hands gripping her head with fiery force, his fingers pulling her hair vigorously, his entire burly body shuddered.

His head rolled from side to side.

She sucked long and hard.

A primal Tarzan screech tore forth from deep in his throat.

'Oh, my sweet Princess.' He groaned again and again as spurts of semen, warm and briny like salt water, pumped into her mouth in several short spasms.

Oh, sweet victory. Even with her hands bound this Princess was the master bitch. Hell, she'd made him cry out already and she was just warming up.

Spitting his relaxed cock from her mouth and allowing her head and neck to relax in his strong hands, she couldn't help smiling at the rapture on his face.

Oh, he was a happy little soldier, very happy.

'Untie me,' she commanded.

But the Warrior wasn't surrendering anything yet.

Still on his knees, the authoritative jerk leered down at her before slowly lowering his lips to hers. Straining against her bonds, Martha kissed him, taking his lower lip playfully between hers, moving her tongue to meet his. Did he like the taste of his seed in her mouth? Like the smell of it?

He did. It made him smile. He had great teeth, a great smile.

As he rubbed his cheek against her half-closed mouth, his brawny hands stroked the back of her head and neck. Slowly he relaxed and slipped down to sit at her feet. He looked away, dismissing her.

What the hell?

The Princess immediately jerked against the belt holding her; it was still firmly attached to the headboard.

She remained his captive.

'That was good, Princess. That was the one you owed me from this morning.'

He sounded a little winded and extremely content. God Almighty but he was gorgeous, all pumped up and macho beautiful. The Warrior was clearly pleased with himself, and her too.

'Good, huh? You think that's good?' She laughed.

All she had to do was tease him a bit more and he would be begging from her hand. Then she'd give him the slip. It was all a matter of perfect timing.

Wiping his juices from her mouth along her arm, Martha cleaned up the skin on her face. All in all, the sexual game between them was going well. She was winning.

'Release me, Lee. It's time for me to really do you *good*.' She used her sweetest voice.

'No, Princess. Not yet.' He flashed his pearly whites at her as his fingers ran through his now moist hair.

What a sexy dog he was!

'You might try to run away. You're good at that. Fucking and sucking the guys senseless and then slipping away before they can catch their breath. I know all your little manoeuvres, Princess. Gus has had me trailing you a long, long time.'

Unsure how to react, Martha merely shrugged in silence and tried to compose herself into quiet beauty.

'I know everything about you. This having a life, job, and a husband to answer to is a whole new lifestyle for you, Princess, huh? What Frost called that cold snowy fork in the road.'

His almond-shaped green eyes remained in shadow as he stood and reached for his discarded pants. He did have a body of a god. From one of the pockets her Warrior withdrew a prescription bottle full of white pills.

'Your new husband has a little wedding present for his white Princess.' He shook the bottle at her playfully.

God Almighty, he'd brought her clean prescription drugs. Oh, sweet victory. Now, this was good.

Now. She needed one now and he had it.

OK. Except for the damn food and belt/power things, her new life with Lee was suddenly looking pretty good from her bound position on the bed. With much relief and his assistance the Princess popped a few pills.

Again it was like night and day. His manner changed entirely.

Once more he played the gentle helper, bringing her a cold bottle of water from the bar, holding it for her while she drank, wetting his hands and then using them to wipe her body down with the cool dampness. Oh yes. He was mean, but as a master he knew how to take care of his belongings.

Treat her bad. Treat her good. And keep her coming back for more.

The Princess belonged to the Warrior. She was his new possession. His booty.

Hot damn! Life was looking good for a thrill. The total power-tripping Joaquin Xavier Lee had rescued her from hell with nice clean pills and good sex.

The master Warrior was her new god. If he shoved food at her and demanded she beg in bed, and in return was willing to supply her with good, clean prescription drugs, the Princess would eat, beg, and suck his balls for a thrill ride.

No problem. Why not? It was a job, wasn't it?

Sure enough. And with a dangerous partner.

Could she deal with the dangerous partner? Maybe. She'd have to pay attention. It wasn't going to be easy. It'd require her focus. But in the end the Princess decided she needed to put on twenty pounds anyway and would risk whatever.

Food. Sex. Drugs. Bondage.

It was dangerous. She'd have to surrender and be his captive.

He was a Warrior. It would be a war.

His dark side sent disturbing chills racing across her skin. She took a deep drink of the cool water he offered.

She'd have to rethink their game. A safe escape must be carefully planned. She wasn't sure about all this spy shit at all.

He used that deep tenor voice of his in a comforting, disarming tone. 'You've been doing drugs a long time.' It was a statement, not a question.

She nodded. 'Started stealing cigarettes and drinking when I was six. I'm sure you've heard the same old a-girl-and-her-drugs stories.'

Sliding his moist hands under her ass with one swift lifting motion, the Warrior startled her a little when he paused only to lubricate his finger before stroking it back and forth across the crack of her ass. Oh yeah?

Her head bumped hard against the wall in surprise as he physically lifted her into the position he wanted.

She was helpless. Not good. Princess not happy here.

But Lee continued to talk to her in that deep sensual whisper of his. Oddly enough, she liked it. 'You're not much of a serious drug addict. You smoked one cigarette on Lankersheim over a day ago now. About twenty-four hours ago you killed three to six Martinis. The champagne this morning was like water. As your employer and boss, I'd say you were doing better than good.'

His voice carried a note of honest admiration that she appreciated. If she looked at it his way, the Princess was behaving very well. Alarm bells. The snake in the grass kept up the smooth talking in that deep luscious voice.

'Of course, I'm not sure how many pills you've had. Still, you're not what anyone could call a serious junkie.'

The Warrior stuck his index finger inside her, and the warm and moist muscles in her ass responded. His attitude grew slightly more playful. Not good. She remained quiet and motionless and listened.

'A Princess who's married to a working man and who has her first real job can't be expected to adjust to the new lifestyle overnight. I understand more than you think, Princess. If you try to go cold, clean, sober, you'll end up doing serious time in a clinic. We can't have that. Your body needs drugs even if you changed your mind tomorrow. I know all about you, remember?'

Bells. Warning bells.

The tricky snake was trying way too hard to be nice and compassionate. Alarm ran up her spine and her brow lifted as his finger probed further up her ass. She'd never liked men who controlled their women with drugs or physical abuse.

Food and drugs.

Punishment and reward.

Command, completion, and then reward. The classic how-to-train-your-puppy manual on human behaviour. Basic cult-control 101 stuff. In the future, she'd have to pay closer attention to his demands and little gifts.

'I don't need drugs. I like them. It's my choice. Not a habit. I've cleaned up lots of time. I was once totally straight for eighteen months. Totally healthy. No tobacco. No booze. No pills. No pot. No drugs of any kind. I thought I'd die of boredom. Absolutely murdered my sex drive.'

The Princess wiggled again, this time to let him know that his whole new anal thing wasn't working for her.

However, the pig ignored her protesting little wiggle and from his position of power shoved his finger further up her ass.

Ouch!

It was painful, but she knew better than to wince. The beautiful Princess remained unimpressed and tried to ignore the Warrior's crude assault.

She turned her attention to the pill bottle next to her hip and silently read the label. The prescription was his. Frowning, she caught his green eyes watching her. But it wasn't a threatening, violent kind of look.

OK. Trouble.

He indicated the bottle with his little eyes. 'It's good for a Princess to be sleepy. Sleepy good. I took a few myself to help me through the ceremony this morning. Princess, I got a newsflash for you. I don't want to have a wife. I'm not the marrying kind.'

Digging in her heels, the Princess lifted her hips up and got her ass away from him, removing his annoying finger as she physically outmanoeuvred him. She was quick and escaped the little power trip of his.

The glimmer of a smile appeared in his almond-shaped eyes at her victory.

Not wanting to irritate him, she kept her voice calm

and composed herself, trying to look beautiful. 'So, this marriage and job-partner thing is all about the money for you?'

For the first time he allowed her to run her nails over the knotted belt that held her captive to the bed. Damn. He did know how to use that belt. She'd never let him use it again, so he'd better be enjoying the hell out of it right now.

But the dirty dog didn't appear to be enjoying it. He moved off the bed, settled himself in a comfortable nearby chair, directly in the cool flow from the air conditioner, and flashed her a big smile.

'Money is a big part of it for both of us. But unlike you, Princess, I can really build something with that kind of cash. If I can successfully sit on you for one year, then my entire life could explode into a blaze of glory.'

'You've taken on a real risk, huh?' Her seriousness surprised even her. 'Placing all your hopes for the future on my good behaviour?'

He gave her an odd look. 'Haven't you?'

Frustrated with the belt situation, the Princess nodded in agreement.

Withdrawing behind an all-business, all-professional façade, Lee searched his bag and produced that familiar folding manila file. 'Paperwork. As a private investigating team we deal in the information business. We gather, pass, and deliver all kinds of information. You're a working gal now. Welcome to the trailer park, Princess.'

Only the calming effect of the pills saved Martha from a panic attack. She relaxed and didn't try to fight the belt. Instead, she stretched out on the bed, posing her naked body in the most provocative pose she could. 'Is this going to be boring? I can't do boring, boss.'

'Put your Princess childhood behind you, bitch. It's gone. And I can guarantee your new life as Mrs Joaquin Xavier Lee will be anything but dull.' Lee chuckled and pulled papers from the file. He was such a jerk. And he was so physically beautiful.

Oh, Mama. Not good. Trouble.

'We're mailing a set of our wedding photos, a copy of our State of Nevada marriage licence, and your employment agreement to Stan. My attorney's name is Stan.'

With her lower lip out in a Princess pout she teased him a little. 'Is Stan a good attorney? Because you're going to need a damn good one to collect.'

Although her tone was light and flippant, she wasn't joking. Men always underestimated the wrong women. Lawyer or no lawyer, between her and Margaret, this guy didn't have a chance in hell of ever seeing a dime.

But the dirty dog only smiled at her and responded in deep, earnest tones. 'Princess, you think I don't know that? I'm not some dumb boy-toy who you can use in one of your scams. I'm smarter than you. And I'm your husband. And partner. And –' he paused to give his words emphasis ' – remember, I know all your dirty little tricks.'

Suddenly the pouting Princess found herself twisting her wedding ring nervously. Rings of bondage. This was not good.

She'd only been married a few hours and this control freak already had plans on how to physically control her and later spend her millions. Not a great thrill. It wasn't her money; it was Margaret's. And she wasn't about to let any supremacy-hungry creep get his hands on it.

Warriors play rough.

She was a master bitch at rough.

Princess smiled at him sweetly and tried to sound sincere and honest. 'I wouldn't have agreed to marry you if I thought you would be anything but a challenge, Lee. Besides, I wouldn't marry stupid, no matter how desperate I was. Marriage changes everything for a woman.'

Without softening his facial expression Lee prepared the mailing.

Closing her eyes and taking a deep breath, the captive Princess seriously considered popping another pill. She'd surrender to him for now and would take the time needed to plan her successful scam and escape him. It was sure going to be one hell of a thrill ride.

A challenge. A thrill.

Maybe.

The power-hungry dude had his battle plans in place, didn't he? Maybe as far back as his arrival in Big Gus's office, he'd played her. He'd returned the family jewels and then trapped her into holy wedlock.

He was a smart little general. He'd used the puppy manual successfully with women in the past. Emily, huh. What was the deal with the ex-woman?

The Princess began to put all the pieces in place. Either Julie or Norm had indicated that Emily was a partner in the agency.

Bad. Emily had hurt him bad.

His defeat that night came rushing back to her.

A revenge fuck. Shit.

In the morning, right before he left.

She'd given him a pity fuck. And he'd fucked her in revenge.

She was only the toy. The pawn. Emily was the major player in his war, not the Princess.

Revenge, huh?

Revenge always mixed with jealousy. Was the bitch the jealous type? Crap!

OK, so the thrill life with Joaquin Xavier Lee was going to be big, dangerous trouble – but nothing an experienced Princess couldn't handle. The royal court has always held its intrigues, complete with its fools and discarded parasites and lovers.

'Can I send my sister Margaret one of our wedding photos? You look so cute standing next to Elvis.' She flashed him her best Princess smile and used her upper arm to pinch her beautiful tits together.

Noting and approving of her little tit action, he smiled back cheerfully. 'Well, so do you, Princess. That little white dress really showed off your Dolly Parton figure.' The dirty dog shook his dark curly locks and chuckled softly. 'It's amazing how any woman as small and thin as you are can have such full, round, beautiful, all-natural tits! Emily hates your tits.' The dog chuckled and smiled in delight again.

Fuck. Revenge. Damn.

'May I keep a picture for my wallet?' The Princess understood. One picture was worth ten thousand words. Yes. Trouble. But what words? And to whom?

Damn it! Her skin tingled and her nipples grew painfully hard.

'You don't own a wallet.' His deep velvet voice remained flat, totally lacking any expression, which told her immediately that she was right. She was in trouble. The photographs were a danger. They would have to be destroyed, and quickly.

'You got a wallet?' the Princess asked sweetly, playing her gorgeous tits with another little struggle against the belt.

She was in so much trouble.

Lee frowned at her.

She continued in her sweetest wistful voice. 'I want to be married to the kind of man who carries pictures of his wife and their wedding in his wallet. Feel free to show it off whenever.'

'I'll do that and make all those bar-stool Warriors jealous.' Lee actually grinned.

Then to her surprise he pulled a black, flat, long wallet from his bag. He placed three small pictures in a protected leather slot. The respectful way his rough hands handled them made her feel weak. Oh yes, there was something evil about those photographs.

Smiling and twisting her shoulders so her stunning tits jiggled sensually, the sly little Princess asked, 'Don't I need to send a copy of the pre-nuptial agreement to my family lawyer?'

'Done. But there is one piece of paperwork you need to take care of personally.' He rubbed his chin. 'Say something like, Dearest sister.'

Every muscle in Martha's body tensed, but she didn't move. Lee wasn't fooled by her composure. From the glint in his eye she knew she was now in for the con. He continued rubbing his chin as if in great thought. 'You should say, Dear Margaret, I married a fine, honest man today who gave me a job as one of Charlie's Angels.'

The belt was cutting into her flesh but the Princess remained calm. 'How do I spell Joaquin Xavier?'

The smiling little tyrant put the papers aside and further dictated from his chair: 'Tell her that the happy couple will be living in Nephi, Utah.'

Her mouth and tongue went dry. 'Oh, no. What happened to Vegas or LA? Nephi? Isn't that a small black hole somewhere near Mount Nebo, that strange rounded mountain off the Interstate?'

Smiling, he left the chair and began to creep up on the bed. 'Hotbed of bedroom polygamy activity. Over seventy thousand of them in Juab County alone. Devoted followers of *The Principle*.'

Her skin prickled as his rough hands encircled both of her ankles. Not in the mood for one of his power sex games, Martha tried to keep him talking about business.

Oh, great! Polygamists.

The realisation that she might be expected to interact with lecherous religious freaks bothered her more than his rough hands, which were slowly massaging their way up her inner legs.

'Polygamist colonies in Manti and Nephi have grown steadily in the last two decades. Lots of new little sects sprouting up throughout the west, sects established by generations of religious pioneer blood, born when it was all Brigham Young and Reed Smoot territory.' Leaning down, he kissed her navel before circling it with his tongue.

He was lecturing her about cults? Did he know her family history, or what? Daddy had been a living prophet.

Damn! Cults. Male pigs dominated cults. Women were lower than possessions. Dirt on the floor.

Nope.

She didn't find his move sexy at all, so she kept the conversation going.

'You want me to join a polygamist cult?'

Once again he kissed and bit her belly and then licked and nibbled his way down towards her pussy, using his big rough hands to stroke her hips before inserting a finger to feel her wetness. And, baby, she was wet just like that.

His rough hands felt so good.

He was a sexy dirty dog with the body of a god.

'You will do exactly as I say.'

To reaffirm his point, he gave her left breast a firm slap.

The sting made her gasp.

He slapped her other breast and then used his fingertips to twist the tight end of both her nipples. Pain. Ouch.

The nasty Warrior paused long enough to lick his fingers. Then he tweaked her nipples again. Ouch! When she squealed a painful protest, he simply straddled her body and used his weight to hold her down. He would have his way, and there was nothing she could physically do about it.

And unfortunately, right now, he was into slapping her and pinching her and manhandling her.

Ouch. Rough was good. Mean was painful.

His coarse, crude hands assaulted her upper torso. The Princess was his captive and he was massaging and examining every inch of the flesh he possessed.

Pain and reward.

He slapped her hard, then smoothed the stinging and painful flesh with a warm and tender caress.

Oh yes! Oh lovely. Oh, baby.

This power control thing of his had its exciting moments. Her flesh tingled and winced painfully under his abuse. It hurt and then it felt so good.

Huge bruises were already appearing on her wrists. The more she strained, the more pain she felt, and the more reward the bastard offered. Pain first and then pleasure.

Oh no. He was good at it too. Too damn good. Trouble.

Trying to change the focus of the game, the Princess tried talking to him, tenderly, submissiveness always in her tone and posture.

'So, you really did marry me for my family money, connections, and church pedigree? Ambitious to be a king?' The Princess was successful in her teasing but his green eyes told her not to go there.

Startled, she read the message in his hands.

Ownership. Control. Power.

Tart. Whore. Maybe. Bad girl that she was. But she was still a Princess and he was nothing but a working dick from the Valley.

His sexy green eyes never left her flesh as he moved his weight down along her body to a position where he inserted first one then two fingers into her pussy and began shoving in and out with harder and faster thrusts.

Responding with wetness, the captive Princess closed her eyes and let him play. It felt good. Very good.

While her breasts ached with an echo of pain, his fingers worked in and out of her pussy and then stroked the area around her G-spot; his lush sexy voice fell almost to a hungry whisper. 'Oh, Princess, you've no idea how many of us live in hell. Abandoned.'

Ouch. Pain. Ecstasy!

Using his rough thumb he drew circles around her moist clit, his smaller circles stimulating the very tip while the wider circles alternated directions.

He had her juices flowing good now.

Then he pinched the tip of her clit hard.

Ouch. Ecstasy. Pleasure.

With great mastery his unyielding touch forced squeals of agony and delight from her. As she grew more and more wet, he smiled and stroked the length and breadth of her small, sensitive clit. His magic fingers worked her with firm rhythmic caresses, brisk flicks, hard, then light, then alternating. Pain and pleasure. Inflexible and subtle. Pain and pleasure. Sting and gratification.

Oh yes. Pain and pleasure.

Her entire body strained against the continuing torment and then basked in the joy of stimulation.

Light and fast. Hard and soft. Pressure and release. Opening her eyes and dropping her head back and to the side, she captured the first glimpse of him in the mirror.

Oh God, he was gorgeous. He was a god himself, a fucking magnificent Warrior of incredible beauty and strength.

His eyes were open and focused on her flesh's every response. His broad shoulders and muscular upper body flexed and released. His sweat gave his glorious skin a light glow. He was so beautiful. Entirely focused on her flesh, he failed to notice her eyes. She watched him.

His skill and concentration on his labour pleased her. He wanted to make it good for her. He liked her pleasure.

And he would have her pleasure.

Forcing it. Inhaling it. Devouring it.

Her pleasure belonged to him.

His middle finger moved to separate her inner lips while his second and fourth fingers held them apart as he slid his middle finger firmly over her G-spot.

Her clit twitched.

Oh, baby. Oh, baby.

The climax was building.

A series of strong pulsing circles around her clit drove her wild.

God, this man was good. His touch was phenomenal.

The more her clit twitched, the lighter his touch grew. The more sensual the circles, the more intense the flicking. The more her body strained against his strength, the more yielding his touch became.

Losing herself totally to the taut passion the Princess, whispered a word of warning to her tormentor. 'You're going to need a fucking great lawyer, Lee. Because you're never going to see those millions.'

He slapped her. Hard.

Licking her lower lip, she tasted blood. Salty. Warm. Blood.

What the fuck? He'd hit her. And hard.

The Princess swallowed warm blood.

Every muscle in her body fought full force against his assault and the bondage, against the leather belt and the weight of his exquisite body, against the torture and delight.

The Princess cried out in exquisite pain as the bastard carried on working his rhythmic finger circles, rubbing her clit ever so slightly harder in time with her hip thrusts against his hand.

Oh yes. Oh, baby.

'Princess, before we're finished, you're going to beg me to take the millions and your damn family jewels. And you know why?'

She could barely breathe. Gasping for bodily deliverance she managed a whisper. 'Why?'

'Because I know just how to fuck you, Princess.'

With a sudden and intense brutality his other hand attacked, thrusting two, then three fingers all the way up inside her, circling, exploring all of her, plunging against her tender inner tissue, faster and faster, harder and harder, until her body and spirit tensed in total immobility. His other hand caressed and worked her clit.

God! She couldn't breathe. She couldn't move. She was his.

God! Yes! Release! Now!

Pain. Pain. Pleasure. Pleasure.

Release, please – release.

He increased the pressure and rhythm of his assault, accelerating her into a high-pitched wail of an orgasm that rippled through her entire body, rising and falling again and again.

She jerked. Her entire body juddered.

For a long time her body convulsed in violent, agonising liberation. Gradually the rhythm of his powerful hands slowed to meet her subsiding gyrations, but instead of stopping he continued to stroke her softly.

The flesh on her entire body burned and glowed with the force of her come. Adjusting his position, he leaned over to kiss and bite her hardened nipples. His hard cock rested against her smouldering flesh.

He was beautiful. He was great. He was magnificent.

Digging in her heels and lifting her hips, the Princess willingly offered herself, spreading her legs wider to his exploring fingers. Oh, he was good. The smell of her pheromones filled the room. Oh, he was very good.

Slowly a glimmering sense of her surroundings returned to her. Awareness of anything past her own sexual gratification was a struggle. The bed was drenched in her female juices. Blood remained in her mouth. Her breathing was laboured, and her lungs burned.

And he never stopped.

Sometimes his magic fingers were in and out of her, fast but soft, and then he'd rub her G-spot with tremendous force.

Pleasure and pain.

One moment his fingers were fucking her with long,

slow, sensuous strokes – and the the next, he was brutalizing her.

As her juices continued to flow, he shifted his position and, digging his fingers into her ass, he lifted her hips up to his mouth.

Oh yes.

The Princess thrust her clit hard against his mouth as he worked the tip of his tongue back and forth across her. With each lick, each flick, each nibble, her pussy pulsed to meet his astonishing tongue and lips. Her bruised wrists fought the belt that held her taut. As she was reaching the peak of another orgasm, Lee stopped cold and pulled away from her.

Standing, he casually walked away from her as if she were a piece of nasty dirt. 'Keep it wet, Princess. I'll be back after I've showered.'

'Oh, you sick mother!' she screamed after him.

A Princess didn't have to tolerate this crap. His abuse and little control games were definitely not working for this American white-bread royalty.

What a cruel monster he was. Twice now he'd left her on the brink and unsatisfied. This was nasty and cruel.

A fucking malicious, thick-skinned, nasty son of a bitch. Fucker. Bitching bastard.

Did she need this shit?

She heard the shower water in the bathroom. He wasn't really going to leave her strapped to the bed, panting, moments away from a great climax?

Damn!

'Joaquin Xavier Lee, get your ass back here,' the Princess commanded as loudly as she could.

He ignored her.

Working her way to her feet, she now managed to bend her head over and use her teeth to help her fingers free herself from the bondage of the leather belt.

Grinning and appearing highly pleased with himself, Lee returned to stand in the doorway, stroking his still rigid cock while she attempted to work herself free of the knotted belt.

'Why, Princess, using all three of my names in that tone of voice? I swear, you sounded just like my grandmother.' His massive muscular shoulders shook in a fake quick chill.

'You're one sick slant-eyed half-breed.' She was so furious she couldn't even think of any more nasty, degrading names to call him. As soon as she was free, she was going to claw his little green eyes out.

But his smile didn't disappear; only the pitch of his voice changed. 'You're married to a man of mixed colour now. Your lily-white Princess existence is in for a rude awakening, bitch.'

'You think?' Martha managed to work one of knots loose. In a few more moments she'd be free of her bonds and then she was going to rip this merciless bastard a new asshole.

But Lee didn't seem concerned about her progress with the belt. His shadowy green eyes never left her as the pitch of his voice dropped lower and echoed with even more potency.

'Playing with men of colour, fucking them, and marrying one are not all the same thing. As you'll discover when you introduce me to your highly respectable family members and rich country club friends.'

Finally freeing one hand, she twisted the other clear of the belt.

She was going to kill him.

Panting, standing abused and naked on the soiled

bed, the Princess paused, licked her lips and sucked clean the dried blood as she carefully studied her new husband for a moment.

He was ready for her to attack. He was so damn smug. He thought he was smarter than her, stronger than her. He thought he knew her every trick and that she was totally under his control.

Ha.

The Princess, panting, ready to spring, didn't.

No. She could wait. Revenge was a dish best served cold, right?

OK. She'd wait to destroy this power-hungry dick and show him who was the master and who was the bitch in their partnership. Oh yes.

Tossing her head and rubbing her shaking fingers through her short blonde hair, the proud Princess raised her chin high in defiance. 'With your permission, I'll pop a few more pills while you make an appointment for me at the spa downstairs.'

Surprised at her words, sudden calm, and control, he arched an eyebrow slightly. He wasn't fooled.

But there was absolutely nothing he could do until she took action. He was now the helpless waiting victim in their torture game. She'd get him. She'd do him. She'd do him right.

Puzzled, Lee stared at her with a quizzical expression. 'As you wish, my Princess.'

'I'll require a soft touch, quiet pampering, a long bath, waxing, wrapping, massage, facial, manicure, pedicure, and a hairstylist. And you, Mr Joaquin Xavier Lee, my darling husband, will pick up the tab because that's what husbands do. Pay for it.'

'OK, as long as I can watch.'

And so the Princess began putting his plastic to work. She charged and charged and charged everything to him. Under his direct governing company at all times, she spent a small fortune at the spa and then another whopping load in the boutiques.

He watched, talked on the phone, and paid.

To his credit, Lee never commented or complained when presented with a bill. In fact, the Princess was a little disappointed with his indifference.

The phone in their suite, as well as his cellular, rang non-stop. Even when he accompanied her down to the pool and admired her new purple G-string bikini, he had the damn thing in his ear. He lounged in the shade of a pool-side umbrella and continued to bark orders to the callers while his pampered Princess sunbathed. Clearly Lee was a workaholic.

Boring.

The Princess spent most of the week in their suite, being force-fed, drinking Martinis, popping pills, and silently observing her new husband while he fucked her. He was physically gorgeous, but oddly inhuman. And except for that first time in the dumpy motel, he always bound her during their rough sex. She had the battered body to prove it.

5 The Last Vegas Ballet

'Stand here,' Lee commanded one evening as the red summer sun lapped at the mountaintops in the west.

Rising from her posed position on the bed, the obedient little Princess immediately and gracefully went to him. His eyes never left her. Never.

That was because she was gorgeous, and she knew it.

Besides, she was totally tweaked and amusing herself with sexual play.

He'd placed a high-backed chair before a floor-to-ceiling mirror on their walk-in closet.

'Take off the robe.'

Oh goody. A new game – one that hopefully didn't require her to be hog-tied.

Dutifully she let the silk garment slowly slip from her bare shoulders to the lush carpet.

Oh, she felt good. Good pills. Good times. Good sex.

But whenever she reached to touch him like now, he stepped away from her.

'Don't touch. Listen to my voice. Look in the mirror.'

Turning her head, she admired the profile of her great tits and ass. Damn. A full week of healthy food and pampering and the Princess was working her way back to her beautiful statuesque self. Apart from all the bruises, she was looking damn hot.

With crude force he gripped her shoulders and set them square to the mirror, the chair inches in front of her.

'Look,' he commanded with a deep roar.

She looked.

Good. She was looking magnificent.

Naked, except for her wine-dark nail polish and the spy toy/necklace, Martha smiled coyly. And it felt good to be beautiful again. It was so delightful to be loaded and having fun.

Lee appeared busy momentarily with his laptop computer over on the dresser and she felt slighted. Ignored.

Her lower lip curled out into a Traci Lords pout.

Her hero had given her a new stash of pills just an hour ago and she was feeling no pain. Sleepy. Pampered. Sexy. Beautiful. And no pain.

Life was good.

This was the life for a true Princess.

'Now keep your necklace to the mirror at all times or I'll have to smack you around a little.' He was using that sexy playful tenor voice of his just the way she liked it.

'Yes, master.' She continued her coy little pout but giggled sweetly.

But she felt too good just to stand there quietly before the mirror, naked and admiring her own physical exquisiteness in the gorgeous fiery light of the sunset.

Time for fun and games.

'Now what can I do for you, master?'

He always got a kick out of the *master*. Nothing made him happier than to think he fucking controlled her.

Ha.

Forgetting the power pout, the Princess licked her lips and twisted her wedding ring.

Bondage.

The bruises on her arms told the whole world that she was his slave. And he liked it that way. She didn't care. Rough was good. Rough was safe. Rough wasn't emotionally demanding, only physically.

Besides, she could use rough against him later if she needed a cop to help her escape his clutches.

Quickly he stripped off his clothes, making her smile.

He was fucking gorgeous.

To her surprise Lee didn't come near her, but instead took a relaxed position on the bed, where he could watch both his computer screen and her reflection in the mirror.

He almost whispered, 'Did you take some pills, Princess?'

She purred in the affirmative. Oh, life was so very sweet.

'Lift your arms.'

She did.

'Higher,' he demanded.

She complied and dazzled him with her marvellous tits. Twisting and turning slightly, always keeping the eye of the necklace towards the mirror, the Princess began her poses.

Oh yes. Daddy had paid for modelling school, and the money hadn't been wasted.

Days living with his intense food-pushing had called her body back to life. She was thin, still too thin to really be at her most glorious, but all the same she looked fucking great.

Growing bored with the standing poses, the Princess mounted the throne from behind. First she put her right leg over the back of the chair, and then her foot slid into the cushioned seat.

'Take it slow, Princess. Show it all to me.'

The lust in his rich tone forced her to smile. Oh, sweet success. The Princess ruled the castle.

Extending her right leg again, she lifted it, higher, higher. Hell, Daddy hadn't paid for all those ballet lessons for nothing.

Her painted, pointed, and polished toes were above her head. Flexing and curling her waxed and manicured feet, the Princess threw her head back slightly and gave him her *Swan Lake* pose.

His big hands went straight to his cock.

Yeah, clapping. Glorious. He liked her.

Leaning forwards she shifted the leg behind her and then, ever so slowly, lowered her ample breasts to the back of the chair, posing her pussy directly at him.

His hands massaged his swelling cock. It worked for him. She smiled.

In one swift, graceful sweep, Martha mounted the back of the chair, swung both feet into the seat, and threw her knees open to the mirror.

Now posed on the back of the chair, her pink pussy opened to the mirror, she let her long slender fingers leisurely stroke her inner thighs.

'Take your time, Princess. Take your time.'

Arching her back, she dragged her fingers through her short bleached hair and broke into a pout. Her lower lip extended.

Beautiful.

Even she had to admire the stunning reflection in the mirror. She was a pretty Princess.

A happy, drugged-to-the-gills Princess with a very happy sugar daddy. Life was good, as it should be.

The desert sun burned suddenly golden.

Shadows of the mountains began to creep across the desert sands. She paused, taking in the scene surrounding them. They were surrounded by luxury. In every niche there were decadent reminders of wealth and power; expensive accoutrements of the bath and body that he'd purchased for her cluttered the area.

It defied all logic. Just days ago she'd been broke, shattered, totally isolated and desperate.

Now, the thick vanilla scent of her massage oil rose from her mollycoddled skin. Only a little over a week ago she'd been a lost and defeated Princess. But then she'd been abducted by a strange and powerful Warrior with almond-shaped green eyes, a deep voice, and a taste for the nasty. Her whole existence was now limited by the boundaries of his whims, his superb surroundings, and the drugs he gave her. She was dedicated to his seduction.

This was surreal for her.

This was a new fancy cage.

This was her new life.

She had no self-control or free will. Her sole purpose was to wait until her all-powerful Warrior chose to use her. Oh yes. Fed, pampered, drugged, and back to living the good life of a Princess.

'What do you feel?' His deep rich voice startled her from her sleepy numbness.

'Contentment and desire.' She turned. She had to see him.

'No,' her master sharply objected. 'Turn the eye of the necklace back towards the mirror. Now only I can see everything in the mirror and I'm recording.'

Up off the bed, he suddenly stood directly behind her, his warm breath caressing her neck. The air was suddenly saturated with the scent of his sexual arousal, thick and ominous. Their eyes met in the mirror, hers large, open, and sky blue, and his narrow, shaded, and green.

Both full of lust.

The rough calluses on the palms of his hands sent shivers through her warming flesh. Running his possessive hands over her, he adjusted his voyeur view. Bending slightly over her, his fingers stroking, he whispered deeply into her ear. 'What do you feel?'

She purred in response.

Caressing her, he insinuated his finger between her buttocks.

She melted with his expert touch.

Unprepared for the feeling of silk material sliding down between her open legs, she opened her lips and started to take long, deep, panting breaths.

He pressed a white silk scarf against her pussy.

'What do you feel, Princess?'

As he leaned forwards into her, his firm chest against her back, she rolled her hands towards her breasts so that all was visible in the magic glass.

Magic, hard hands, strong and possessive, working on her, feeling her, brushed up against the silk covering her pussy. Her clit tightened.

Lee took a long deep breath, reared back, and rammed his huge hard cock against her butt crack.

The Princess was excited.

He was going to use her, indulgent in his own self-pleasure.

Exploit her. Possess her.

He knew it. She knew it.

It was exciting. She felt alive.

Possessive. Erotic. Pure. Commanding. Voluptuous. She pinched her tits while his fingers stroked her. The silk between her legs grew damp with her wetness. Their eyes met in the mirror. Without warning, he jerked the silk from her and wrapped it around his neck, the scent of her passion just below his nose so that he could inhale deeply. And he did.

The lustful sex scent enveloped them both.

Halfway between a groan and a growl, his body contracted against hers. Rooted there, poised with his thick hard cock against her butt, his powerful shoulder, chest, and stomach muscles flexing in torment, he needed her.

They didn't speak.

She wanted penetration, his cock deep between her legs, forcefully taking possession of her.

Drawing in a hissing breath, she felt the heat of the sunset disappear. She shuddered.

He smiled faintly and mouthed something to her – something she missed. He pulled himself away.

She groaned.

'I've never known a bitch more willing to spread her legs than you are.' His hard brutal voice slapped her hard.

Ouch.

Their eyes met again in the mirror – his challenging, daring, and hers startled and slightly wounded. He smiled grimly, slipped the silk from his neck and draped it over his own protuberant cock.

She watched his big hand work the delicate cool silk over himself, deliberately, tauntingly sliding the fabric downwards stiffening his cock more before finally tying it loosely around his neck.

The Princess paused, then lowered herself to a sitting position with one leg angled outwards. Undulating her hips invitingly, she sighed and moaned at him. Barely brushing her taut nipples with long dark fingernails, she panted hard and pleaded with her eyes.

She wanted him to take her with his relentless primitive force – possess her, pump her, hump her, ride her, and ferociously ram her.

Instead his fingers traced intricate patterns on her

body. His hands moved freely, intimately, possessively, exploring every inch of her flesh.

Revelling in the sensation, Martha moaned with pleasure when his hands lifted her buttocks, positioning her hips so that the reflection of her hot, wet pussy was captured by the eye of the necklace.

'Don't move,' he whispered.

But she did. The long fingers of her right hand delved into her open lower lips to stroke her clit. She gasped when both his strong hands cupped her full tits and stroked the burgeoning nipples with his thumbs.

Arching herself against the massaging caress of his hands, the feel of him, she moaned and ground her hips. He tormented her nipples while she crammed her fingers tightly inside herself. Shivering with pleasure, the feel of his powerful virile hands on her flesh, the scent of wanton sex smothering them, she felt her body vibrate with passion and knew she was ready.

Oh, baby. Oh, baby.

His arms gripped her tighter.

Then, growling, he nudged her forward so that she fell off the chair and to her knees. He literally tossed the chair across the room, lifted her under her hips so she was perfectly placed on all fours between him and the mirror, and without another word took her.

Hard and hot. He pumped her from behind. The sensation grew more and more intense. Her butt shimmied with his every stroke, pushing up against him, encouraging him. His rough hard hands grasped her hips and helped her pump. Powerful strokes sent them both into a savage lustful fury.

Inviting his thrusts, the Princess whimpered a sigh of acquiescence, of submission. Her body vibrated against his hardness. He lifted her hips higher, spreading her legs further apart, driving himself, forcefully and painfully embedding his cock deep within her, filling her, pounding her.

The heat.

She couldn't move. He possessed her.

He was the centre of her universe, her reality. All pleasure and pain came from him. All sensation radiated from him.

His thrusts were sometimes long and slow and hard against her softness, the enfolding heat of her pussy. Wanting it. Wanting him. Pumping it. Pumping him. She let loose unintelligible little sounds of delicious surrender at the back of her throat in rhythm with his thrusting.

He ground his hips against her long and hard, his cock still deep within her, tormenting her, tantalising her, gyrating tauntingly now, wanting her, punishing her, taking her again and again, shifting her hips to take his cock more fully, more intensely. Pumping for it.

She begged him for release.

'Please, Joaquin, please. Fuck me!'

Her urgency made her twinge and spasm as she continued to grind her pussy against him harder and harder.

He came back into her, hammering brutally, holding her tightly when her thrashing threatened to separate them. In one heart-stopping, shattering explosion they were both left breathless.

A stillness, a silence filled only with their animalistic panting, followed. Still joined, he lowered her hips, kneeling and relaxing his chest momentarily over her back.

Their eyes met in the mirror, hers blue, sated, and happy, and his eyes guarded, and cold.

She angled her hips and pushed downwards to

embed him more deeply within her as they both relaxed.

'Oh, Princess.' He almost chuckled. 'You do me right.'

Supporting himself with his knees, he let his hard hands soothe her sweaty flesh. It was only his cock connecting them now, and she revelled in the feel of the filling length and depth of him. Lovely. Oh yes. Exquisite.

The scent of their sex permeated the room. The sunlight was gone. She reached out for him in the darkness as he panted, his heartbeat thudding through her from his cock, his lathered body just barely touching hers.

He caught his breath.

His hands cushioned her butt, settling her, pushing her downwards and guiding her until she could feel his pulsating cock stirring back to life in her hot, wet core.

His body was rippling, undulating, grinding against hers again, tantalising her by moving his hot cock so hard and so deep within her.

Slowly he rode her, up and down, up and down, all around. She reared back to feel him more fully, more deeply, and to allow him to possess her more completely.

His entire body melted around her, through her. In the darkness they collapsed together onto the thick carpet, still connected by his throbbing member in her pulsing pussy.

Oh, baby. Oh, baby. Good drugs. Good sex. It was a good game.

But that's all it was to her, a game.

Huddled against his rock-solid chest, she took his powerful arms and wrapped them around her. He kissed her shoulder ever so lightly.

The Princess was happy now.

The Princess was content. And sleepy.

She awakened hours later, on the carpet, naked and alone. Lying very still, she slowly and carefully took stock of her surroundings before she moved.

He was gone. Only the devastating aroma of their sex remained behind. The suite was empty.

She was alone.

The thrill was gone.

The controlling bastard was gone.

She could escape!

Hell, she could cut and run right now.

But she no longer wanted to run. Yawning, she stretched her body and took her nails to the carpet. The air-conditioning was on full and she was cold. She loved being cold. It was never cold in Hell.

So she popped a few more pills, crawled between the crisp clean sheets, and rested her head on the soft pillow.

It was the last time he fucked her.

The last time he fucked anyone.

The pills were great. Sleepy, blissfully sleepy didn't even begin to describe the bliss she found dreaming on his pills. Beyond exultant. The Princess was floating in a painless heaven.

6 Dead Man's Curve

The air-con had made the sheets on the bed luscious and divine. The pills had eased the horrors of reality. Her every sexual desire and appetite had been fulfilled, and now her entire body lay relaxed, well pampered, and happy, happy, happy.

But she wasn't so happy that she didn't realize almost immediately that the man's hands on her naked body didn't belong to Joaquin Xavier Lee.

A stranger in the night?

How exciting.

His hands were rough and slightly callused, but not as hard or demanding or anywhere near as possessive as her husband's. This man's touch lacked the roughness and lusty hunger necessary to stir her from her happy floating sleep. These new hands were strong but compassionate, and too tender and considerate to unleash her sexual fury.

She ignored him and enjoyed the drowsy happiness.

He stroked her naked body with admiration and cooed softly in her ear in Spanish. His breath was hot in contrast to her flesh. She liked him immediately, whoever he was.

Oh my, yes. A stranger in the dark.

From her distant blissful sleepy place she was vaguely aware of the stranger moving around the suite. He was packing. Occasionally he would stop in his labours and run his long slender fingers across her shoulders and breasts.

'Martha,' he cooed to her. 'Martha, wake up.'

But the Princess didn't want to surrender the pleasantness of floating in nothingness. She'd been a very good girl and deserved this prize. Why was this man ruining her fun? And she was having fun, floating free, naked, and satisfied in her sleep. She didn't want to be bothered with a stranger or sex or reality. All she wanted to do was to glide through the painlessness.

Later she had a vague awareness of shouting. The stranger was arguing with someone – a woman. Two women. Then harsh, unwelcome female hands jerked her upright in bed and dragged her into the shower.

The cool water made her nipples tighten, and her flesh shivered with arousing sensuality, but her mind fought her body and she remained happily drifting without the bother of the real world.

The first recognizable jolt of nasty reality happened later. How much later? Martha had no idea. It was that icky hospital smell that did it, that pulled her back into existence again. She was seated on one of those uncomfortable hard plastic chairs in a hospital hallway, holding a warm cup of coffee between her trembling fingers. The floating suddenly ended. Taking a deep breath the displeased Princess frowned.

What the hell was this all about?

Who was hurt?

Why was she here and not in her comfy bed?

It slowly dawned on her that someone must have slipped her an upper and brought her here. The Princess's cherished lethargic downers had been violently and cruelly assassinated by someone else's drug.

Yucky! No. Not nice.

With her heart pounding wildly and blood rushing through her entire body, Martha was now wide awake and suffering from an intensely dry mouth. Her tongue was a hairy thing without movement.

What the fuck?

Although she was dressed in her new silken underwear, a tight, beige linen dress, and designer open-toed heels, she had absolutely no recollection of dressing, or leaving the hotel suite, or travelling, or anything else. She didn't remember anything except the stranger's hands stroking her beautiful tits.

What was happening?

Now she was frightened. She looked up and down the corridor for a clue.

Nothing – at least at first.

Then, out of the corner of her eye, she saw something on the other side of the swinging door.

No.

Mysteriously, once on her feet she had no sense of dropping the coffee that splattered on the tiled floor, or the tiny hot droplets burning her toes and ankles. She somehow rushed forwards, through the swinging doors.

It was incredible.

It was horrible. Terrible.

Although she had heard a woman screaming, the Princess hadn't been aware it was herself until much later, when her throat was sore – much, much later, when the horrible reality at the hospital was far behind her and she was safely wrapped in a warm blanket, nestled in Harvey's strong arms before a roaring campfire.

Harvey was the stranger. He was a *vaquero*.

They were alone now, somewhere north of St George, Utah, in one of those canyons with the large round white boulders nestling oddly against the dramatic blood-red sandy cliffs. The stranger held her close and mumbled comforting things in Spanish. Somehow it was better in Spanish. She didn't want to concentrate on words, or meanings. Only the comfort. Like great music in a strange tongue.

Her body was racked with tension. Martha trembled with an uncontrollable cold the likes of which she'd never known before. She'd always loved the cold. But now, no matter how much wood he piled on the campfire, she couldn't feel warmth. Brrr. Cold. She was cold through and through.

Harvey was a mature Mexican cowboy type with distinguished silver streaks in his short black hair and moustache. He claimed to be Joaquin Xavier Lee's partner and best friend. He could speak English, but more often spoke in Spanish, saying little she understood.

The Princess was not happy now. No. No. No.

Not pleased.

Staring into the flames Martha saw the beaten and slashed body of her Warrior husband, lying in the hospital bed. Someone had beaten him damn near to death and then taken a knife to his flesh. In the dancing light of the roaring cedar blaze she saw him lying there, defeated, destroyed. Even if he survived, it was all over for him.

He would never be a god again.

He would never be a Warrior.

Hell, he would be lucky if his brain ever worked well enough for him to do much more than drool.

There had never been anyone like her Warrior before in her life. No one.

Surprised to discover that she was going to miss him, Martha sighed in regret. Violence in America.

Her Warrior had possessed the body of a god and had made her come like a freight train. In the middle of one her breakdowns and freak-outs, he'd offered her a job, a chance to get money from Margaret, and he'd proposed to her. Married her. Slapped her around and loved her. And what was worst of all, he'd made her feel for him.

Not good.

Never feel. Not for a man. Not any man. They were never worth it. Never. People weren't worth it.

But in the flames of the fire she kept seeing herself reflected in the mirror as she knelt on all fours before him, begging him to fuck her from behind. Begging him to lick her and bite her and suck her and fuck her. Fuck her hard and nasty. Fuck her rough and make her submissive. There for a moment, in the heat of all the fucking, he'd convinced her that he was her almighty, strong and powerful, sex god. She'd believed he could protect her from the unseen horrors lurking in the darkest recesses of her life. Rescue her.

But no. Damn it. Poor Joaquin would be better off dead.

She swallowed and struggled to bury all memories of Joaquin. The pleasure and pain he'd made her feel was no more. Damn. Feeling. That's always where the pain lurks.

Suck 'em and fuck 'em and leave 'em.

Rough and nasty. Quick and hard.

Fuck 'em and exit.

Never look back. Never think back. That was the mantra of her life. And whenever she broke that mantra, it was always disastrous. Like now.

Her ears were still ringing from the cocktails of drug she'd had before leaving Vegas with the *vaquero*, Harvey. What was she going to do now?

The compassionate and caring *vaquero* gently rocked her back and forth, squeezing and caressing the length of her, humming some old-world Latin love song. Harvey seemed like such a strange name for a Mexican cowboy. He'd probably bought it either at the border or later in East LA. It didn't matter to Martha. She didn't even want to know his name and she sure as hell didn't want him to break into English. No way did she need to have any more of the details explained to her.

What she needed was a good fuck.

Yes. All she needed was hot sex.

Warm her blood up. Bring life back to her body.

Yes. Sex.

And Mexican was the special for tonight.

While the *vaquero* continued to soothe her as if she were a child, with gentle stroking and soft words, the needy Princess took his hand firmly in hers and led it to her gorgeous tits.

Make me feel better, big cowboy.

He hesitated only a moment before he massaged her nipples. Oh *si, si, señor.*

When his endearing and comforting mumblings in Spanish annoyed her, she simply told him to shut up.

He did. Real quick.

Good.

Opening the blankets surrounding her, she reached out for his warmth. One yank and his zipper went down, another and his cock was in her hand.

That was what she needed: a good cock.

He did nothing.

His cock, however, was throbbing and bone-hard immediately. Rolling towards him, she inhaled his masculine scent, now almost smothered by the burning cedar of the fire. Oh yeah, Mexican tonight.

There was a good cock in her hand. What else did the Princess want?

A big cock in her mouth.

Sliding her tits along his body, she rained hot kisses all over him while clutching and manipulating his throbbing organ until she grabbed the root of it tightly in her hands. She took him in her mouth and sucked his ridged tip. There was more and more of him. He thrust in short, erotic little movements. She sucked him, all of him. Sucked and sucked until urgent groans accompanied the first salty taste of his creamy drops. She sucked and sucked and pulled him deep into her throat, pulling all the spunk from him until he was bone-dry and sagging.

When she released the *vaquero*, his dark eyes still flamed with desire. Grasping her chin, he turned her mouth to his and, slanting his mouth over hers, he devoured her lips with his kiss. Her body writhed against his, easing her now wet and wanting pussy back and forth across him. He lifted the skirt of her dress and she spread her legs.

When he delved his fingers around her moist silk panties and into her, she moaned, pulling her thighs together to imprison them there.

He pressed his fingers tighter. She drew in a sharp breath.

'You are Joaquin's wife,' he cooed passionately in English.

Oh yuck. Why the hell did she keep finding the talkers? Didn't any guys just like to fuck without conversation any more?

She ignored his words and communicated her need. With his dark eyes still smouldering with fervour, he slid his fingers still deeper into her, forcing her to hiss with pleasure. As she slightly relaxed the pressure of her thighs, he twisted his fingers and shoved.

Deep breath.

She wanted it; she needed it. Opening her legs to

allow him better penetration, she gyrated against his fingers, against his whole hand, working frantically with his rhythm. He pushed harder and harder. Her pussy responded.

It was good for her.

She came, shuddered, and relaxed.

Yum, yum.

The *vaquero* didn't release her. Instead he wrapped the warm blankets around them both and she rested in his warm strong embrace. He adored her. She knew it. Could feel it.

Yuck.

'If you were mine,' he whispered passionately, 'I would kill anyone who touched you.' He was so freaking sincere.

What the fuck? Blind devotion from a guy who claimed to be her husband's best friend and partner? No. No. No. Not what she needed.

'Do us both a favour, big *hombre*,' she murmured softly. His dark Bambi eyes continued to adore her. 'Don't speak any more English tonight.'

With the heat now returned to her body, she dismissed him. He felt it. Oh yes, she remained in his strong arms but Harvey knew she had used him and was now finished with him. He understood.

He wasn't totally stupid. He knew his place.

But still, to his credit, he didn't release her. They rested together until the flames of their campfire had died and the cold night had passed. With the morning sunlight, he took her, a rutting cock in a willing pussy, pumping it, driving it in with lots of Latin lusty passion but no force. No fire. No flame.

In the bright light of morning, Joaquin loomed powerfully between them. This old Mexican cowboy was screwing his best friend's wife. They both tried to push that detail aside and just enjoy the now, the fuck, but she was more successful than he was. However, the ugly reality that his best friend and partner might be dead in a hospital bed in Vegas didn't stop Harvey from fucking her.

No, he wanted the Princess.

And he took her.

And there it was. Even though that meant betraying his treasured friend, his partner, he took her. His ethics were nagging at him but he fucked her anyway.

A man of shallow character.

She wasn't impressed. Not with him. Nor with the fuck.

When they'd finished and packed up their few camp belongings, they headed south, back towards St George. She found it odd that she didn't have even the slightest memory of the old dented pick-up that might once have been either blue or steel grey. But she assumed he had driven her the three hours from Vegas to the campground in it.

The golden angel Moroni gleamed on top of the white temple in the beautiful morning sunlight. Disappointed that the *vaquero* was now wearing his brown cowboy hat pulled down to hide his guilty face, the Princess played the martyr.

'I need coffee,' she announced.

A dark shadow passed over his face. Maybe it was his voice, or perhaps it was his attitude, but suddenly a chill ran down Martha's spine.

This was not good.

'Something bad happened. Are you going to tell me about it?'

He shifted gears and nodded before speaking again. 'You belong to Joaquin.' He almost choked on his words.

She almost snorted. 'I don't belong to anyone.'

But Martha suddenly felt sick as she watched a tear run down the rugged cowboy's wrinkled face. Hell, he was going to unload and talk her to death. Nothing was worse than being trapped in a pick-up with a talkative, guilt-ridden Latin man.

Damn, damn, damn.

'It was supposed to be easy money. We were picking up a guy who'd jumped bail when everything went bad. It was Emily's fault. She went crazy, mad, totally furious, and walked out, leaving us all without backup. Frank got killed taking a bullet for Joaquin.'

Emily? Again, with this Emily babe?

The Princess didn't want to hear it. But what the hell? She told him what she knew.

'Joaquin loved Emily. She dumped him. It broke his heart. He only married me to get his hands on my family's money. And –' she paused '– maybe to piss her off a little.'

Harvey stared at her as if she were a freaking idiot.

'You don't believe that?' He almost spat the words out.

'Sure I do. That's what happened. I was there.'

He shook his head in disbelief.

Annoyed, Martha frowned. 'No? Then why don't you tell me what really happened?'

So he did. He told her an incredible story. An unbelievable story. A horror story. All about a handsome Warrior, his love for a Princess, and a wicked witch named Emily.

Bad news.

This *vaquero* guy was a real downer. The faster she unloaded him and his ugly stories, the better. But better than what? Being broke and alone?

What was she going to do?

Then it hit her, almost like the chime of distant bells. She'd play the private dick game. Yes, of course. It'd be fun. A thrill. A rush. All she had to do was wear the stupid necklace and point her tits at religious freaks. Crap, she could do that. Whatever the agency needed from her, she could deliver; she could worry about the finer details later.

What a rush!

The Princess wasn't walking away from that kind of easy money and such an entertaining game.

In fact, she could do it better without Joaquin, because those crazy, power-hungry cult guys were always burning with the passion of the Lord and fucking with the force of the Devil. Hell yes. She'd play along.

Get laid. Get money. Get thrilled.

'Harvey, I've heard enough. Take me to Nephi, then get lost.' Her harsh tones jerked his face towards her.

'What? No. No. You can't be serious.'

'But I am.' She flashed him a Princess smile. Was he going to give her a hard time? No. She'd hit him hard with guilt and have her way. 'Remember, Harvey, I have a husband damn near cut to death to support. No doubt we'll have medical bills. So as his wife, I can either earn some money doing the Nephi cult thing or sell my body on Sunset Boulevard. Which do you think he'd prefer?'

Harvey winced in real emotional pain. 'No. Don't you understand anything yet?'

'I understand that someone had better be on the other end of this necklace signal to save my ass if I get into trouble, or I could get killed, or worse. Far worse. End up like my dear husband, your best friend.'

Guilt. It worked every time. His facial expression said it all.

Victory! She had him by the balls. Guilt, the weapon most women choose.

So her new job was dangerous.

Well? More nervous than she wanted to admit, Martha flashed Harvey a confident smile.

'I'll be fine. After all, these cult crazies *are* part of my extended family. What do you think they'll do when I show them the bruises on my body and tell them all about my violent new husband?'

'They're treacherous people.'

'As treacherous as members of the agency?' the Princess added, and then licked her lips as she gathered her thoughts. 'I'll go in, be friendly with my idiotic family, and let the necklace do the rest. Isn't that it?' She sneered at him. 'Joaquin is my partner. And unlike Emily, I'm not going to hurt him.' Then to really make him feel bad she added, 'I'm going to be a great partner.'

Poor Harvey looked exhausted. 'You fucked me.'

'You fucked me,' she corrected him.

That was the nail in the coffin. He drove her the four hours north into Nephi without any attempt at further conversation.

After parking the old Ford loaded with household items in the parking lot of a Victorian bed and breakfast, the *vaquero* lowered the brim of his cowboy hat and quickly disappeared on foot. The Princess swallowed hard and fingered her necklace.

7 When She Was Good, She Was Very Very Good, But When She Was Bored, She Got Weird

'Listed on the National Register of Historic Places, the Whitmore Mansion in Nephi, Utah, opens its six bedrooms, two bridal suites, and one family suite, each with private baths, to the public for tours and lodging. Recently renovated to reflect its original Victorian beauty, the 1898 sandstone mansion features carved gingerbread designs and quaint turrets with curved glass windows.' The Princess immediately fell in love with her new palace.

Sweet. Yes. Delightful. Charming. The Princess paid for an entire month in advance with the agency cash Harvey had given her, before happily moving into one of the bridal suites with her pills, her fancy silk underwear, and the rest of the Vegas booty.

Yes indeed. Life was suddenly very good. Exactly the kind of small out-of-the-way palace she could enjoy while playing respectable and living on the agency allowances until the cash flow came in from Margaret. Oh yes, the Princess was feeling mighty fine. Joaquin and Big Gus's agency was paying her to hang out here? All right.

Beat the hell out of working on the chain gang. Woohaw.

Martha could do this new spy job, undercover con, private-dick thing. No problem. It was just another con game. Wear a necklace and point her gorgeous tits in the direction of cult members. If she'd known she could find legit cons that were this easy, she might have considered it years ago.

Really?

Naw. But it was a fun new game. A cheap new thrill.

'Welcome to the Whitmore Mansion, Mrs Lee.' Her modest hostess noted the poor Princess's bruised body and offered a kind of quiet sympathy as she explained that guests were invited to gather each morning in the dining room for a delicious breakfast.

Small towns. Gossip was the air they breathed. It was definitely too easy. Before dark everyone respectable in Nephi would know about the abused little Princess shacked up in the Whitmore Mansion looking for safety and protection.

She wouldn't have to do a damn thing.

Given time, members of her extended family would come looking for her. This was a beautiful con. And Joaquin thought this up, huh? Good enough. Maybe she could really get into this new reputable Mrs Lee thing for a year, so she could collect from Margaret. Sure. No problem.

Maybe.

If the respectable con didn't mean boring. The Princess didn't do boring.

The first hurdle in this new con game? The law. Oh yes, the law would come by with questions. From experience Martha figured that first thing in the morning the man with the star would arrive to check the situation out. The locals didn't want any trouble. Not the kind of trouble a battered female stranger brought to their tiny decent hamlet.

And as soon as the law found out who her deceased Daddy was, they'd tell the fine upstanding Church leaders, who in turn would no doubt inform the appropriate members of her extended family living among the nearby polygamists. The family would be by to rescue their wayward Princess.

'Totally brilliant, Joaquin.' She shook her head in amazement. 'Simple. Easy. Clean. The ideal reputable pastime for a Princess like me.'

Absolutely superb. His whole approach was so very straightforward and so faultless. So *flawless*. It amazed her. If he was looking to find someone hiding within the cult, no doubt the All-Seeing necklace around her neck would do the trick.

Oh, that dirty dog. Joaquin really knew how to take advantage of a gal's meltdown. Wow. He'd pimped her for his glory quick enough. His use of her was so perfectly low-key. For the first time, Martha realised she'd married a very brainy con artist. So, good fucking and excellent instincts might not be his only virtues, huh? Sweet.

Evening drinks and a light snack were provided for Martha and the other guests as they read in the parlour or chatted out on the veranda. The entire palace and staff provided her with the most luxurious of accommodations in the centre of the quiet rural central Utah community. *Happy Days*. *Pollyanna*, even.

Nephi might be in the boondocks, totally a Mormon Mayberry, but her mountain valley palace was divine. Life was excellent.

She had more cash than she could possibly spend in a mini-hellhole like Nephi, and at least a month's worth of clean prescription drugs to help her continue the unpleasant withdrawal from the Miami drug storm.

And no attachments. No demands. And plenty of time. Time was on her side. She had a year to kill. Maybe that was too much time. But the good news was that now, thanks to Joaquin, she had an answer. That old 'What am I doing with my life?' quandary no longer nagged at her. Because now she had an answer.

A good one too.

Getting into the whole new Mrs Joaquin Xavier Lee gig while becoming *Princess Perfect* was a good thing. Yup. She could do this.

OK. The time had come to dump her drug dependency, get totally clean, and go absolutely straight.

Boo hoo. The Princess enjoyed drugs. But *hasta la vista*, drugged comfort.

Carefully considering everything that hopping on the drug-free bandwagon meant, the Princess relaxed in the huge claw-and-ball bathtub of her honeymoon suite. Too bad the groom wasn't there to scrub her back.

Oh yes, the Princess loved warm soapy bubbles. Intense headache fading. Body tension slowly relaxing. 'Aaah,' she sighed in delight. 'Oh Joaquin, baby. How I wish you were here.' She almost giggled as she massaged her throbbing temples. 'I'd do you good, baby. I'd do you damn *good*.'

Except that her once handsome Joaquin wasn't actually there. No one was. Bad luck. She'd need a sex partner or a decent vibrator soon, if not immediately. Then she might be able to face the drug-free months ahead. Only one year to go until Margaret delivered the big bucks. Maybe. Getting clean would have been a lot easier with Joaquin around. Sex with him had been a good distraction.

Married, huh? She was a married woman.

Mrs Joaquin Xavier Lee.

A husband? Wow!

Steady-guy things had never been a popular concept with Martha. Poor potty habits. And she wasn't into sharing a bathroom. Her steady-guy things were always restricted to her mark in a con.

Tonight, soaking in the warm bath, she sighed again in straightforward regret; Joaquin possessed possibilities as a husband, lover, and business partner. Legally, he was her new steady guy. She felt frustration with his absence. Remorse. Lament. Sexual disappointment.

Big sigh. Forget Joaquin.

Now Harvey, on the other hand, had been a good carry-her-through-to-the-next-highway-exit fuck. Sex with him had been agreeable, but meaningless. Common. Just another cock on the road. Not a primo fuck like Joaquin. No surprise, the Princess yearned for more primo. Much more. After all, a true Princess just didn't primo fuck with a Warrior god like Joaquin Xavier Lee and then stop. No. No. No.

Wasn't going to happen. Playing nun was never fun. Not good. Boring.

Not Martha's favourite lifestyle choice. She needed to feel alive. Yes, alive.

The Princess was no dummy. Daddy had sent her to enough shrinks through the years to understand the basic concept behind twelve-step programmes. Duh! Replace the addiction. Step by step. Replace the negative with a positive. Give up drinking yourself shitless every night and instead attend rehab meetings and support groups to suck down caffeine and tobacco, while working at signalling others for help. Replace the bad thing with a good one.

Stupid. But it worked for most people.

Simple. Stupid. And horrifically challenging.

However, the Princess figured she was ahead in the game. She already knew herself. Very few surprises any more.

Getting clean? Perfect addition to the game. Great for appearances. The poor lonely Princess hiding. Seeking salvation for her sins. Kicking drugs. Dumping alcohol. Eating healthy. Exercising. Keeping the Word of Wisdom.

Woo. Word of Wisdom healthy. Interesting challenge.

Margaret would love it.

OK. She'd live the Word. All part of playing out Joaquin's con. Unnerving.

'Oh, Joaquin, you charming anaconda,' she moaned aloud, sinking further down into the comforting warm water full of beautiful bubbles before laughing aloud in begrudging respect. Oh yes. Joaquin Xavier Lee was good. Very good. 'You damn dirty dog.'

But time was now a new friend. A new confidence emerged. She'd play and ultimately win. She'd earn Margaret's millions – and take the master.

She'd need a major body makeover to match the terms of Margaret's agreement while earning the sympathy and respect of the local goody-goodies for the con. Margaret wanted her bad little sister to transform into Princess Perfect. Word of Wisdom perfect in both mind and body. Oh yuck. Oh dull. Oh pooh. Word of Wisdom yucky – nasty.

'Fuck it, I can survive this.'

And win. Oh yes. She would live the Word and play out Joaquin's con. Reflecting on him now made her ache. Remembering the primo sex in the Vegas palace made her nipples tighten. Hot damn. But the pleasure and thrill of his hard body were now long gone.

Adios. Happy trails. Dark hole. No need to relive that fuck.

Her Warrior god had vanished. Lost. Not by choice, but simply viciously ripped from her. Destroyed. Abrupt. Unexpected. Gone.

'Oh, Joaquin.' Martha whispered his name in the darkness in lamented worship.

Violence.

Bam! A bolt from the blue.

Crack! Shock. Numbness. Then reaction. Different for different people. The Princess and the best-friend *vaquero* had been physically sickened at the violence done to the mighty Warrior Joaquin Xavier Lee. Sick. Actually she'd been throwing up and hysterical, that kind of sick. A shocking kind of sick. Amazingly sick.

It troubled her.

Nevertheless, sick shit happens. In America, violent shit happens. Often.

Death on the highways, brutality in the streets, and even in the behind-the-green-doors of American suburbia, it happened. Daily, often, and wholly uncontrollably violent.

The best fuck she'd ever had was from a bank teller who'd been held hostage in a now infamous North Hollywood bank robbery. During the extended shoot-out the No Ho cops dashed to the local B&B Gun Shop on Magnolia to borrow weapons. The law didn't even pack enough weapon power to take those bad boys down. The bad boys wore Superman bullet suits and packed a damn arsenal. Automatic weapons pumping out thousands of dirty bullets in a heartbeat. Bonnie and Clyde nasty.

Blood. Death. A whole, ugly, nasty, brutal, Round-heads vs the Younger and James brothers scene. The experience had left the terrified guy with a six-hour hard-on, and fortunately the Princess had been there to help him through his crisis.

Violence. It was the American way. Praise Old Glory, apple pie, and the National Rife Association. Ah, yes. Born in the USA! Where a man could still be judged by the size of his gun and how he uses it, instead of the size of his penis.

Remember the Alamo. Teddy Roosevelt. And Hiroshima.

Oh, Yankee boy, *be* bad. Yes, very bad.

Obviously diverse individuals reacted differently at different times to carnage, but when the Princess had seen the magnificent Joaquin beaten and cut beyond recognition in an ICU hospital bed, something had snapped inside her. Her Daddy was dead. Margaret demanded Princess Perfect. Big Gus fought for life in the Valley. Nevertheless, it had taken the violence done to Joaquin to finally freeze her blue blood, freeze it frigidity cold. Dead cold. Turned Martha into a total Ice Princess. She needed heat to survive.

Life. Immediately.

Heat with Harvey in the canyon had thawed her out some, reminded her that she was still alive. Living. Breathing. Touching. Flourishing. From time to time, everyone needed reminding.

Everyone. Warm blood pulsing. Pumping.

As far as she was concerned, sex was the fastest and best way to feel life thrusting throughout her entire body.

Life. Sex. Passion. The best part of living.

Passion following violence was usually hot for her.

The Princess imagined sex in a foxhole to be a raging inferno. Even so, no fiery inferno tonight. Damn it! After her long and comforting bubble bath, the imperfect Princess went naked to the canopied, four-poster bed. Alone. All alone. Sniffle. Sniffle.

The huge elevated bed, and for that matter the entire suite, smelled of roses. Turning off the bedside lamp and curling her toes beneath the clean, lace-trimmed sheets, Martha let her hands gently massage her lovely tits. She relaxed in the dark, her headache fading. Frowning, she remembered again the so-so sex with Harvey in the canyon. Although their sex had served as a quick fix, it had hardly satisfied her.

No. Alas, the Princess's Daddy had called her 'A low-life sex junkie. Without ethics or morals. Without any personal respect or discipline. Without control.'

Maybe she was. Or maybe Daddy had been a religious prude who failed to acknowledge anything but Victorian sexual ethic as gospel. Maybe.

Or maybe it was nothing more than a simple life-style choice for her. Maybe.

With only a hint of the bubble bath's scent on her skin, the Princess let her fingertips make lazy circles around her navel and flat stomach. Totally rejecting the memory of the panting Latin-lover Harvey she instead reflected on the violence done to her handsome Joaquin. It wasn't pretty.

Even if he recovered, he'd never be the same.

Gone was his perfect muscle control and idyllic body.

And the strength.

The fierce control. The sweltering passion. The magnificence. The exhilaration. The pleasure.

No more. What a waste.

Stroking her nakedness she sighed in honest regret and closed her eyes, longing for the feel of his rough callused hands on her again. She could have fucked him further. But more than likely, he'd never fuck again.

Poor baby. He was part of the walking wounded now.

But that didn't mean the game was over. No. He might be wounded. But he wasn't defeated. Not yet.

Oh no. Time for a living, breathing Princess to take their game to the next level. Time was on her side. Because by the time he got up out of that hospital bed, Princess Perfect would be so far ahead, it would all be over but the crying.

Although quickies with Joaquin's guilt-ridden partner may have left her sexually wanting, the bizarre story Harvey told her about Joaquin had proved most interesting.

Revealing. Remarkable. Curious. If true.

Harvey claimed Joaquin was a true voyeur, and that was the major reason his career had been so successful. Watching from the shadows, perfect profession for a voyeur. Her Daddy had paid Joaquin big bucks to watch his wayward Princess. Watch her. Shadow her. Keep track of her. And report in. He'd been watching for years. Years! Like almost a decade. Since she was a runaway kid.

She couldn't pin down how she felt about it.

And Martha never spotted Joaquin's shadow?

Oh, he was damn good. Because she was a pro. And he'd outplayed her. Was Harvey telling the truth? The whole truth? Nothing but the truth? Or just the truth as he knew it.

One man's truth wasn't necessarily another's reality.

'I know all your dirty little tricks.' She could hear his voice in her head. Well, at least he'd been honest.

Her skin tingled. Too creepy. Eerie. Sinister. Paranoid material enough for this Princess's diary.

But regrettably Harvey's truth not only had her serving as the focus of Joaquin's financial livelihood and personal live entertainment, but also as his personal film star. Harvey said that whenever possible Joaquin recorded her – her wild adventurous and very active sex life, all for his own private viewing later. Invasion of privacy happening here. Insult happening, maybe? No. Not exactly. More like straight-up anxiety.

Still, the repulsive truth grew more sinister.

Through the years Joaquin ultimately grew obsessed with his job, obsessed with watching her. With her. The Princess. Martha. Her. He'd turned *her* into his private sick fantasy. And his only lover. Soon his intense passion for her crippled all his other relationships. It sounded totally unbelievable. Very Wes Craven. Hitchcock even. But, for some odd reason, she believed it. Or at least part of it.

Maybe because Martha understood obsession.

Not everyone did.

According to Harvey's truth, the handsome Joaquin had never fucked the mysterious and vengeful Emily. Not once. Nor anyone else for years. Unbelievable. He'd watch, not just the Princess but other people. Always watched. Never participated. Never touched. Never allowed contact to happen.

Instead, he'd touch himself later, alone, either from the shadows, watching her, or in private with footage of her.

Weird and wonderful.

So he'd preferred to watch her fuck other people than have sex with someone himself?

Wow. Strange choice. But not her choice, or her responsibility.

His. His alone. Joaquin nurtured one of those personal stalker/prey wacko things with her, huh? *One Hour Photo* creepy and beyond.

As the Princess concentrated on Joaquin, she

caressed herself, circling gently with her fingertips. And what was truly scary? She hadn't even been suspicious. Bloodcurdling concept. Not only hadn't she ever spotted him lurking about in the shadows, not once in all those years, and *that* was horrifying enough, but she didn't even get the thrill.

Watching? Too *Rear Window* for her.

What a waste of life. All those wasted hours, weeks, months, years, spent watching her. No one was that interesting. Not even the Princess.

She didn't understand the fascination. Nope. Watching was certainly no substitute for living.

No couch potatoes or internet jockeys here. As far as Martha was concerned, watching was only foreplay. She needed action, delivery. Life.

No one was going to live her life for her. No instant replays purchased on life's moments.

Live now. Live in the moment. That's all there is.

After much reflection, Harvey's truths helped Martha re-evaluate Joaquin's more brutal appetites and a certain amount of the bondage shit. It was his manner. His style. His touch. Developed with her after years of fantasy sex.

His choice. With her. And it had been primo. He'd done her good. Done her primo.

Hard to believe that anyone not into touching could deliver such primo. That level of skill developed only with practice. Recalling now how often he'd backed away from her touch made some sense if Harvey's truth was reality, and so she somehow forgave him. For what, she couldn't identify.

But she could tell what it was doing to her. Forgiving made her tingle. Strange mind and body rush. Tingling.

Oh, baby!

Prickling with the newborn tingling phenomenon, Martha fondled and hugged herself while struggling to recall every detail of her sex life with Joaquin. Control. It had all been about power control. His. Hadn't it?

This was the main problem with Harvey's story. For a guy who was supposed to be totally into watching, he'd sure taken up manhandling her fast enough. Bondage. Control. Power. His. He always got his way. He was the boss. He was the husband. He was the *hombre*.

'This marriage is a business partnership. I'm the husband. I'm the boss. You'll do what I say,' he'd command with that sexier-than-hell voice of his. 'Trust me.'

His tenor tones whispering to her when she needed comfort.

'Trust me,' played again and again in her head.

Trust, right?

Like he was some fine upstanding trustworthy person. Yeah, right. Business, huh? Well, he was the one who made their business partnership personal. He'd showed up with a pre-nuptial agreement all worked out and ready for her to sign. Oh yes. He was the boss, the husband, and the con master.

He could be cruel. Tying her up whenever he left the room or whenever he decided to suck and fuck her. And when they'd left the suite together, always together, he'd smothered her. Manhandled her. Controlled her. He'd say, 'Remember, I know all your dirty little tricks, Princess.'

When she'd whined and complained, he responded with, 'I'm working here. Relax, Princess. Eat something. Take a pill. Trust me, Princess.'

Right. More like, 'Let me con you, Princess.'

'Trust me,' he'd say again and again.

Lying in her warm comfy bed, she imagined his rich voice and her body responded. 'Trust me.'

She missed his voice. He had a damn sexy voice.

It felt *good* to think back on their primo sex in the luxury of her rose-scented and canopied bed. Obviously her new handsome husband carried tons of baggage she hadn't seen; too much for a ravenous Princess with a lust for life and cheap thrills.

No men with baggage. Too heavy. She had enough luggage of her own.

More of Harvey's story. This part she believed. The Emily chick loved the handsome Joaquin regardless. They'd developed one of those kinky but strangely mature sensual relationships. She'd masturbate regularly for him and fuck other guys and gals while he watched, in what Harvey described as attempts to lure Joaquin into her web and trap him. Apparently it had sickened her, but she'd done it anyway.

Someone needed to drop a house on this Emily chick.

It was obviously an immature ploy designed to excite the voyeur into sexual activity. Silly. Childish. Unsuccessful. Evidently Emily didn't know much about sexual appetites. Nope, the wicked witch didn't sound at all smart to the Princess. The witch desperately tried everything and anything to make Joaquin touch her, fuck her, make love to her. Desperate. Unsuccessful. And oh so very irrational. Stupid bitch.

Nope. The Warrior never fucked the witch. Apparently he should have.

Because if best-pal Harvey could be believed, and the Princess was the only one Joaquin had touched, then no wonder the witch had lost it. Betrayal. All those wasted years. Yoo-hoo, fellas, female fury fuelling up in torpedo tube two. Extreme battle conditions.

Were all men totally brainless about women, or what? Bad luck Emily finding out about Martha like that. Shitty bad luck.

'Access to the wrong agency computer,' Harvey had admitted sullenly.

Damn bad luck. Stupid All-Seeing necklace. Think about it.

Since Joaquin's proposal in the Vegas dump, the All-Seeing had been sending the Princess's life back in full living colour to anyone with the computer access code. Voyeur heaven happening. Had Joaquin known that the witch had the access code to the All-Seeing?

Harvey didn't know. While in the old truck on the way to Nephi, Harvey had told her that 'Emily took one look at you sucking Joaquin's balls and went into speechless shock. Later, she snapped.'

Revenge. He'd fucked her for revenge.

Now Joaquin was fucked. And better off dead.

Revenge was such a nasty bitch. An immense, malicious, treacherous bitch. A true Lizzie Borden with an axe. Lorraine Bobbit with a butcher knife. Amy Fisher, the North Island Lolita, with a gun.

Only revenge is best served cold, right? The Princess hadn't slept through Shakespeare. No way. 'With my last breath, I stab at thee.'

Revenge. All her instincts told her that if, and when, Joaquin ever made it up on his own two feet again, the Emily bitchy witch was in big trouble.

Oh yes.

The bitch would be going down.

He'd take her down. And out. Revenge. Sweet iceberg revenge.

Arching her back slightly the Princess's fingers glided a tango over her lower lips. She needed pleasure. Life. Picturing the gory mass of bloody meat that had once been her husband, boss, and lover Joaquin Xavier Lee, Martha found her G-spot. She was alive.

Alive. Passionate. Pulsing. Sweltering. Concentrating on him. Recalling his body. Imagining his touch. Wham! His macho scent and taste rushed forth from her memory banks.

'Joaquin,' she screamed out with passion. 'Please, Joaquin, fuck me. Please. Oh, Joaquin,' she begged, just the way he liked it.

Sensory rush. Recall. Sensory and memory total recall. A little trick she'd picked up in acting class. Oh yes. He was there, with her. Joaquin was present, in her mind's eye and pleasuring touch. She could smell him. Taste him. Feel him. Her hands were his hands. Her touch, his calloused cruel touch. He was fucking her. Tormenting her. Oh yes. *Fantasy Island*, baby. Recalling his tremendous sadistic control, she imagined destroying it. Then she found satisfaction, and sighed in contentment. It was good. But . . .

She missed him.

Ouch!

She missed him? Damn straight. Martha told herself it was only natural. Nothing to worry about. After all, he'd continually smothered her since the moment they'd first met, and had taken complete control of her life, shoving food into her, bathing her, dressing her, and primo fucking her. What Princess wouldn't miss that kind of controlling monster?

Adorable monsters. Go figure.

With her sexual tension successfully released, the Princess relaxed and admitted to herself that she really did grieve for her dirty dog. Her grief wouldn't last, however. The emotional crap would pass. It always did.

She'd set it free, a trick that had always worked for her. And what the hell? He was gone. No regrets. She'd loved the thrill ride. A Princess could find another thick-dick mutt in any sewer or at any animal pound. Right?

Besides, the Princess didn't miss Joaquin Xavier Lee *exactly*, only the thrills he'd provided; that wasn't quite the same.

8 Elvira Does Mayberry

The next few days saw the Princess floating through a fairyland of beautiful antiques and polished wood. She forgot about the All-Seeing necklace, working for the agency or seeking out her family. Instead, she tried very, very hard not to swallow pills.

While her body trembled and revolted, and her complexion paled, Martha concentrated on emptying her mind and feeling nothing but sexual pleasure. She pleasured herself. Frequently. Often. Repeatedly. It was a very serious mind game.

She was sick. Very sick. Mind control absolutely necessary. Vomit management learned immediately. The drug withdrawal was nasty. She dumped all of the emotional and physical withdrawal reality, turned it off. Off. Off. Off. Nothing. A little trick she'd picked up somewhere in a yoga or mediation class or from a shrink. First nothingness. Numbness. All pain liberated first. Freedom. Freedom from the painful. Then, slowly, pleasure. Careful. Yes, a little bit at a time. Turn on pleasure. Yes. Enjoyment. Let sexual pleasure slide on through the mental numbness barricade into her reality consciousness.

The trick was to let only the *good* slip through.

The Princess mastered the trick but nevertheless the first three drug-free weeks were an agonizing hell for her. She was sick. That was to be expected.

'I can survive this,' was once again her mantra.

Only soon the poor Princess's magic fingers grew

weary. A vibrator and/or sex toys were an immediate need.

Difficulty. Calamity. Unsophisticated community.

No adult toy shops were available within over three hundred miles in any direction. Sex shops are not welcome in God's county. God, the angel Moroni, and his saints don't need a dildo. Not in the American Zion.

Only the Devil does.

Unfortunately, she was a fucking demon behind the Zion curtain of Mormon Utah. No one-on-one adult shopping available. Crisis happening.

Urgent high-priority problem. If she ordered from a catalogue or online then she'd need a credit card and a delivery address. She'd stolen Joaquin's credit cards, along with his wallet, and a little over a grand in cash. She was his wife. Husbands paid for it.

And if the hubby's plastic didn't work, then she'd pick a wallet. But she didn't really want to do that. Credit-card fraud tends to tick off the big kahuna. The Perfect Princess couldn't get arrested for a whole year. No mug shots. No jail cells. Not with millions at stake.

And then there was a delivery problem. Unfortunately, plain brown packages arriving for her at the Whitmore Mansion would quickly raise the eyebrows and imagination levels of the local goody-goodies. Not that she wasn't willing to feed their imaginations. She was. After all, the good wives, wide-ass widows, and old biddies had to gossip about something over the backyard fence. Right?

Cluck. Cluck.

However, Martha needed to be careful and not go too far. The conservative, religious, and family oriented community would certainly run her out of town if she slipped up too much too soon. Vigilance. She needed to be discreet. Guarded. She didn't want to be forced out of town before she was ready. Not if she wanted to get her hands on Margaret's millions and to work Joaquin's con.

It wasn't until after she'd applied for a post office box in the Main Street office that the big man with the star finally showed up in full uniform and wearing weapons on his belt to ask her questions. Postmen are notorious gossips. Now the law appeared most concerned. A post office box indicated that the Princess wasn't just visiting their good town, but staying.

Tourist, maybe. Citizen, never.

Oddly enough, Martha told the local law and his state and federal posse-pals Joaquin's story. Not necessarily her story of course, but enough to make her uneasy. Telling any kind of truthful story wasn't her style. Nope. Truth and men, particularly lawmen, didn't happen in the same brain concept. Never!

But ... one step at a time.

With the devious assistance of the Whitmore hostess, the law had cornered her off guard about midmorning in the posh main floor parlour. Warming mid-August sunlight spilled in through the fancy cut windows and across the highly polished oak floor. The last of the summer hot weather hung on. She'd kicked off her sandals earlier, and now wore only a white T-shirt, a pair of white short-shorts that let her butt cheeks show, and a pair of classy gold and opal earrings purchased in Vegas to match the All-Seeing.

They had questions. They wanted to hear her story.

Her story was a simple one.

Smiling sweetly at each hero in a uniform, the Princess licked her lips ever so slowly. 'My husband worked for my Daddy for years and years. Following Daddy's death, we met. Magic happened. We connected. Joaquin ignited something in me. Twenty-four hours later, we eloped.'

'Las Vegas?' The Juab County Sheriff, wearing an immaculately pressed beige and brown uniform with gold braid trim, got out his notebook but didn't write anything down. She nodded in the affirmative.

The other Utah State and Federal badges frowned at the stupid Princess and her impulsive, irresponsible behaviour, but then winked at each other in some shared joke. Lawmen. Men with stars. Badges. Shields. These trustworthy Warriors and gunslingers possessed Miss Liberty's authority to poke around in people's private lives and make *some* judgement calls because they were proud, brave public servants, paid to protect and serve. Public heroes. The Princess didn't much care for the protect-and-serve-the-public hero type.

Nope. They made her itch. Public-hero types got off way too much on all the heroic stuff necessary in their dangerous protecting-and-serving lifestyle. Truth. Justice. And that macho laying-down-your-life playing-hero mentality. Unlike her private-dick husband and his partners, these grand Warriors of Utah State and the extended nation didn't put their lives on the line for the big bucks of private investigation or celebrity and corporate security. No. These honest, bribe-free gentlemen of honour played Warrior for other reasons. Righteous, scrupulous, reputable reasons.

Yuck. Mind-numbing.

These good-old-boy heroes were all decent fellows. Dependable. Family men. Not a bar-stool Warrior, drug addict, or dirty shield among the lot of them. Clean. Squeaky clean. Small-town religious clean. Hygienic. Uncontaminated. Unpolluted. Unsoiled. Not just sanitary, but purified.

Mind-numbing macho-man lifestyle adjustment needed.

This Princess of passion found public heroes boring.

Their little wink-wink game pissed her off for some reason. Wink. Wink. Wink, huh? OK, playtime.

The Princess was into the game. Scratch and sniff.

Heaving her gorgeous tits up in a deep sigh, and using her best silky Dorothy-in-Oz voice, the Princess attempted to answer all their persistent questions concerning her ugly bruises. When her taut nipples had every hero's full attention, she began to pace, wiggling her cute ass around the sunlit parlour as she explained.

'Honeymoon sex. We had fabulous honeymoon sex. Spicy. Tempestuous. Steamy. Sweaty. Bumpy. Surely you gentlemen are familiar with honeymoon sex?' Her tongue rested on her lower lip briefly. 'Wild and wonderful.'

Oh yes. The goody-goody badges blushed slightly. But no winking. Instead, resting their hands casually on the handles of their pistols, they smirked knowingly at each other. Oh, they understood.

The Princess rolled her innocent blue eyes and sighed deeply. Leaning her eye-catching tits forwards into better light, and as if in distracted thought, the Princess tugged ever so slightly on her spaghetti-strapped white T-shirt, flashing each hero just enough boob to boost their blood pressure before continuing her slow sexy stroll around the polished Victorian parlour. Oh, baby. The Princess wasn't wearing a bra.

She was good. So good. The he-man pistols they were packing in their trousers were loading up.

Let's hear it for the infamous diamond pistols!

Braless! Silk thong panties. White. Baby, virginal white in the sunlight. The beautiful Princess was almost naked. A simple titbit that each hero's penis-pistol suddenly acknowledged.

Attention. Oh yes. Only the light summer fabric trimmed with delicate baby lace, stretched tightly across her now perky nipples, shielded her dazzling round voluptuous tits from their full view. Slowly, she curled the tip of her tongue back from her lower lip and into her mouth, a move not totally wasted. A few of the heroes caught the delicate tongue action, although most still had their eyeballs glued to her magnificent tits.

Great tits and a terrific ass truly are a gal's best resources. Oh yes.

The law wanted her to say something bad about Joaquin.

'Clearly you were injured by his callous behaviour, Mrs Lee.' The badge's sympathetic tone carried a hint that he might be more than willing to protect and serve. He would save her. Lead her to salvation.

'Masochistic men often experience trouble with establishing boundaries, or control. Do you wish to apply for a restraining order?'

'Excuse me?' The Princess shifted her weight from one hip to the other and gave the public heroes her best sweet little if-I-only-had-a-brain Valley Girl bit. Opening her big blue eyes wide, she tilted her chin slightly down, and blinked in fake confusion. It worked. Holy crap. Did it ever work! The big heroes with guns were thrown slightly off balance. Was she for real?

Oh, this was fun. Comically nasty. Not boring at all. Why was this crap such a thrill?

The Princess knew she had to be a bad seed.

The hero with the biggest pistol folded his flabby arms across his massive soft chest and kept his voice low, but his tone slightly threatening. He shoved big glossy photographs of her naked body on the Vegas massage table. Wow. The bruises looked awful, worse than reality.

'We don't tolerate wife-beating around here, Mrs Lee.'

Gasping like a truly shocked convent-educated schoolgirl, the Princess brought her fingertips to her lower lip. 'I don't understand. What *are* you suggesting?'

They had Las Vegas video surveillance tapes. 'Your husband isn't welcome here.' Another, more youthful badge blurted out with too much bravado, 'And if Mr Lee shows up here or dares to try any of his sadistic bullshit in our town, we'll arrest him. Understand?'

Slightly ticked off, the Princess bit her lower lip and carefully considered her words. 'Joaquin Xavier Lee is a fine, honest, hard-working gentleman. During all the years he was on Daddy's payroll, no one ever found fault with his performance. He's very smart. I trust him.'

'Then why are you hiding from him?'

'I'm not.'

'No?' All the heroes scoffed in disbelief.

'No!' Even Martha was amazed at how serious and tough she sounded. Standing up to the law. Doing her Miss Tammy's stand-by-your-man thing. Hilary Clinton, stand back. 'I'm hiding from the person responsible for him being damn near dead meat.'

The public heroes didn't react. Deputy Dawg faces.

The sunlight shifting through the filtering leaves of the trees outside faded slightly. The Princess worked her tits one final time in the last of the light by taking a deep breath, holding it, and then sighing deeply. Using her most patient voice, she asked, 'Haven't any of you ever experienced authentic, unbridled, unexplainable, fanatical lust? Passion?'

The heroes didn't respond.

'No? Then, let me explain it to you. It's insanity. Mr Lee and I are both very passionate individuals. Our sex together is amazingly hot, and sometimes our passions run wild. It gets rough. I like it rough. Particularly first thing in the morning.'

Oh, now the good moral public heroes responded. Barney Fife style. They frowned to cover their blushes. Blushing and scratching. Itching. Good.

Before Martha made her grand exit, storming up the grand staircase to her glass and lace turret bedroom in an insulted huff that would make her acting teachers cream, she made it very clear she adored her new husband. Everything sexual, rough or not, was acceptable between married, consenting adults. Anything that happened behind their bedroom door was their business. Unfortunately both the pain and pleasure of her honeymoon sex in Las Vegas had come to an abrupt end.

'While moonlighting one night, doing some bounty-hunting work, my new husband was taken down by some serious bad guys. Frightened, I wanted to escape and hide while he recovers in a private hospital. So I came to the safety of Nephi to be near my extended family.'

That was her story. And the Princess was sticking to it.

Sad story too. Boo-hoo yarn. Beautiful rebellious Princess, a poor victim here. It was a good tragic tale. A true Nephi story. Damn. It was good enough for cable. But they didn't believe it. The public hero types rarely believed her. What a waste of the truth.

Anyway, the suspicious law checked her story out

with the Vegas cops and sure enough, all was well. One of the heroes made a special trip back to the Whitmore to assure her that she'd be safe in Nephi. Damn. Telling public heroes the truth was something brand new for her. A cheap thrill. And it worked so well. Joaquin's con was proceeding perfectly. Excellent.

But that wasn't all the good news. No. When the local law checked further and discovered exactly who her recently deceased Daddy had been, the community heroes took an abrupt shine to her. They too would protect and serve. Oh yes. The law and the respectable citizens would save the poor stupid naughty Princess from her unwise life choices; for at least as long as she was in their community, anyway.

But make no mistake – they wanted her gone.

Small-town cops and city officials are always extremely territorial, and the ill-disciplined Princess had invaded their space. She smelled like trouble. She walked like trouble. She was trouble.

And they didn't like *trouble* in their town.

They wanted her gone. Gone. As simple as that.

But they couldn't force her out. Not until she did something stupid on their watch. Hence they put a shadow on her to wait and watch for that stupid move. She'd acquired a stupid shadow. Brainless. But a rush.

Another cheap thrill.

9 The Monster's Ball

Her vulgar posing and sticky-finger ballet was the most amusing game in the whole boring town.

Main Street in Nephi was totally empty by dinner time. If the town had sidewalks, they could have rolled them up until dawn. Hell, only Main Street had a kerb and gutters. Not a soul stirred outside their homes in the sleepy rural town much after dark, except maybe to attend a sanctified Church function or crummy PTA event. The nearby Interstate traffic could barely be heard in the distance.

One September night when Mount Nebo stood majestically profiled against the stars in the autumn night sky, Martha couldn't stand her lacy gilded cage any longer. Quickly bored with her own performance before the huge bedroom mirror, the Princess took the erotic ballet to another level. She took it outside, to the street, developing an innovative rumba of sexual midnight hide-and-seek.

Naked except for one of Joaquin's dark shirts that hit her about mid-thigh, she slipped past the shadow, which wasn't all that tough for a clever girl, and slithered out to play in the dark. Masturbating in parks while encouraging voyeurs to watch or even join her in her pleasure had been one of her favourite adolescent amusements, but she hadn't done it in years. But with no one in Nephi out and about to watch or encourage her, she put a different spin on her usual game.

Maybe the All-Seeing couldn't actually see her without a mirror, but it could hear her. Talking dirty sympathy. So, inspired, the Princess supplied a hushed, whispered, running voice-over of the night. Oh yes. Carefully selecting each word, describing every aspect of her bodily pleasures, she slid quietly through the chilly darkness of the streets.

Lust in the dark shadows. How vampish.

The sexual ballet moved to the streets where she shared everything with the autumn mountain air and her silent distant partner. All her hand movements. Each drop of moisture. The twitches of anticipation and stimulation. Every fragrance. All the vibrations. The exhilaration of the wild fresh canyon winds on her wet warm pussy. The texture and fragrance of her sex juices on her fingers. The taste in her mouth.

Her pleasure.

The Princess enjoyed sharing her cheap thrills in great detail.

Oh yes. Good rush.

The silly childish game worked for her. A positive. Or a negative?

A positive.

An insanely imprudent and dangerous positive to keep her away from the genuine negative.

Dancing in the dark, Martha slithered all over town without anyone seeing her. Occasionally, but only rarely, she'd spot someone in the night. When she did, they never saw her in the shadows. It was fun. Freaky funhouse fun. It was a diversion. It was a cheap thrill.

In the small city park, on people's front lawns, or balanced up against their cars in the driveway, the Princess touched and pleasured herself, and enjoyed the risky adventure of it all.

Would someone peek out their window and catch her?

If so, she'd lose the game. And Margaret's millions.

Would she be arrested? If so, the same thing would happen. She might even lose Joaquin's con game.

Ah, but what if someone unexpectedly showed up and wanted to play too?

A playmate!

Spine-tingling thought. Very fun fantasy.

She worked it. Fantasy fucking. The new reality.

Even though the whole entertainment was absolutely stupid and totally self-destructive, Martha found playing it great fun. Often she'd stay out until dawn.

The small Mormon town of Nephi was picturesque in the fresh morning sunlight. The strong mountain winds had recently chilled, forcing the tree and shrubbery into vivid and dazzling colours. Mount Nebo was decked out in the most astoundingly rich shades of autumn. Striking. Pleasing. Incredible. Absolutely beautiful.

The Princess loved autumn.

Careful always to slip back into the Whitmore before the good people awakened, she'd watch the sunrise from the arched window in her turret room. After the demanding dark street dancing, the aroma of baking muffins drifted up to the Princess in the turret room from the Whitmore kitchen, stimulating her appetite.

She was slowly gaining weight. But good weight. Muscle weight.

Unfortunately, as the state deer hunt approached, the Princess grew totally bored with solo games and ballets. Thinking about Joaquin and cooing, 'Fuck me, Joaquin,' for hours was suddenly depressing.

Her head hurt. She felt sick and shaky. Her prescription pills were gone. Depression set in.

To replace the depression and the drugs, she struggled to find a new thrill, a diversion, a challenge. Action. Reaction. The Princess longed for human contact. Life. Thrills. She decided her new depression could be cured with the exciting buzz of a strange penis.

Penis power.

What was a Princess to do? Hell, after weeks in little old Nephi, it was clear that sexy thrills weren't coming to find her, so she'd have to go looking. Ah, but what was the best place to seek?

The truck stop near the Interstate.

Yeah, let's hear it for the truckers, baby!

No. No truckers. Not yet. Too damn tempting. A trucker would be like a super big test. One she'd fail. Without a doubt, she'd hitch a ride with the first trucker with good drugs and a hard cock. Yup, she'd be gone with one of the hunky knights of the road. Disappear. No. No truckers. Not yet. Too much temptation. She was still way too weak.

No. If she wanted hot cock for a night, the best place to hunt was in among the locals. Because as every good Princess ho knows, a hard cock is available around every corner. All a pretty Princess had to do was look. This town was full of lusty religious freaks looking to add one more woman to his earthly and celestial harem.

She'd suck'n'fuck a polygamist and then he'd invite her back to the cult to meet his good wives. Who knew, maybe a threesome was on the horizon. Yeah! Good plan.

She now had a plan. All right.

And maybe the All-Seeing might enjoy watching everything. A threesome and an audience? Hot damn! Could a bad girl really get that lucky? Oh yes. And Joaquin was paying her to work this con?

Even in her depression, Martha admitted that, so far,

the working and cleaning up her act thing wasn't all that bad. It had its moments.

Fearing the attention, or trouble from the law, her extended family among the local polygamists had remained at a safe distance from her so far. But Martha knew how to use their connections to go pretty much wherever she wanted. The Princess decided to go looking for the power of a cock and the Lord among the polygamists.

A hard cock fed by religious fever.

Might be a good time.

Oh yes. Bring on the hard preacher man.

The north wind kicked up hard, bringing the smell of the winter soon to come. The glorious colour of the leaves now dimmed and faded, leaving the trees mostly bare against the wind. Since childhood, Martha had always been able to smell the glaciers of Canada on the northern wind tearing through the western Rockies of Utah. The extreme cold was coming very early this year; she could smell it, along with the local evergreens. Unfortunately the Princess had no winter clothes, only the stuff purchased in the summer Vegas heat. Slight problem.

The cooling wind made her titties stand to attention. Dressed only in sandals, her shortest, backless blue sundress, and silky white thong panties, the Princess purchased a brand-new red mountain bike and pedalled all over town exploring. Hunting.

Tally-ho! Great fun. The cock hunt was on. What a rush.

The wind whipped lively autumn harmonies from the surrounding mountain passes as she pedalled all over the area. The exercise felt good. Between the bike seat and the silk thong underwear, the exercise was soon working her good. Woo.

Blood rushed through her entire body.

A light glow appeared on her flushing skin but was immediately cooled by the wind. Aaaah!

Slowly the depression began to fade. She felt cleaner. Younger. Alive. Life was good.

Paved streets without curbs and gutters, family homes built in an era of charm and manners, and noisy children playing safely in the big yards of Nephi were a century away from the loud, crime-ridden streets of Los Angeles, Miami or New York. The Princess waved at everyone in the yards. They waved back. She wiggled and pointed her perky tits. And the All-Seeing saw them all. The private-dick job was almost too easy.

Nephi was a safe, small, conservative family town. Yuck. Nauseating. Boring.

Everyone knew everyone. Everyone's relatives and ancestors knew everyone else's relatives and ancestors. The graveyard was full of friends and family, not the headstones of strangers.

Horrid. Disgusting. In-breeding climate control necessary.

Talk about invasion of privacy. Her All-Seeing was nothing compared to the community's eyes and ears lurking behind every bush, stone, and blade of grass as she pedalled along the many streets and into the surrounding country roads. Sick motherfuckers in constant quest of vicarious sinning. They all watched her and gossiped.

1984. She watched them do it.

The good and respectable community members shunned her. But she didn't care. Because she'd walked out on similar people and a similar religious commune years ago.

Can't ever go home again. Not to Daddy's house.

Why would anyone want that?

Why would anyone who'd escaped this kind of community mind control ever return? Ever?

Wacko. *Scream. Psycho. Friday the Thirteenth.*

The Princess was not dumb. Joaquin wanted to locate someone in Nephi's religious cults? Not a challenge. A smart gal needed to look at only two things, the laundry and the market. The dirty laundry was the most promising.

Who washed what, when, and how often, would show a smart Princess everything she wanted to know about the population. Who buys what food at the local market, how much, and how often, also might be a pointer, but not as accurate. The food supplies in rural farming communities like Nephi weren't totally dependent on the local commerce, particularly now the harvest was complete. In fact, the market purchasing could often be misleading. However, there was nothing ambiguous about the number and size of items of underwear on the backyard clotheslines. Between her bicycle rides and some quality time at the only local coin-operated launderette, she'd quickly located the majority of the cult population.

Dirty knickers never lied.

The local launderette was on the corner of 800 South and Main Street. The Princess decided to stop paying the Whitmore staff to wash her things. She took up doing her own laundry. Yuck. Cinderella here. But it was good for the con, so she suffered. Sniff. Sniff. Princess tears.

After a long and particularly rewarding bicycle ride one afternoon, Martha was on her way back to Whitmore Mansion to collect her dirty laundry when she spotted it.

Oh yes. She was good. So good. Nobel Prize good.

Down along the west side of south Main Street,

nestled between the Forest Service building with the flag flying in the breeze and an old cement factory, she found it – Ray's Café. Yup! She had this private-dick shit down.

The hub of the cult hive was located.

Even a stupid blind atheist could see the joint was some kind of front for the local religious freaks. For someone like the Princess, born and raised in small-town Utah, the telltale signs were subtly all over it. Might as well hang out a sign – 'Zealous spiritual games held regularly within'. The whole stinking atmosphere smacked of merciless male dominance, kinky mind games, and holy-rollin'.

Hallelujah! Praise the creepy. And bend over the altar, cute stuff. Glorify God. Damn the Devil.

And take it from behind.

Ray's Café, a yellow building with a red neon sign, was attached on the north to what appeared to be a closed salvage company. No surprise that the café obviously wasn't trying to attract any of the tourist or trucker business. In fact, it didn't appear to be open for any kind of public business, only that secret cult shit. Absolutely sure she'd found the inner sect's paradise, the Princess parked her new bike and slowly wiggled her great ass towards the mischievous saints of the angel Moroni.

Get thee behind me, sinner.

Slowly and carefully Martha strolled around the building, flashing her All-Seeing tits at everything surrounding the place that might be of interest to Joaquin. She found all the ways in and all the ways out. Then, turning her tits towards the now empty farm fields beyond, the All-Seeing transmitted the lay of the land. This was the place. Drum roll please.

Cult headquarters. Ta-da.

Commune control centre. Holy rollin'. A-reelin'-and-a-rockin'-and-a-rollin'-till-the-break-of-day within. Ding-a-ling. Praise God in all his glory. And the preacher men made in his image. Halleluiah, brother. Oh, brother.

Ray's Café had vertical parking slots in the front and along the south side of the building. There was nothing much beyond the building except the colony of traveller and tourist business stops several miles down, where the road met the Interstate. The town centre lay to the north, where the valley narrowed and the mountains shot straight up.

All right.

The Princess was into the espionage entertainment. It made her feel hot. Sexy. Young.

Charlie's Angels stand back. Bring on the Oscars. The Princess was quarterbacking the new con. With her full-on Cameron-Lucy-Drew-mode in gear, she entered Ray's Café, swinging her hot ass for all to admire. Hot damn. She *be* working it now, big boys.

She was beautiful; her nipples were pert from her bike ride in the cool air and her usual pale complexion was now flushed with an impressive healthy glow. God, it was good to be royalty.

Once upon a time, there was a true Princess born of regal Pioneer blood. Her Daddy was a living prophet. And today was the cult's lucky day. With confidence the Princess went forth to greet the holy-rollin' peasants.

The place wasn't empty. Several men sat at the counter and most of the booths contained women. Bible school was obviously in session. No one spoke. Every eye was on her. She felt so sexy, healthy, and totally feminine. Rush happening. The excitement tickled her fancy. Made her wet.

Ever so gently Martha let her upper arms squeeze her gorgeous tits together as she waltzed on in to assess the scene. No dishes. No cooking smells. Only people smells, human sweat, and grubby odours; only black New Testaments open before the women with a splattering of adult men.

It was quickly clear who was the alpha male.

Smoothing her short little skirt in false adolescent modesty, the pretty Princess approached the skinny tall guy behind the counter who, without saying a word, made it obvious he wanted her to know that *he* was the head honcho. Oh yes. He had that power-hungry arrogance to him and the costume of a holy-roller: dark work pants, long-sleeved blue shirt buttoned all the way to the top, accenting his protruding Adam's apple, and a heavy dark vest.

'Good afternoon.' Playfully, she flashed him her best cheerfully innocent oh-aren't-I-pretty Princess smile and slowly panned her All-Seeing tits around the entire joint. She counted twenty-three women from the ages of eighteen to about fifty.

Oh goody. Dick Tracy time.

She scanned them all, sending them straight from her pretty titties to Joaquin's computer. Stand back dimpled babes, Lucy, Cameron, and Drew. And kiss Tommy Cruise with the floppy hair. The Princess was cooking good on the whole *Mission Impossible* thing now. The All-Seeing captured everyone's face, young and old. It was so freakin' easy!

God, it was good to be regal.

Unfortunately, the adult response she received wasn't cheerful or welcoming. 'What do you want?'

Ouch! Oh, he was a mean one. Nasty even.

Licking her lips, she flashed him her innocent baby-doll smile. 'My name is Martha Lee and I'm looking for work as a waitress.'

The skinny macho-tense religious freak relaxed, dismissing her with, 'Sorry. We aren't hiring.'

Of course not. She struggled to smother a giggle.

Cult labour. Slave labour. Zombie labour. Oh yeah. Excitement pulsed through her entire body. Before these dull lifeless women the Princess commanded centre stage. Bravely she stepped up to the counter. She was about to do her acting coaches proud. Star power! There were more people in the back who, interested, were now peeking through the swinging kitchen doors. Ever so casually, she jiggled her tits. Gotcha.

She was so damn hot.

Gotcha again. And again. All the dull mindless faces were captured by the All-Seeing.

She was so freaking great at this new job thing.

Another heavier holy-roller with a slightly receding hairline came to the counter to admire her tits. He looked her up and down carefully.

Mind-fuck. He was mind-fucking her.

And she was good. Very good.

He was more than appreciative.

It ticked the head honcho off. He frowned and, while his mind-fucking companion worked her over, he checked out all her nasty bruises. Even after all these weeks the bruises were still yellowish, still ugly and visible. Her skimpy dress hid nothing. Even an inbred idiot could see the poor Princess was battered and bruised, on the run, and hiding out from a big strong bully. His attitude softened.

'Where's your husband, Mrs Lee? Why has he deserted you and left you alone to find work?'

What an idiot.

The Princess played the scene beautifully. First, she gave a big sigh, heaving her incredible tits up and down, and waited, giving time for everyone to admire her before she twisted her wedding ring. Oh yes, she be smart and stylin'. She be a royal bitch. 'My husband and I have temporarily parted company.'

Too much.

Damn it. The holy-rollin' head honcho had an immediate hard-on. The huge peak in his pants couldn't be easily hidden. Tsk-tsk. Can't have that. Not in front of the decent people. Frustrated with his arousal, the head honcho lost his cool front. 'You run along, Mrs Lee. We don't have anything for someone like you.'

Acting most distressed and terribly disappointed, the unfortunate Princess once again licked her lips slowly and nodded in quiet understanding. He was hard and she was happy. The All-Seeing had to be ecstatic. So, trembling slightly for effect, the Princess left the café.

With her heart pounding, Martha was dizzy with her small victory. She'd done it. Entered the crazed dreamland, fed the All-Seeing everything, and left without anyone the wiser. Hot damn. She was so *good*.

There had to have been between twenty-five to thirty other people in the back room, all in their places with dull, lifeless faces. Now this job, this legal con game, was really fun. Roller-coaster dangerous kind of fun. A cheap thrill happening.

Hell yes! The Princess was into working now.

Fun. Fun. Fun.

Money. Money. Money.

Regular people actually made money playing these legal cons? Wow! Why hadn't someone invited her to the party earlier? She might even have gone legit earlier.

Feeling elated by her first small success the Princess returned to the Whitmore and, exhausted from all the cycling, slept through the rest of the day and the entire night.

10 **Tiptoe Through the Sagebrush**

Still warm from her victory the day before, the Princess awoke early and decided it was a dirty laundry day. As much as she loved the Vegas wardrobe, she was freezing to death. Autumn in the Utah mountains was no tropical picnic. Snow was on the horizon. She'd wash and pack away her lovely summer things.

But then what would she wear to the Ugly Bug Ball?

Main Street Nephi was a galaxy away from Rodeo Drive. Hardly a shopping-spree nerve centre for a Princess. After a lovely breakfast in bed provided by her thoughtful hostess, the Princess dressed herself in her shortest denim shorts, a lacy pink tank top, and then covered herself with Joaquin's shirt. Leaving the big shirt unbuttoned, she rolled up the long sleeves and smiled.

Joaquin had given her this shirt. Once. A long time ago. Far, far away. In a No Ho office. She sighed.

Martha gathered her summer clothes together and placed them in a storage cardboard box thoughtfully supplied by the Whitmore kitchen help. Balancing the box on her bicycle she headed down Main Street.

Main Street Nephi was bustling, if three trucks with campers, two cars, and about five huge RVs or motorhomes could be called traffic. Hunters. Getting ready for the upcoming hunt. State holiday. Hell, the entire state didn't bother to hold classes in public schools the day before the opening of the annual deer hunt. No reason. No one showed up. Everyone old enough to qualify for a tag took to the mountains. James Dickey freaky.

Local hunters came into town to pick up supplies. All the other responsible, respectable adults appeared to be employed elsewhere. Children were now occupied in school. Local homemakers were still busy at the home nesting thing. Only the elderly and the hunters were shopping.

And the Princess.

She even bought several of the same items the hunters were buying. Numerous items of long thermal underwear, tops and bottoms, in all the colours available, which was mainly white and grey. Heavy socks. Hiking or mountain boots. Plaid wool shirts, one red and black, one green and blue. And a thick heavy sweatshirt with a hood and a front muff-pocket for cold hands. Grey. Not hunter orange. No Paris black available.

Dull practical wardrobe. Now she'd fit right in with the other cult classics. Barfing here. What a Princess needed was mink. What Martha got was thermal.

But what the hell? A gal has to do what's necessary to survive. And she was freezing her titties off.

Carefully adding the white plastic sacks filled with her new purchases to the summer laundry box that she balanced on her handlebars, Martha slowly pedalled along with almost no difficulty. The weather had turned a nasty cold.

At the corner of Fourth South and Main Street the Princess suffered a serious stroke of mischievous genius. Ray's Café wasn't the only so-called restaurant in Nephi. To improve her game face Martha parked her flashy new bike in front of the Mi Ranchero Mexican

Café and rested the now overflowing box on the ground. The smells were great. Salsa. Refried beans. Tamales. Chicken with lime sauce. Now this was a real café.

Food. Real food. She loved the smell. It was hot.

Unlike Ray's Café this restaurant was full of hungry people looking for a good filling meal, including the few immoral locals who actually dared break the strict Word of Wisdom and consume coffee with caffeine, along with several car travellers, and a few lusty-looking truckers. Every eye watched the summer-clad Princess sashay forwards to apply for a waitress position.

Hell, even an ugly dog wearing thermals and granny panties could attract admirers in a place like this. A Princess with great tits and a beautiful ass would have to beat them off. All right. The Mexican café was busy, neighbourly, and full of life. She liked it immediately. Yup! A smart gal could get fucked in a place like this.

But although the owner was friendly, he was also suspicious. She sensed that he would never hire an outsider even when she made it deviously obvious that she was willing to exchange sexual favours for a job.

'Got all the help I need right now. Thank you.' The owner was polite but clearly not interested. His tastes seemed to run more to a big, burly, hairy trucker seated near the back window. Hell, she couldn't blame him. She could enjoy a ride with the truckers herself.

Truckers were among her favourites.

Once, when she was still a teenager, she'd hopped in an eighteen-wheeler outside Chicago and fucked the driver and his partner for two thousand miles. What a ride! Made her nipples hard just remembering it. Nothing like blowing a knight of the road in five tons of metal while ploughing up the highway at top speed with his partner's dick up her ass. What a rush. Yes. A total thrill!

Oh, how her Daddy had hated truckers.

The Princess saw truckers as the true knights of the American highways, and members of that last great American wolf-pack. Mostly alpha males, all hungry, all lonely, all horny, all constantly hunting, prowling, and moving on, all cruising the lifelines of commerce, willing to help a pretty Princess in distress at any time. Oh yes. She could do a big burly trucker about now.

Unfortunately the truckers appeared more interested in the sweet, blond, apple-cheeked young man clearing a nearby booth. Bad luck. Shitty bad luck. Obviously her luck needed to change. But it wasn't looking good.

The sweetly pitched cook's bell chimed. A working waitress rushed to pick up the order. A bell. Hell's bells. Maybe her luck would change now.

The Princess missed church bells.

Not one Mormon steeple was ever erected with bells. Neither the respectable Latter Day Saints or the cult spin-offs believe in church bells. Bad medicine. An entire community without bells of faith, hope and inspiration? Not good. Nope, this small dinner chime was the only bell she'd heard in weeks, no months. No church bells. Not since the morning she'd met Joaquin. Not one damn good-luck tinkle in all of the Mormon Zion. Bad luck.

Disappointed, but oddly encouraged, the Princess returned to her bike and box and continued down Main Street. Several blocks further south, attached to the laundrette, was the Country Kitchen Café. She was cold, and therefore considering making a grand entrance and applying for a job, when she saw the clientele leaving. Damn tourists with families. No. No. A waitress would really have to work in there. Not what she had in mind, thanks very much.

While the washers filled up with water the Princess sorted her loads. The mission was two-fold. Wash and fold, and kill time. She took her time with the task. Flipping through an old celebrity magazine without really seeing it, she fingered her hair and waited for the homemakers to arrive for laundry inspection.

Damn, the Princess needed a bleach job, a cut, and a stylist bad. The dark roots of her hair were now longer than the Miami blonde tips of mid-summer. Ugly fashion statement. The cut had grown out great, but could use some touch-up help. No place in Nephi for repairs. Like she'd let some small-town Sandy Dee actually touch her hair. They only had three hairdos going for women in this town; light, dark, or red Elizabeth Taylor, Tammy-Tell-Me-True Debbie Reynolds braids, or the perennial favourite, mousy Mia Farrow. A mature lady with cash could choose.

The Princess chose to abstain.

Then her luck changed.

It was the bell. One of the truckers had followed her from the Mexican café. Smiling, the Princess slipped into the back restroom with chipped and peeling green paint to wait. He followed. Yeah! Forbidden sex in a public restroom. All right. Cheap thrill happening.

The trucker locked the restroom door behind him.

Yeah! A stranger. A danger. A thrill. Briefly and awkwardly cuddling her he smelled of bitter coffee, diesel fuel, and stale cigarettes. Thick through the middle and with absolutely no ass, the guy was no action hero. It didn't matter. The Princess was very happy to meet a friendly knight of the road. As long as he had a thick cock, it didn't matter what he looked like. She closed her eyes and fingered the cock beneath his faded Levi's.

Bad luck.

Small cock. Not what a Princess fantasised about, but maybe he had other virtues. Maybe he knew how to eat pussy. She was starved, ready to devour and be devoured. Suck. Nibble. Eat. Send in the hungry hairy beasts.

In her mind's eye she pictured her beautiful, proud Joaquin with his majestic shoulders and narrow green eyes. His mouth explored her neck and shoulders, forcing her head back slightly. She arched her body to his touch.

Oh yes. Would Joaquin be aroused watching her with this nameless, speechless trucker?

The trucker reached beneath her pink tank top and slipped her bra up so he could fondle and kiss her spectacular tits. She felt beautiful. Her eyes opened briefly. The trucker's brown eyes met her gaze, breaking her trance. All wrong. She closed her eyes again.

Someone rattled the locked restroom doorknob. He pulled her hard against him and she responded to every nuance of his touch, a touch that grew steadily greedy. Was her handsome wounded Warrior watching?

Was he hot?

Closing her eyes she whispered, just loud enough for the All-Seeing, 'Joaquin. Joaquin. Joaquin.' Breathing deeply she backed up to the sink and hopped up to sit on it. The trucker removed her denim shorts and thong panties, and she spread her legs. The nameless trucker knelt before her and began to lick, slurping noisily and plunging his tongue in and out, this way and that. The Princess bit down on one of her fingers, making soft purring noises. What a delightful relief to have some-one else working it for her.

'Kiss it, baby. Kiss it,' she commanded.

And he did, making loud slurping, groaning, kissing sounds as she completed small gyrations, her orgasm building. Twining her hands into his greying hair, she opened her eyes and watched. The sight of his tongue fucking her gave her a thrill. Oh, baby. At least the guy had a good tongue and knew how to take orders.

Someone knocked on the door.

'Occupied,' she shouted.

Another knock. He looked up at her.

'Occupied,' she repeated louder as he stuck one, then two, then three fingers into her cunt, smacking up hard against her G-spot as his tongue returned to sucking her clit. Oh yes!

More knocking. The damn knocking seemed to drive him crazy, and his pressure and tempo increased. All right. It was good. It was fine. It worked for her. And with a long low guttural groan, she came all over his face.

He loved it.

The knocking stopped.

'I could eat you all day, all night,' the nameless trucker whispered blissfully.

The Princess smiled sweetly down at the knight. 'Sorry. I've got a jealous husband with a very bad temper and a posse of wannabe gangster friends.'

Sighing with disappointment, the trucker fondled her pussy one last time before washing his face with cold water from the sink. She slipped back into her shorts and waited.

'I'll be back along this way in a few days,' he volunteered.

'Not interested. But thanks for the quickie. It was fun.' He was clearly disappointed.

Too bad.

As much as she'd love to enjoy the good knight's wicked tongue again, casual sex in the restroom of a laundrette on Main Street in the middle of the day with a nameless trucker smelled too much like a jail cell. This year, the Princess was allergic to jail cells. Too bad.

'If you change your mind . . .' he offered.

But she shook her head, smiling and making it clear that she was dismissing him. The poor guy didn't even get jerked off. Checking to see if the coast was clear, he left first without another word. The Princess heard his rig pull away. Martha loved truckers, and she sighed in sincere disappointment. Boo-hoo.

Whoever had been at the door had obviously left in search of another toilet. Alone and now facing the small dusty mirror above the sink, the Princess smiled as she admired her own reflection. 'Was that good for you, Joaquin. Did you watch it, baby? Did it make you hot?'

Martha fluffed and fingered her hair. Damn, she was beautiful. Giggling her best little-girl giggle, she placed a hot kiss on the surface of the mirror. 'Wish you were here, Joaquin. Wish it were you, baby.'

Without another word, she returned to the dirty laundry. Cinderella time.

While she was folding her underwear a local heavy blonde woman entered and smiled at her.

'Travelling? Where you from?'

The Princess smiled at the frump. 'Oh, I'm not travelling, I'm here to stay.'

'In Nephi?' Noticeably surprised, the big blonde

woman loaded thirteen washers with male adult work clothing. Damn, she must be doing ten guys. The frump hurried to continue their friendly conversation. 'I mean, why would anyone leave the excitement of Los Angeles to live here?'

Two dull-faced, loud women in their mid-twenties rushed through the glass door with sticky red stuff on their faces, lugging more laundry bags. Laughing like children, they joined the frump and began loading more washers carelessly. Oh yuck. Miserable little maids hanging on, sucking the life out of the poor overworked first wife. The Princess gave the demon seeds her best kind Princess smile and aimed the All-Seeing at their ugly little faces.

'My Aunt Lou Ellen always told me that Nephi was the perfect place to raise a family. I've recently married and I'd hoped to make us a home here.' She lied so well.

Instantly the Princess hated the two little maids. Obviously the younger and more attractive sister-wives felt laundry labour beneath them. Well, let the stupid young things enjoy their merriment and disrespect. Age has a rapid effect on cult women. First the second, then the third, then the fourth, or even the fifth wife rapidly age living the true Principle. But somehow the mature husbands, the lords and masters in this Holy Kingdom, never seem aware of their own advancing age or sagging guts. Funny how it works that way.

The first wife may grow old or dull or worn in time, and so then a cult male with the proper cult credentials, who has received the right revelations from the Lord, may take another wife; usually a younger one with life enough to replace the elder wife in the master's bed while gradually becoming nothing more than a slave for all her elder sister-wives and the demanding cult lifestyle.

These repulsive female-things were loud and sticky and demanding and horrible and the Princess was allergic to them both immediately. Back, Satan seeds. Back. Back. Hiss. Boo. However, in true Princess form, she flashed the miniature she-monsters her warmest Princess smile, worthy of an Oscar. Damn, she was so good today.

Applause please.

When the frump with the min-monsters finished loading another entire two rows of washers with dull female clothing she actually spat on her fat, worn fingers and with much too much force wiped the red sticky stuff from one of the maid's faces as if she were a grubby child. 'We are sisters. They are young.' The frump attempted to apologise for the poor manners and repulsive immature behaviour of her sister-wives.

The Princess smiled. 'I understand.' And she did.

'We are eight. I'm the eldest,' the frump went on.

'Eight?' The Princess didn't try to hide her surprise, only her horror. Crap. What was the frump, a glutton for punishment? Crazy! What woman in her right mind allowed her husband to take seven other women as wives? Mistresses, maybe. They wouldn't have legal claim on the guy's financial assets. But wives? No. No. No.

Husbands paid. And unless this husband was a freakin' prince from old money, there was no way he could support eight wives with even the basics, let alone a true Princess. What total idiots. Although the frump was heavy, she didn't appear forty or unattractive yet. Why had she fallen to so many so quickly? Dumb!

'To live the Principle is a blessing. One that insures us a place in the highest Celestial Kingdom.' The frump preached with great conviction. 'Aren't you interested in returning to live among the Faithful and perhaps, one day, if worthy, becoming a sister-wife?'

Taken back by her directness, the Princess could only perjure herself and nod in the affirmative. 'One day. If I'm worthy.' She managed not to choke on that big fat fib. However, Martha did feel her nose growing longer. She touched it to make sure. But the frump didn't notice.

Immediately the light in the frump's eyes changed. 'My name is Jane Jensen.'

And for the remainder of the time in the laundrette the Princess shared secrets with Jane Jensen. She listened and smiled. Long after her few frilly garments and new rugged autumn clothes were cleaned and neatly folded in her box, she stayed and folded labour clothes and listened to Jane share the local gossip. It was wonderful. The bitch knew dirt about everyone and was willing to share.

The Princess returned to the Whitmore in a wonderful mood.

11 **Please, Mr Postman**

To her surprise, after the second weekend of the annual October deer hunt Martha unexpectedly heard from Joaquin. On a chilly Saturday morning, she received a letter in a care package containing a variety of vibrators, an activated cellular phone, and money from him – enough cash to actually make her consider skipping town and dumping the whole legit con thing. But his letter!

His letter was so ... eerie. The Princess read her husband's letter numerous times. Frightening.

As eccentric and as intimidating as it was to Martha, her whole new Mrs Lee thing appeared to be really working great for Joaquin. According to his letter he was 'recuperating very slowly' from his injuries and now that 'the infection' had disappeared, he was improving more rapidly and hinted that he might actually be somewhere nearby, but didn't indicate where. However, he did assure her that he was monitoring the All-Seeing constantly and raved about how successful she'd been at her new undercover gig.

Not in so many words, because he was obviously concerned someone else might read his letter and figure out that she was up to something. But it was there, in a sort of code that was clear to her. What's more, he flat-out said how proud he was of her.

Proud that she was Mrs Joaquin Xavier Lee. Pleased and surprised that she hadn't skipped out on him. Full of pride that she was working his con. Proud that she was 'committed to our partnership'.

He wrote the words. He was proud of her.

Proud of her! Proud? Huh?

No one had expressed pride in Martha much past her kindergarten years, and certainly not since her mother's death. His praise made her stomach hurt, made her anxious and uneasy.

But it also made her smile. Made her feel sexy. And young.

With a scrawling pen he wrote that she was an absolutely ideal Mrs Lee. Wow! Ideal wife, huh? Well, how about that? Ideal.

Oh, really?

So the Princess was now accomplished at something besides just having a good time.

Joaquin also raved about her masturbation captured in her boudoir mirror. The All-Seeing allowed him to witness all her creative sexy moves – a performance he entusiastically reviewed. He praised her grace, creativity, and beautiful body, encouraging her to continue to masturbate for him. He loved it. Shit. He'd written her a damn love letter.

Anguish. Yuck. No. Stop. Halt.

The Princess felt dizzy and slightly ill. What the hell? She was just trying to be nice to the wounded Warrior before she sued his ass for alimony. And now he was sending her vibrators and money and love letters?

Too weird.

But a good weird. One she intended to use to her advantage. The game between them wasn't over yet. As much as he loved her solo performances, he also indicated that he'd appreciated her cooing his name to the trucker. No jealous husband, him.

Except for the assless trucker who now made occasional unannounced appearances at the laundrette, the Princess wasn't getting any one-on-one sexual action of any kind. Boring. But Joaquin appeared to understand her sexual frustration with living alone in Nephi, and sympathized with her need for physical contact with the trucker. Talk about an understanding partner.

But then, why should he object? If Harvey's truth was gospel, then Joaquin had always enjoyed watching her with other men. Why would that change now they were married partners?

Evidently it hadn't.

For some odd vindictive reason, Martha wished it had. She wanted it to bother him. She wanted him suffering with jealousy. Weird, huh? Yup. Somewhere deep down inside she longed for his resentment. But resentment wasn't happening.

Why would it?

As per her husband's request in the letter, next time the almost assless trucker arrived and sucked her pussy in the restroom of the laundrette, she peed on his face and chest.

The trucker loved it. The guy went fucking nuts. Unloaded in his trousers.

Then, wild with gusto, he licked, nibbled, sucked, and finger-fucked her through multi-orgasms, and in appreciation she peed in his face again.

Ecstasy! With a major grin the trucker left without even washing off her piss.

Martha could only chuckle and smile. Took all kinds.

The trucker made her pussy happy. And in thanks, she'd pissed in his face. Which he LOVED!

It worked for the two of them. Both enjoyed their end of the sexual experience. And out there, somewhere in cyberspace, Joaquin enjoyed it too. Everybody was happy. Life was good.

Simple. Easy. Too easy.

Joaquin had known. How could he have guessed the trucker's sexual preference? He hadn't guessed. He knew. The sneaky jerk had known somehow. It didn't matter. But still, it did make her curious.

Joaquin's love letter changed everything. It made her fidgety. Restless. Twitchy, even. She didn't trust him.

One afternoon, while helping Jane fold clothes at the laundarette, Martha shared her love letter in a pathetic attempt to get another perspective on her own reaction. With all of the glee of an adolescent girl in the school restroom, the Princess read sections of Joaquin's letter aloud to her gal-pal Jane, omitting the best parts, of course. Jane was impressed.

'He really loves you.'

Loves her? Did he?

Martha didn't know how she felt about that concept. Love, huh?

'I can tell you care for him too. However, and it isn't my place to say, but –' Jane hesitated only a moment '– for your soul you should reconsider this marriage. Whatever joy you might find with this heathen can never compare to an eternal life within the glorious bounties of the Celestial Kingdom. It's good you've returned to live among the Faithful and heal. This man from the outside only contaminates your everlasting spirit. You must find redemption and salvation only through a proper marriage with a worthy man – one who will hold you, not just for the short years upon this earth, but for all eternity, happily sealed to each other forever.'

Forever? Puke. What a concept.

The same dick hanging around forever? No thanks. Not in this world, let alone in the next.

But the gal-pal frump was right about one thing. Martha was healing. Her drug addiction was slowly and painfully being replaced by her cycling and getting into the whole new Mrs Lee, private-dick mentality. She was doing the mind and body thing well. Trying to live the Word. Taking baby steps.

The frump openly praised and encouraged Martha's efforts. Of course, Martha had to share the 'agony' of her drug withdrawal with her new and best gal-pal. It was good for the gossip and the con. Tell the frump one dirty titbit and by noon the following day, everyone in town had heard 'in confidence' the gruesome details of the wayward Princess's personal struggle to regain salvation.

God, it was all so freaking easy.

October became November. By the time the first snow flurries arrived the Princess was actually pedalling between twenty and forty-five miles a day. Everything and everyone along her routes captured by the All-Seeing. Between the long bike rides and her trips to the laundrette, Martha was damn sure that there wasn't a cult member in the Nephi or Manti area whose face hadn't found its way before the All-Seeing. Yeah, baby. The Princess was talented.

All hail the Princess and the All-Seeing.

The Princess was so great at her new job. Very clever. Skilful, even. But bored with it.

The secret-dick thing no longer felt like much of a challenge. The thrill was gone. So one night, while playing with her new vibrator in front of the tilted standing bedroom mirror, Martha shared her frustrations with her mysterious husband.

'I'm bored, Joaquin.'

And she was.

'I don't do boring. Boredom will destroy our plans.

Help me.' She pleaded with Joaquin via the bedroom mirror and the All-Seeing. 'Baby, it's the call of the wild. I'm fighting the old wandering-star thing bad. I'm bored. I want drugs. I want a primo fuck. I want. I want. I want,' she whined.

And she did.

'And I'm weakening,' she admitted.

Later, after the vibrator had worked its magic, and the Princess had showered and was pacing around her bridal suite dressed only in long, silky sage pyjamas, applying vanilla-scented lotion to her skin, the Princess heard it.

Ringing. Bells? Yeah! Wait. No. Ringing. Say what? Ringing again. Ringing in her room? Wait. The cellphone? It never rang. Anyway, it'd never rung before. Ringing. Ringing again. And again.

Surprised, the Princess actually had to search the lower drawers for the damn thing before she could answer it. Must be a wrong number. But hell, even that would be a cheap thrill if the voice on the other end was masculine.

'Hello.'

A long pause.

'Hey, Princess.'

Her stomach hit her ribcage. Shock. Saliva in her open mouth. She could barely breathe. Rich tenor tones. Her physical reaction was instantaneous and powerful. Immediately wet, her nipples tight and pert, she wanted him. Required him. She wanted her dirty dog Joaquin. Now. He was there. His voice. He was real.

Unable to speak, and panting slightly in wonder at her own extreme body response to his rich voice, the Princess held the phone to her ear and licked her lips slowly. Her hands shook. Wow. She was excited – ready, even. This was great. Electrifying.

Oh, baby. Oh, baby.

After a brief moment of silence a command came from the thick voice. 'Look at me.'

Huh? What? The Princess twirled around in a kind of gasping confusion. Only the small crystal lamp near the bed behind her lit the Victorian boudoir. Turning to the smaller oval mirror over the dresser, Martha flashed him her best Princess smile. It was so good to hear him. Just breathing, even.

There was a long pause.

Staring into her own reflection she finally managed to speak first. 'Where are you?'

'Watching. Always watching.'

Reaching out with her fingertips to gently touch the mirror glass, the Princess quivered. 'I need to see you.'

'No.' It wasn't a cruel or harsh command, but just a simple 'No'. Nevertheless, a clear command and flat refusal. 'No,' he repeated again. Her entire body ached. Her temperature rise made her pant with heat. Hot damn. She wanted Joaquin. Her body screamed out for his touch.

Through all the months of solitude and fantasy, nothing had prepared her for an actual conversation with Joaquin. Not one where he'd speak. Not like this. She hadn't fantasized about the magic his beautiful voice might command over her body. Wantonly wanting him, she swallowed and backed away from the mirror, accidentally knocking the rose potpourri to the oak floor. The dainty porcelain dish broke, sending the scent of roses floating out into the night. Suddenly flustered beyond control the Princess couldn't think. She could only feel. Only hunger.

Her body hungered for him. His touch. His voice. Oh, Joaquin. Oh yes. Phone sex tonight, baby! Yes indeed. Now. This minute. His rich, deep voice. Please. Please.

It's been way too long. Tears unexpectedly rolled down her cheeks.

What the hell?

Get a grip. Grab hold. It was only phone sex after all, not primo fucking in a five-star palace. But she'd take it. Gladly. Yes. Oh yes. Anything. She was beyond starving. Taking several slow, deep breaths the Princess attempted to calm herself before the upcoming sexual feast.

Joaquin spoke quickly to her now, his words rushing together. 'I thought I knew all your sneaky little tricks. But this is a new one, Princess. You're sure full of surprises.' He paused, waiting for her to respond.

The Princess couldn't. His voice forced her body to tingle. Running her fingers through her hair, Martha turned from the dresser mirror and moved slowly to the circular window seat, where she collapsed and sat cross-legged. She was ready. Phone sex. Yeah! Phone sex. Now in the shadows, with her reflection muted by the low light in the tall mirror, she studied her own expression and waited for the sexy flow of his tenor tones to flow through her pulsing, burning flesh.

Unfortunately the reflection wasn't absolutely pretty. The room, the low crystal mood lights, the white lace, and the voice on the phone were all beautiful. Perfect. But the reflection of the Princess in the mirror wasn't. Regrettably she hadn't seen a hairdresser or manicurist in months. Not since Vegas. Suddenly aware of how common and unkempt she might appear to him, the Princess could only shake her head in flustered confusion without speaking.

Instead he spoke. 'I never figured you'd stick.' Something respectful and appreciative echoed in his voice. 'I'm glad you did. I am. But surprised. When Harvey said he found you at the hotel, I figured you'd been too drugged to move on. But then you demanded to go to Nephi. The things you've done since. The chances you've taken. I'm very proud of you.'

Proud of her. Tears flowing from some deep hidden spring within made her face look swollen. She quickly wiped them away. Why did he keep saying that?

'Princess, we need to talk.'

Talk. Oh yeah?

It was so Joaquin. Here she was trembling in sexual anticipation waiting for phone sex, and the guy wanted to talk business. She licked her lips before touching her aching tits. OK. He could talk about whatever he wanted for as long as he wanted, as long as she could hear his tenor and know he was watching. His voice made him real again. No fantasy. Real.

Yeah! Viva AT&T.

'Talk to me, Joaquin. I'm ready.'

Pause.

Something hidden deep in his silence made her suddenly edgy and insecure. He wasn't talking, only breathing heavily. What could she say to him? Damn it. She should say something. Something smart and witty. Something. Something nasty? Maybe something rude. No, something hot, sexy and teasing. But she couldn't. Instead, leaning back, she rested against the cool window-pane beneath the lacy drapery, caressed her own tits, and waited, listening. Waiting for his deep sexy tones. Her entire body trembled in eager sexual expectation.

After a long silence, he spoke calmly. 'You said you were going to be good at your new life. And you've been great. Proud to call you my partner.'

His voice. Oh yes. Oh, baby. He had to keep talking. Her body didn't need to hear the words – only his tenor was necessary. Tingling. Throbbing. Aching. Wet. Hungry. Needing. Her hand moved to find her clit beneath the sage silk. Oh yes. The Princess smiled and managed a soft, 'Partner, huh? Not wife.'

'Partner and wife.' His tones were affectionate. Oh yum. Yum. Yes. How rich and warm his voice felt. Her fingers found the spot. Oh, baby. Talk dirty to me, big Daddy. 'You're looking good. Damn good. Like a true Princess.'

Say what? No. Yes. Wait. There was something. Something. She tensed all over in expectation. It was hiding. Beneath the silky sexy tones it lurked once again. Her body remembered too. First the pleasure. Then the pain. Why was he finally phoning her after all these weeks, months even?

Pleasure? No. The magic mirror and All-Seeing provided him with pleasure. She wasn't stupid. Pain. It was out there lurking behind his commanding presence and sulky tones. Pain. Hanging still in the silent rose-scented night.

Pleasure. The pleasure of his voice. The pleasure of his words of praise. The pleasure leading only to the pain. Pain. OK, bad boy. Bring on the nasty pain.

Long pause. Shifting the phone from one hand to another, the panicky Princess ignored the upcoming pain to focus only on the pleasure she might find in the brief moment. He was working up to hurting her. She could feel it. Pain was coming. That was only to be expected. But first, the promised pleasure. Please.

She touched herself, closing her eyes. Her hands were his. He was there in the silence between them. There, touching her. His voice. Please, his voice.

Silence. More silence, and then, 'No. Princess, stop. No. Not now.' His tone suddenly grew abrupt and businesslike. Her stomach twisted. No pleasure. Oh no. No. She screamed inside as she plunged into agony.

'Our clients are also extremely pleased. What's more, the State and Federal law enforcement agencies have scheduled their move. It's bad publicity to take screaming pious nuts away from their religious freedoms during the holy Christian holidays. Round-up is set for mid-January. But that doesn't mean you can't leave Nephi now. You can. Now. Or whenever you want. The job there is done. It's over.'

Over? Leave? Say what?

No. No. No. Princess Perfect wasn't leaving her pretty little Victorian palace. Not when she was on such a successful roll. Or was she? No. No, she wasn't ready for it to be over. Unacceptable. A dark agonizing bolt from the night.

And what besides the job was over?

OK. Chewing her lower lip, Martha managed a nod into the magic looking glass. 'Good. Come and rescue me. I'm ready for you with or without a white horse. I'll pack and be downstairs.'

Static. Pause. Silence.

Well, this wasn't going suitably, was it? Proudly, the Princess rose and paced about her elegant turret, chewing on her thumbnail. Damn.

'Joaquin, you *are* coming to rescue me, aren't you?' Silence. 'Joaquin.' Her disappointment burned in the way she said his name. 'Joaquin.'

'They need a deposition from you in Salt Lake City. Basically, all you've got to do is swear under oath that you wore the necklace and gave me, your husband, the right to record everything it transmitted. You won't even have to make a court appearance. They'll remove the necklace for you. I'm giving you a divorce. You're free. It's over.'

Divorce? Free? Over? Say again? He was conning her. She could feel it. Not good. No. It was too uncomplicated. Too freakin' easy. He was up to something nasty. Why was she suddenly so disappointed in him? She always knew he was a snake, one that enjoyed wrapping himself around her, cuddling her and warming her. Binding her. Squeezing. Until it hurt. Hurt good.

She kept her voice sweet. 'All right. I understand. We'll connect in Salt Lake City. Tomorrow.'

Silence. Pause. 'No.'

No? He was dumping her without even a weekend quickie. Damn, damn, damn. What a nasty dirty dog. Son of a bitch. He had what he needed, now he didn't need her. Shit. She couldn't leave Nephi alone. She didn't know how. She felt her panic rising. She needed him to need her.

What the hell?

Putting on her best Princess face, she struggled not to allow her rising alarm to show, and managed to smile sweetly at her own reflection and the anaconda behind the magic glass. 'Joaquin, we can't do Christmas in the damn Valley. I hate the Valley. So, my darling *husband* –' she tried to stress the word *husband* and sound cheery '– please let's go to Sun Valley, Idaho, and do that macho Hemingway fucking-in-the-snow thing for a few weeks. Are you up to it? I'll do you good, baby.' Smiling into the mirror she gave him a little tit and tongue action.

Silence. Her stomach churning, she felt sick.

'Not going to happen, Princess,' he said at last.

'Why? You're out of the hospital, aren't you?'

'Yes.'

'I want to see you.'

'No. I don't want you to see me like this.'

She stifled a frustrated scream. 'I'm your partner. You've those husbandly duties to perform. A wife has rights, you know.' Pacing gave her sudden courage. 'I am Mrs Joaquin Xavier Lee. Keep that concept. So don't try playing the vain martyr whose beauty was unjustly taken from him with me. Forget that sour song, dude. Since I was a kid I've loved Victor's Monster and Beauty's Beast. We're partners, Shrek. I'm your Princess and together we'll fuck and make waffles in the morning. But not in a swamp. In Sun Valley. With room service. For the holidays. Sounds good, huh?'

Silence.

Panic rising. 'We're partners, Joaquin. Until fucking death kind of partners.' The Princess stopped pacing and directed her words into the unkind mirror. 'In sickness and in health partners.'

'No.' He was hard.

'No, what?' She waited before the magic mirror for his voice.

Silence. Long silence.

'Joaquin?' the Princess begged as sweetly as she could. Her tears flowed unnaturally. She wanted him to want her. She wanted him to be her hero. Backing up to pose her healthy, perfect body with the great tits and ass directly in the magic mirror, Martha hesitated only a moment before stripping off her sage silk. Standing totally exposed in the low crystal light, her new healthy body more than made up for the common hair and nails. She was a Princess, a Princess of great value, and he wasn't throwing her into the sewer.

She was gorgeous. It gave her confidence.

'Can you see me, Joaquin?'

A short pause. 'Yes.'

One word. One word and she knew. He wasn't weakening. He wasn't coming to get her. Crap. She was alone. A frightened Princess in a Victorian tower without a good fuck or protecting Warrior. No. She'd been a good girl. She deserved better.

The wounded Princess put it out there to him.

'Your letter said I've been your ideal wife. Haven't you enjoyed watching everything? Listening? All these long weeks, months, hasn't it been good for you? Joaquin, we're partners. Not bossman and agency employee. Partners. And this is about more than Margaret's money. More than any business agreement. More than lovers. Partners. I'm a freaking great Mrs Joaquin Xavier Lee, so don't even go there, dude. Because it's the truth. I've been good for you.'

'Truth?' Now the whispering tenor was quick with a warm response. 'Princess, not even Hollywood could have figured a more textbook way for you to play me.' A warm, rich flowing sigh was followed by a short pause. 'Yes. You're my perfect wife and Princess. But . . .' His tenor cracked.

'Rescue me.'

'No.'

'You can.'

'Yes. I could. But I'm not going to.'

'Joaquin.' The Princess fell naked before the magic mirror, and begged in her most sweet and lovely manner. 'Please, Joaquin. Please. Don't abandon me. Not now. Please. I trusted you. Don't treat me mean.'

Silence. From experience she sensed her failure.

Reality set in. He was dumping her. OK. Good. She didn't need him. She didn't need anyone. She was a Princess. A poor abandoned Princess, once again all alone and scared.

Dread rising.

The Princess wasn't stupid. She saw it all before her now. He was playing his pre-nuptial card this holiday season. The old pre-nuptial con. If they didn't remain together for the year, he got the family jewels. Nice gift. Well, Merry Christmas. The scumbag held the legal claim to take her precious jewels and then disappear.

Why was he dumping her? Why? Hadn't she been a good little Princess? Hadn't she? It didn't matter. It never mattered. She'd been conned. As his reward, he'd take the family jewels. How could she ever face Margaret again? Oh no.

No.

That dirty dog. That dirty nasty hound dog. Oh no.

Livid poise happening here.

'OK. So this is how it is between us, Joaquin. Warrior style. Mercenary. I understand.' Pissed-off royally now, the Princess threw her head back in defiance and stared into the magic mirror. Their game wasn't over until she said it was over. And, baby, it wasn't going to be over until both the family jewels and Margaret's millions were in her hands. Fuck this guy.

No excuse. The gloves were off. The Princess bitch had arrived and was about to play the game by new rules.

'Can you see me, Joaquin?' she demanded again in a whisper.

Pause.

Flashing him a sexy come-fuck-me smile, she almost giggled. 'I can feel your eyes on me.'

'Yes. I can see you.'

'Joaquin, baby, look at your Princess. As partners we agreed you'd babysit me for a year. Hey, I've been a good girl and easy to sit. I deserve better from you, Joaquin. Let me see you.'

'No.'

'Why not?'

No answer.

'Look, I'm eating and living the Word here. Playing

183

Princess Perfect. And it hasn't been painless. You know me. I'm totally without job skills or morals. You said trust me. And I did. And now you're discarding me? You damn dirty dog. No wonder Emily tried to kill you. You're one sick son of a bitch.'

Pause. No response from him.

Hot tears of anger rose from the raw pain deep in her gut. The family jewels. Her grandmother's elegant pearls. Her mother's magnificent emeralds. The diamonds. Shit. Not the diamonds. No. The Princess wouldn't surrender one more thing to Joaquin. Certainly not the family gems.

Their game wasn't over until the Princess said it was. And it wasn't over. The year wasn't up. She wasn't through with him. Ignoring his silence, the Princess continued. 'Joaquin, we both know you've no grounds for an annulment or divorce. One year. Trust me, you said back in Burbank. Then you pimped me out for your professional and financial gain. I understand the pimp business. I've held up my end and remained loyal, partner. We agreed one year. Trust me, you said. I signed all your papers. Trust me, you said. I married you. Trust me, you said. Trust you? I did. And I do. One year.'

Pause. The jerk wasn't talking.

'Don't do me nasty, Joaquin,' she growled in open resentment. 'Don't make me beg or treat me cruel. This agreement has already taken a terrible toll in blood and misery. You won't leave me, Joaquin.'

She relaxed against the wall, framed in the low luscious crystal light.

'You won't abandon me because you're having way too much fun torturing me. Controlling me. Pimping me. Bondage is a dangerous game. So, chew on this, oh great one, I'm your lawful wife, not some dumb mark in a cheap con. Don't even consider turning on me, partner. We're partners. Got it? Partners. For a year.'

Silence.

'A year, Joaquin, do you understand me?'

Silence.

Biting her lower lip, the frustrated and frightened Princess stepped back from the mirror and touched her great tits. 'Joaquin,' she mewed softly, her insides churning. 'I'm your wife. I'm Mrs Joaquin Xavier Lee. Don't leave me, baby. Don't –'

He hung up. A dial tone buzzed in her ear.

What the hell? Fuck. Fuck. Fucker.

Slamming the useless phone down on the bed she fumed. 'I'm Mrs Joaquin Xavier Lee,' she shouted at her own reflection. Enraged, she grabbed the silk pyjamas from the floor and tossed them into the mirror in an attempt to smash his watching face. But the silk only fluttered harmlessly to the floor, the delicate sage colour reflecting the crystal lamplight and mocking her anger.

No, no, no.

Tears flowed. 'Nobody uses me. Nobody.' Unable to control her fury or her hot tears she paced naked, shouting out in anguish.

'I've been too good to you. Haven't I?' she roared again and again through the tears. 'I'm a damn great Mrs Lee. A wonderful Mrs Lee. I'm *ideal*. I'm the best damn partner a jerk like you could ever hope to find. You're not fucking me over, Joaquin. You're not.'

She was infuriated. Furious. Burning with poignant pain and bitterness, she seethed. Unable to stop the hot tears, the Princess picked up the elegant silk and, using all her strength, pulled. The flimsy garment gave way at the seams. She shredded the pyjamas and collapsed naked, except for her tears, on the canopied bed.

This wasn't over. No. It wasn't over.

12 **Thank Heavens for Little Boys**

After Joaquin's phone call everything started to go wrong. When presented with December and January's rent the hostess at the Whitmore Mansion continued to appear pleased with Martha's presence but explained tactfully that both bridal suites had been reserved for the holiday months.

Therefore, with a forced smile, the Princess moved into a less expensive, smaller room on the second floor, which didn't have a view of Main Street but did have a big pine tree complete with a squirrel's nest outside her new bay window, and a huge standing mirror. The Princess loved her new mirror. She could no longer flash her tits unobserved at all the Main Street traffic from her turret but, hey, she had a gorgeous mirror.

Too bad she was giving up dancing. No more dancing for the freaky Joaquin. No more. He'd pissed her off. She wasn't leaving town. She wasn't giving a damn deposition in Salt Lake City. And she wasn't going to lose the millions or the gems.

Nope. The Princess was sticking. For the first time in her life, she was sucking up her own misery and going for the big prize. Or in this case, the prize, the jewels, and the millions.

The Whitmore hostess was also concerned about the *vaquero*'s Ford truck, and demanded it be moved. The old thing was an eyesore. Harvey had left the old Ford pick-up with her last summer. Not that she could drive it. She couldn't drive anything with a clutch. But he'd mumbled something about Joaquin's great secret plan, and about the truck having a hidden surveillance lens. But she figured the stuff he'd told her in the old Ford truck was only part of his happy-couple-beginning-a-life-together con. The Princess promised to move the old thing to appease the hostess, but didn't, because she couldn't.

Next problem. The drug-free thing wasn't working for her any more. No matter how much she'd eaten and exercised and masturbated, her body was still in withdrawal. She felt shitty. Lonely. Lousy. And bored.

Knowing that Joaquin was no longer on her side made a huge difference. If she'd been in a bigger place, a more sophisticated community, the poor Princess could have adjourned to the local bar and remained drunk until the ugliest of her symptoms disappeared. Nothing in her agreement with Margaret said she couldn't drink herself shit-faced – only that she couldn't get arrested before, during or after getting shit-faced. However, Mormon communities didn't encourage bars or drinking in public places. Hard liquor was sold only during restricted business hours at the one licensed state store on a carry-out only basis. Utah state law restricted beer to a 3.2 per cent alcohol level. Watery piss. A woman alone couldn't make a purchase without drawing social criticism. No drugs, maybe. But no liquor and no drugs?

Crisis. What the hell was she going to do now?

Joaquin's betrayal had hit her too damn hard. It shouldn't have. But unfortunately it did. Martha grew more and more restless and more and more bored. And with the boredom came depression. And loneliness.

The week of the Christmas holiday, the Princess

awoke totally depressed with a horrendous throbbing headache. Forgetting breakfast, she pulled on one of her thermals, a pair of new denim Levi's, and her warm bulky sweatshirt. She had a plan to make everything better. With extra cash in her front pocket she intended to jog on down to the Interstate off-ramp colony and buy drugs.

The Princess wasn't exactly admitting defeat. Not yet. But she needed a little help. Just a trifling aid. Figuring she still had enough time to clear out her system before Margaret's required drug-testing, the Princess surrendered. Only a small defeat. Mini setback. She had time to clean her system. Months. Time was on her side. Joaquin had said that his legit con was over. Good. Because playing Princess Perfect for the cult scrutiny was suddenly too damn boring to tolerate. Too hard. And the poor Princess was in too much pain.

Enough of the going straight bullshit.

Any kind of drugs would do today. Sleepy was better.

But she could compromise.

Money and drugs were not her first problem. The All-Seeing was. Joaquin could no longer be trusted. He was handing over the recordings of her life via the All-Seeing to the law, and the Princess had to stay out of jail. Before leaving the Whitmore on foot she stopped in the kitchen. Unobserved, she wrapped the All-Seeing first in plastic wrap and then in aluminium foil. She tucked the blinded All-Seeing under her heavy clothes next to her skin. Weird sensation. A shadow stepped on her grave.

Her objective was simple. She'd buy anything to take her up or down, from a safe trucker or travelling supplier at one of the gas station mini-marts at the Interstate off-ramp. But she was out of luck. The holiday traffic proved fierce. The badges were out in force. With the strong presence of the Nephi City cops, the Utah State Highway Patrol, and the Juab County Deputy Sheriffs, any contact with 'the undesirables' was clearly undesirable. So unfortunately the Princess had to wait and hope she could time a deal.

'I can survive this.' With her head pounding the Princess chewed her lower lip. Time was her friend. Patience. She spent the entire morning at one of the two chain coffee shops, drinking eight cups of coffee, chain-smoking, and eavesdropping on other people's conversations while pretending to read through every magazine from the mini-mart rack.

More bad luck. The cops watched her. The truckers watched the cops watching her. And the jealous waitresses watched the truckers and the cops watching her.

She got lousy service. Damn jealous waitresses. Stupid public heroes.

Not a prayer in hell of an experienced bad girl finding a little harmless fun in a joint like this. Too many righteous public heroes out to ruin her amusement. Things didn't go well. Too many people watching to even get a good mind-fuck going with one of the willing lonely knights of the road, let alone get a drug transaction happening.

Damn it.

Her life was crumbling into crap all over again.

The trucking and tourist colony at the ramp was a world away from Nephi. Clearly the town council had planned it that way. The tourists and rough pilgrims of the road were kept far away from the innocent good folks of the religious community. On a whim the defeated Princess applied for jobs at both coffee shops and the three chain motels before heading north, back under the Interstate, and along Main Street towards the Whitmore Mansion.

Her biggest score for the day? Cigarettes. Lacklustre, huh? She was breaking the Word of Wisdom. No tobacco. No caffeine. No stimulants. No alcohol. Nothing harmful allowed in the holy temple of the human body. The Word of Wisdom. Jaded or not, she felt like a sinner again. Good.

An unhappy, unsatisfied and sober sinner, but a true sinner. Like her old self.

Watch out fellas, the bad little Princess was back.

Along a lonely quiet stretch of open road, the old sinner's luck changed for the better. She got lucky. Real lucky. Damn lucky. Halleluiah kind of lucky! Praise the Lord and the heathen devil weed kind of lucky.

A trucker rolled up nice and slow and, unobserved, she hopped up into the cab of his rig without him even having to downshift. Damn, she was so good. Once on the open highway and headed north towards Provo she blew him. He had a nice long cock and she sucked him clear down her throat while he whooped and hollered in appreciation. Actually, she sucked him off twice before he pulled over at the Payson exit.

There, he not only showed his appreciation for her fine work in gifts of pills, the heathen devil weed and sugared chemicals, but he also wrapped her legs over his shoulders and fucked her long and hard in the bed behind his seat. It was great. She felt good. And true gentleman and trusty knight of the road that he was, he arranged for her return back to the Nephi exit.

Let's hear it for the American truckers!

True gentlemen. Honest knights of the road.

The return ride provided another wonderful thrill. The new trucker was older and shockingly mature in his sexual tastes. The Princess enjoyed his uniqueness. With great disappointment, her exit came along way too soon. She made him drop her before the off-ramp commerce. Saddened to let such an entertaining sexual connoisseur escape her clutches so fast, the Princess made her way under the big bare trees on foot back towards Main Street and the Whitmore.

Good sex. Good men. Life was good. And drugs. Drugs. She had drugs in her pocket. She wanted to sing it out loud to the wintry mountain wind. She felt alive. Like a pretty party Princess. Hell, Joaquin said it was over. The legit con was done. Oh yeah? Wanna bet?

She'd barely arrived in the privacy of her antique room, and was just about to pop pills and relax, when the hostess knocked on her door.

It appeared that her Aunt Lou Ellen had sent over two of her grandsons. 'Grandma says it's going to snow tonight. She wants us to cover the piano with a heavier tarp or move it indoors,' the older grandson of perhaps nineteen, Israel, explained. He was cute. Real Scandinavian pioneer stock. Blond, tall, thick farm-boy body, and sweet with it. The Princess immediately adored him.

'My piano?' The Princess didn't recall owning a piano. But the new game with the boys was fun.

'Grandma's predicting the storm will last almost a week. She says heavy snows all this winter,' Ian, the younger one of about seventeen or eighteen, offered in pious confidence. 'You should have already covered everything in your truck with a tarp. That piano collected dust all summer. That's not good for a musical instrument,' he scolded her.

Righteous little son of a bitch, even for a future God-maker. Pooh. Pooh.

Both plump, like cousin Horace, the youthful young

men looked like blond teddy bears. The Princess was immediately enchanted. She adored their baby fat cheeks. Shamelessly teasing little boys about their first manly whiskers and spending time to make each one blush was now the Princess's new favourite pastime. Young men were never boring. Never. Not when it was so easy to make peaks in their pants. An experienced Princess wouldn't even have to touch them.

The gleefully amused Princess immediately joined the hormone-pumping men down at the truck in the gravel parking lot to 'discuss' the piano/storm situation.

With great interest the macho farm-boys examined the contents of the seasoned Ford. The Princess noted the younger one actually writing a list while the older brother distracted her in conversation. It was great. They were good. Properly programmed and charming. Cult charismatic. Fascinating. They knew exactly how to handle her, handle the situation, and learn everything whoever sent them wanted to know. She could appreciate their skill because she'd had the same lessons, a long time ago – before Daddy had left the cult to pursue business, before her mother had died, and before she'd been sent off to boarding school. The little men were good. But where was their Fagin?

Someone had sent the little men to her. They were bait. But who was the big catch? And why should she take the bait?

Because it might be a thrill.

OK, she was biting.

'Sister Lee, with a storm coming in tonight it might be wisest to move the whole truck someplace safe and covered.' Taking his role as adviser very seriously, Israel appeared extremely thoughtful – holy-rollin' pensive. The little man was good. Very holier-than-thou. 'We could probably find someone in the family with a barn.'

The Princess beamed in delight at his suggestion. But she had other ideas. Making young virtuous men cream their trousers while she worked them in full respectable view of the religious community was a task no bored Princess could refuse. 'I've got an idea, cousins. Could Israel use this old truck? Maybe you could earn yourself a blessing here.'

'A blessing?' The youngest lifted his head with great interest, the list now forgotten. Oh goody. A young Pope in the making. Power. Women. Religion. All good things to make a little one develop an erection.

The Princess took in a deep breath; both young men helplessly admired her great tits before she exhaled in an exaggerated sigh. Oh yeah, the great tits held a magnetic charm for men of all ages. These babies didn't have a prayer. Poor babes in the woods.

Their young admiration fed her ego but she had no interest in touching them. No little men. She hadn't touched little men even when she was a little woman. No, she liked mature seasoned adult men. But of course, something as silly as age didn't stop the Princess from brazenly flirting with the two heralds of the Lord. And they blushed so delightfully. Cute baby boys, with chubby cheeks and everything.

'The owner of the Whitmore doesn't want this old thing cluttering up her parking lot. The bridal suites are booked for the holidays, you know.' She dropped her voice almost to a whisper. 'Honeymooners.'

Both young men immediately blushed; the older Israel added a little sexy smile. Ah. Martha almost giggled. They understood what happened on honeymoons. Sex. Gasp.

Sex was exciting.

Little men thought about it often.

Like maybe every point two seconds. Or more.

'What are you suggesting?' The younger Ian finally poked his older brother and frowned. Oh, he was a pious little man. Virtuous and beyond.

'Do you boys know of anyone who might rent me storage space? If the truck were empty, I'd let Israel use it until I needed it back next summer.'

'Me?' The older one's surprise couldn't be masked. 'Are you suggesting that you'd let me use this truck? As my own? Me?'

Oh my, yes. The personal and sexual freedom of the open road did it for a young guy every time. He was coming in his shorts. One constant in America: a man, his penis size and his ride are always connected. She gave him her best appreciative Princess smile and teased him by wiggling her tits just enough for an eye-candy topping.

'The old thing is insured. But before you can use it, we have to store the stuff. I can't pay much. I haven't found a job yet.'

An obvious hard-on formed in the young man's pants as his eyes bounced from the truck to Martha's great tits and back again. Naughty Princess that she was, she couldn't resist adding, 'Oh, and you have to promise to give me one driving lesson a week. Do you think I'm too old to learn to drive with a clutch?'

After much puffing and huffing the excited young men assured her that she was young enough to learn anything. They were family – they would love to help her out, and receive a blessing for a good deed. A bargain was struck. With much ceremony the Princess turned over the Ford keys and was instantly rewarded with their undying devoted lust.

'This is what I can pay for storage.' She handed the

boys twenty bucks. Halt. Oh no. Houston, we have a problem.

Now the devout yearning in their eyes turned to deep reverence. Money came between them. It changed everything. A man, his penis, a woman, and money? No. Nasty. Naughty. Righteous heroes that they were, their lust must remain pure. Clean. Money made it somehow dirty. Sinful. They rejected her money. It would only make their erections somehow shameful, not spiritually jubilant. They rejected her twenty pieces of silver.

'We can put this whole load in Grandma's cellar over on First West. I'm sure she won't accept money.'

Wanna bet? 'Well, you tell Grandma I said to pass it along.' The Princess winked at the two and thrust the cash into Ian's pocket. 'I trust Aunt Lou Ellen to put the money to good use. It'll be a blessing for me in return for her affectionate concern and your acts of kindness. I'll count it as tithing.'

The younger man smiled and poked his brother. 'A blessing.'

Well, a blessing. An opportunity to earn a heavenly blessing. That changed everything. Religious intentions made the money and the lust chaste. Oh my, yes. Religion changed it and stamped it with respectability.

Hallelujah. Cherubs singing here.

Nothing can move as fast as an American man around an automobile engine when he holds the keys. The love affair had begun. However, the initial sexual climax was postponed. The Ford's battery was dead. But this only heightened the ultimate thrill. Because the boys would have to jump start it and use the *cables*. Tools! Arf.

Manly men at work they were! Big penis in the house.

At the man and his tools point, the Princess faked a frown. 'Are you sure you know how to do this, cousins?

It looks dangerous. If you should get hurt, Aunt Lou Ellen will never forgive me.' Batting her eyelashes, she signed and let her tits work their magic.

Again, with much huffing and puffing, the two young righteous heroes were finally able to convince the meek Princess that indeed they were macho enough for the task, assuring her repeatedly that they did this kind of thing 'all the time'. Trying not to place too much pressure on them to perform right away, the Princess retired to a wicker rocking chair on the wrap-around veranda to enjoy the fun, letting the boys catch a glimpse of her panties now and then, just to keep them stiff. She even teased them by absently stroking her nipples through her top as she watched. She loved seeing them flush and move awkwardly, adjusting themsevles with a hand in their pants.

As it turned out, moving the old Ford required more than the two willing American boys. Soon four hormone-driven young colleagues and a frail dirty old man arrived to offer advice and moral support.

Absolutely amused, the Princess accepted a mug of warm chocolate from the Whitmore hostess and stretched out to rock at a respectable distance while enjoying her handiwork. She hadn't giggled so much in months.

A cheer of victory resounded through the entire valley when the old engine finally turned over. When the sound of the dilapidated motor had faded from her ears Martha rubbed her temples and tired eyes. Little virtuous boys were fun. But what she really needed was a sinning man.

Did she hear ringing?

Unexpectedly the Whitmore hostess appeared with Martha's cellphone. 'You left this in the kitchen. It's been ringing all morning.'

It was ringing now.

Oh, right. Cellphone ringing.

Knowing damn well she'd left the cell turned off and buried in her underwear drawer, not in the Whitmore kitchen, the Princess smiled sweetly at her lovely thoughtful hostess, who lingered out in the cold where she could listen.

'Hello.'

Heavy breathing. 'Princess, you're all right?'

Genuine concern echoed in his tense tenor tones. Martha glanced at the hostess. The bitch wasn't leaving. Nope. The gossip wanted the scoop.

'What do you want?' The Princess immediately played the poor, put-upon, wife-beaten Mrs Lee routine. Her words and frightened tone had the head of the hostess spinning around. The bitch was so nosy. The Princess sighed and thought about how best to play the scene for the benefit of the gossip. Sucking on her lower lip, she waited for Joaquin's response.

When he finally spoke it was clear that the element of fake fear in her voice had shaken him. 'Don't panic. Something's gone wrong. Listen to me. You're in real danger. I've lost your signal. Harvey and Norm should be pulling into Nephi any minute to collect you.'

'No.'

Silence.

'You're in danger. Trust me.' Pause. 'Martha?'

She tingled. Sensation happening. This was only the second time in their relationship that he'd used her name.

Smothering a small giggle under her pretend tearing, the Princess sniffled. God, she was so good. Thank the Academy good. The poor beaten and misunderstood Princess.

'No. Joaquin, I can never go back to my old life of sin

and self-destruction. I must be worthy. Please, don't pull me back into the evil. Please. Please. Let me earn the Keys to the Kingdom.'

Oh, the hostess was eating it up. Royal. Worthy. Keys to the Kingdom. Oh yes. Picking out a gown for Oscar night about now. The poor wayward Princess only longed to be worthy of being recommended for the temple. Worthy of going to the Celestial Kingdom. Saintly worthy. Worthy. God's chosen path for women in the American Zion.

Yeah, right.

'Trust me, Princess.' Blinded and confused, the poor Joaquin attempted to calm her fears and tears. 'Get as far away from Nephi as you can. Now.'

'No,' she almost screamed, as she continued to pretend to cry. 'No. No. I don't trust you any more. I'm done with you. It's all over. The way to the Celestial Kingdom lies before me here.'

Joaquin's extremely tense voice was almost a hushed whisper. 'It's Emily. Martha, run.'

'Don't ever call me again. I won't be your wife. I'll find a new partner,' the Princess announced firmly, before shutting off the phone.

The hostess beamed with open approval, and gave the secret sign.

The tearful frightened Princess froze. Damn. She recognized that symbol. Incoming.

Then big wham. The world shattered.

Almost immediately Harvey pulled up in front of the Whitmore, driving Joaquin's black jeep at a demon-racing-from-hell speed. The Princess watched. The calamity only took seconds.

Dressed in a heavy plaid wool jacket and wearing his jeans and cowboy hat, Harvey only ran about five steps from the jeep towards the Princess on the veranda before her shadow appeared from nowhere, gun in hand. Harvey was shouting loudly at her in Spanish. The car with the star arrived almost instantly with the sheriff, and then another car with more of the legal posse. And then . . .

Shouting. Harvey stopped and went down without a struggle, first to his knees, fingers laced behind his head, then, when pushed from behind, he went down flat on his belly while they cuffed him from behind.

Stunned, the Princess did nothing.

Everything was surreal, like an action film running in slow motion. There was gunfire. The lawmen ducked behind cars and pointed their weapons towards the city park across the street. More gunfire.

Harvey's hat flew off, spattered with blood. The cowboy wasn't going anywhere now.

Shocked into silence, the Princess allowed the hostess to pull her into the safety of the Whitmore.

A strong male voice from behind startled her. Panicked, the Princess wheeled around. Its face was inches from hers as he spoke. 'Living the Principle isn't easy. Polygamy destroys more people than it saves.'

The extremely composed and calm man preached to her over the gunfire. 'But if a man seeks salvation to the *fullest*, that is exaltation in the Kingdom of God, he must accept the doctrine and live the Principle.'

Holy crap. He'd come for her. Oh no. Horrified, Martha took several steps backwards. His warm words sent chills up her spine. 'My name is Bradford Henry. I've prayed that you might successfully conquer your demons and place your feet on a righteous path.'

Scream. This nightmare couldn't be happening. Not to her. No. The Princess tore upstairs. Even when her bedroom door was safely locked behind her she felt sick. What mistake had she made?

Unable to control her deep breathing, she attempted to calm her escalating terror. She closed her eyes and tried to think. But the sudden nausea continued. His holier-than-hell voice bellowed forth from behind the locked door.

'The Avenging Angel himself, Orrin Porter Rockwell, appeared in a vision and revealed your existence to me. You, Martha, shall be my third wife. The Lord commands it.'

A low dull ringing in her ears. Dizziness. Difficult to remain standing. Unable to grab any sensory reality, Martha covered her ears and closed her eyes. Damn it. She knew it. A Princess should never attempt to con the Faithful, not in this hell-hole like this. What had she been thinking?

Hideous story time.

Panic left her motionless.

It was all over but the crying. The Princess understood she was about to be taken prisoner. Held captive. A true Mormon Princess descended from the dynasty of saints first baptised in upstate New York. Chosen by God. Ordained by the first Prophet. Leader of the Danites. Selected by the second Prophet Brigham Young to guide the Faithful saints into Zion. The blood of Porter Rockwell, the Avenging Angel of the Lord sent to earth to assassinate the enemies of the American Saints, flowed through her veins. Family bloodline had once escalated her Daddy to the position of Living Prophet.

The Avenging Angel's seed. A true Zion Princess.

The wayward Princess had returned to be found worthy.

Returned to live the Word.

Returned to live among the Faithful.

Holy crap. She was in so much trouble.

13 **Pearls of Great Price**

Life within any cult is never what outsiders imagine. Martha couldn't understand exactly what had happened to ignite the killings at the Whitmore Mansion. It didn't matter. Besides, once successfully accepted within any cult, a member never questions. Never. Too dangerous.

It would only bring on the worst kind of punishment: shunning.

For those who've lived an active life within any community, shunning is absolute agony. It drives the sinner to distraction – sometimes to suicide, but most often to mental illness. Permanent madness.

Not good.

And Martha understood how such voodoo worked on the mind. As a kid she'd witnessed the process enough. It was not something she cared to explore personally.

OK. So she was a coward, a wimp. Help.

Regrettably her nasty lustful nature would eventually let her in for some serious disciplinary action. With the All-Seeing still locked around her neck, it was clear she wasn't going anywhere until Joaquin arrived with the cavalry. Hence, before she was plagued with shunning she put some serious thought towards a lesser sin. A sinful distraction worthy of the punishment of isolation, but not serious enough to bring on fully fledged mental torture. She needed a plan.

In the meantime Martha's life within the polygamist

cult began with a submissive whimper and a sober exercise in patience. After the killings at the Whitmore, Joaquin's promised raids didn't occur in January, or February, or even March. No rescue on the horizon. American courts and the lawful exercise of religious freedoms never maintained a faithful standard. Too many elements shifted with the contemporary biases of both state and federal political administrations.

Touchy thing, liberty. Religious freedom.

Utah polygamist cults founded back when the practice was sacrificed for statehood always had an emergency plan in place for when trouble came. Members of the Faithful were divided into units of ten, with unit leadership pre-established. Special Forces had nothing on a good polygamist. It was called survival. Boring. And dangerous.

Martha accepted the survival drills, having been exposed to the same routines as a kid, and for several weeks she kept her mouth shut, her head low, and her eyes and ears open.

Paranoid since birth, most of the Faithful searched for potential antagonists everywhere. Private conflicts erupted. Internal struggles for male leadership had always been vicious.

Blood Atonement. Bodies simply disappeared.

But the male rivalry paled in comparison to the female competition. Religious doctrine placed no man off-limits as a potential partner: therefore the more powerful an alpha male, the more aggressive the females who wished to join him in Celestial Marriage.

Cut-throat competition. Nasty.

Casualties frequently condemned to a form of shunning.

Spine-chilling concept.

The carnage at the Whitmore and the following

unwanted publicity produced a major cockfight among the Faithful alpha males for top dog. Suddenly her new squeeze Bradford Henry found himself in a bloody dogfight.

Successfully returning the Princess to the Faithful as his third wife was considered a major coup because according to ancient dogma, bloodlines were sealed forever. So now, with the Princess sharing his bed, whoever challenged Bradford's right to rule subconsciously and spiritually opposed the Avenging Angel himself. Not many mortals up to that battle. Nope. Suddenly Bradford was a contender for the role of Living Prophet.

So naturally, as his earthly power and influence increased, so too did the competition for his bed. Martha didn't care. The more the merrier. The Princess wasn't impressed with her new stud's sexual performances.

Regrettably Bradford was one of those religious nuts that connected the power of both earthly and celestial glory with the force of his erection. Alas, sex with this mutt was all about God and holy-rolling and spiritual desire and crap. Repulsive. Puke reflex activated.

He'd sermonize at her to get hard. Preaching alone worked his cock up something fierce. During sex he'd continue to spill great words of divine judiciousness into her face non-stop, most of it sanctimonious rubbish she'd heard previously. And, baby, it wasn't sexy or exciting. Faithful wives were expected to partake of sex in awed divine silence and with appreciative humility. So she'd zone out and fantasy-fuck Joaquin through most of his stupid discourses. It worked for her. Made her new life sufferable.

It usually took Bradford several hours of moralizing to work up a good erection. And then when they'd finally get to the part where she fell to her knees before him, he'd place consecrated oil on her forehead, his hands on her head, and beseech the Lord to bless their carnal acts and fill them both with spiritual light. Then he'd jump her. Well then, Bradford was a master at moving himself rapidly towards that great climactic sexual and spiritual illumination, but didn't possess a clue as to how to bring along a woman. For all his carnal fierceness, he was a sexual dud.

Quickly the Princess found herself moving towards brain-dead and sexually famished. Sex with some folks just wasn't worth the effort. No matter how many times, no matter how many struggles to orgasms, it remained monotonous. Dreary, even. No way did sex with Bradford fulfil her carnal desires; it was just too weird and unsatisfying. And unfortunately, under the circumstances, other Faithful men saw her only as a walking Blood Atonement. So no cult love-fest happening. Her restricted contact with outsiders remained far too limited and controlled even to get a good mind-fuck going with a willing stranger. The bored Princess was in big trouble.

And back to her vibrator.

How much was a Princess expected to suffer?

The daily cult grind required mental discipline and sexual patience, while constantly testing her acting skills. Talk about practising the thespian craft – she immersed herself totally in her new role as Princess of the Faithful. No doubt the All-Seeing would eventually recapture the faces of the fugitives and Joaquin would arrive to rescue her. She figured it was all a matter of time.

In the interim she suffered silently, according to the hen-pecking order. The Princess was Bradford's third wife. And in polygamy the first wife commands all the respect while the third wife scratches and roosts only one step above chicken crap.

Bradford's first wife was a naturally blonde, massively round, God-hungry cow named Constance. According to tradition the first wife held final approval or disapproval of all sister-wife candidates jostling for inferior positions. However, Martha's exalted ancestry placed her above any first wife's or single cult member's approval. Mess with this Princess and you messed with the infamous Avenging Angel. Constance was a smart cow; she didn't mess with an Avenging Princess.

Not much, anyway, and never when witnesses were around.

Living arrangements for polygamists varied according to personal wealth. Some men deposited all their wives in one enclosed spacious compound with each sister-wife keeping a separate household. Others maintained sister-wives in different communities. Some even attempted to stash them in the same house, but this didn't usually work out.

However, Bradford gave it a go, moving Martha in with Constance. The Princess didn't enjoy her lowly slave-wife status in the first-wife's household. Not fun. When Bradford was distracted or away for days at a time Constance let her hostile side shine. Martha's lowly state might have proved easier to handle if the second wife, Sharon, had been around to form an alliance or offer sympathy and companionship. Unfortunately Sharon had committed some unmentionable sin, and following five years of community shunning her mind had given way.

Either to hide his embarrassment or to make life easier, Bradford had taken Sharon to some distant isolated ranch where, if the rumours were true, the cult's financial records were also stockpiled. Martha decided Sharon's out-of-the-way lifestyle and possible access to protected paperwork was preferable to her current position. So she plotted to do something that would upset Constance enough to remove the slave Princess from her household, without bringing on shunning or Bradford's anger.

Winter passed. Spring. Easter.

Time for a Princess to escape a queen cow.

Born and raised among the Faithful, Constance came from a long line of polygamists. Oh yes. Generations of women in her family had mastered all the standard tricks necessary to survive a younger, prettier, and sexier sister-wife.

Jealousy wasn't happening.

Not even when Martha inappropriately faked sexual and spiritual ecstasy with Bradford loud enough to rattle all the windows in Constance's house. Not even when the brass headboard banged the walls loud enough to cause cult neighbours to make jests about Bradford's sermons. Jealousy didn't happen, but humiliation did. Eventually Constance felt humiliated. However, she was experienced at seeking wifely revenge without setting off the angry-husband alarm.

Constance actually enjoyed a great status among the other wives of the Faithful. Taking her down required a careful scheme. Enjoying Bradford's successful leadership coup, she was now the reigning cult queen; but she was no true Princess.

Following the huge Easter gathering of the Faithful Martha made her move. Out of sensitive desperation Bradford found himself forced to move Martha, his greatest current political asset, away from the central cult and Constance's household. In order to protect his Princess, Bradford moved her into isolation, away from his or anyone else's direct domination. She had only Sharon for company.

'Why are you in exile?' Sharon asked one evening. The two sister-wives shared an old log ranch house on several thousand acres of slightly rolling red desert. The place didn't even have a name. There was no civilisation on the horizon in any direction, only red dirt, sagebrush and cattle. Living and working only for the glory of Bradford, the Faithful, and God, Martha figured the isolated ranch was somewhere in southern Utah or maybe northern Arizona. Red dirt and sage, was red dirt and sage and all red dirt deserts looked alike to a Princess. Utah. Arizona. New Mexico. Lots of virginal red dirt deserts in America.

'I'm doing penance. My transgression occurred while Bradford and Constance were away in Provo Canyon on a spiritual retreat.' Martha beamed openly in victory.

'I don't understand.' Alone and shunned for way too long, the hard-bitten Sharon's communication skills had sunk to mostly grunts, nods, and pointing with her fingers. For her to actually pull it together enough to string words along for a sentence was a tribute to Martha and her patience.

'Bradford told me to find an old dress in Constance's closet and rip it up to use as rags, then polish all the hardwood in that ugly three-storey atrocity of a house. So I did.'

Not one to waste mental or physical energy forming words, the wiry Sharon merely shrugged and silently turned her attention to the veal milanese, a sautéed breaded veal cutlet with drizzled butter and lemon, that Martha had prepared and now placed respectfully before her.

Unable or unwilling to control her amusement any

longer, Martha laughed aloud and shared more of the story with her sister-wife. 'Actually, I did an outstanding job on that grand circular staircase. Constance examined every inch too. Finally, in front of Bradford she begrudgingly praised me for all my excellent unselfish labour. Things were great, for about an hour. Then after all the bragging she did about their great romantic and spiritually uplifting weekend away, about all the money he'd spent on her, and on how unworthy she was to be blessed with such a loving and devoted husband, who treated her like a true celestial queen, she found the filthy cleaning rags in the trash. Seems that the old dress I ripped up was her wedding gown. Guess it was a hand-me-down from her grandmother. Who knows? It was totally ugly. But she went berserk.'

Sharon didn't speak. But from the immediate light in her blue eyes, it was clear that Sharon had her own issues with Constance the cow. And Martha had earned an ally.

Even as an ally the meek Sharon, the second wife, assumed authority over the third. Holding all the power in their sister-wife relationship as well as the keys to the only working vehicle on the ranch, Sharon reigned supreme. And there was another problem. Unfortunately only the withdrawn and mentally damaged Sharon knew the way out of the desert.

As the third wife Martha held no clout. As a Princess she knew nothing about ranching or animals or how to survive in the swirling red sandstorms that surrounded them constantly. However, being a smart Princess, she did know something about seduction and escape.

Hey, this Princess was a pro after all.

When one heterosexual woman sets out to seduce another heterosexual woman, it's never easy. Nevertheless Martha managed. She'd learned a lot from Joaquin. And so while she assumed he watched via the All-Seeing, Martha put his techniques to work, beginning with expressing concern, practising tenderness, and continually pushing healthy food.

Joaquin's wise ways were in direct conflict with two of Bradford's commandments. The first of Bradford's commandments to be broken concerned Sharon's diet.

Remove the meek from the meat and sources of high protein. Only Warriors ate meat, no one else. Limited grains along with lots and lots of vegetables and fruits made for an obedient flock. Ever met a violent and sexually aggressive vegetarian cult? No. Well, Martha understood the concept.

Peaceful pacifists sprouted from vegetables. Add meat and in turn muscle and sexual energy and naturally combative crap happened. No meat = meek flock.

Second commandment busted? The physical contact between sister-wives without the hubby present. Limitation and restriction of all sexual activities among the meek being restricted to one alpha male also played into standard cult-control issues. You isolated the individual and limited intimate contact to one. Only one. The alpha male. This meant no one had touched Sharon, even casually, in passing, let alone sexually, in over five years.

Poor Sharon, dressed in Bradford's discarded trousers and shirts, laboured from sunrise to sunset outside doing whatever she did on the land and for the animals. After dark she'd return to the rundown ranch house with barely enough energy to cut up and chew a raw turnip as a meal before falling onto her bed, exhausted. Poor abused and neglected baby. As part of her seduction the Princess immediately seized control of the kitchen and fed her. Daddy had sent her to cooking school. She could cook. Really cook.

Every morning she'd rise early with Sharon and begin baking. Nothing like the smell of baking bread to keep the meek and hungry close. At first Sharon never appeared for a midday meal, so Martha delivered it to her – forcing the other woman to cease in her physical work, coercing her into resting for a moment, and pressing her into eating something healthy and filling.

'Eat,' Martha commanded, giving her best Joaquin imitation. 'Eat.'

And Sharon, who was no conversationalist, proved herself a trustworthy and hungry listener. So Martha talked non-stop while Sharon ate. Following Joaquin's example, she complimented the lonely, starving woman. On her strength. On her discipline. On her successful labours.

'I'm very proud we're sister-wives. I like you very much.'

Like all forlorn females, Sharon pretended to ignore the words but secretly relished the praise.

To woo Sharon into the house earlier in the evenings Martha, bored by this time, started baking fancy desserts in the late afternoon, as the burning summer sun started its slow descent to the desert floor. That way the fragrances of dinner and the pretty sweets were the first thing Sharon encountered upon her return.

As weeks slowly slipped by, the aromas coming from Martha's kitchen gradually brought Sharon in from her labours earlier and earlier, until the sister-wives spent most afternoon hours together. Martha always waited on the neglected Sharon like a queen – like she was the first-wife.

Too long shunned, too long in isolation, and too long abandoned, Sharon blossomed under Martha's care.

She was resurrected. Reborn.

Good food and pretty compliments mixed with simple compassionate companionship brought Sharon closer and closer to the house and closer and closer to Martha. And physical contact soon glued Sharon to Martha's side.

She began it simply. A little comforting petting on the hand or arm, and a warm embrace over silly joyous things, were the first contacts Sharon had experienced with anyone in years and years. Unresponsive at first, she quickly warmed to the touch, not by returning it but by willingly accepting it.

Things grew sexier with the nightly massages. Hot oil does it every time. After labouring all day in the summer heat Sharon would allow Martha to massage her weary shoulders and back muscles in the evening. Good diet and simple touch therapy mixed with affectionate, compassionate concern produced miracles – and would have seduced almost any woman.

'Slow down. I worry about you. You work too hard. I mean it, Sharon – you'll put yourself into an early grave. We need help. I'm going to speak to Bradford about it.'

Sharon would blush with pleasure at Martha's sincere concern. The poor creature was ugly and thin, with closely hacked mousy brown hair and the driest of skin. But using the Joaquin techniques, Martha pampered her sister-wife.

And it came to pass that not much later, when Bradford arrived for one of his semi-regular visits, Sharon and Martha were more than friends, more than mere sister-wives; they were almost lovers. As it turned out Bradford, who didn't have a clue as to what might really be happening between the women, was impressed.

'You're a blessing upon her, Martha. A true blessing. Sharon is actually smiling. Reborn.' Proudly, Bradford beamed with both pleasure and surprise. 'The two of you keep such a happy home.'

Damn straight. The sister-wives were on the same side. They shared common enemies, the weird Bradford and the brutal Constance, along with the stifling heat of atonement and the penance of slave labour. But now neither suffered alone. They had each other. Sharing the day. Sharing the night. Sharing secrets. They were good for one another. Very good. Now, by comparison, Constance the cow loomed as only a nagging bitter first wife.

Ah, the Princess was good. Very good.

During the daylight hours of Sharon's outdoor labours Martha masturbated while fantasizing about Joaquin, cooked up tasty miracles in the kitchen, performed the few household chores, and searched for the cult's financial records. Once she'd found the hidden file boxes of paperwork under the false floor boards she spent time, too much time, stirring whatever was on the stove and simply pointing her great tits and the All-Seeing at page after page after page, not even bothering to read most of the documents herself.

Then one day she found a most remarkable file that traced the careers of Big Gus and one Joaquin Xavier Lee, private investigators.

'What the hell?'

With trembling fingers Martha flipped through the numerous records documenting the pair's successful arrests and prosecution evidence. It seemed that Big Gus and Joaquin were quite a pair. They were also responsible for putting away lots of people she knew. Face to face. Her stomach twisted into knots. She knew all the criminals arrested personally, because they were all former associates or marks in her cons. Bells ringing. Hello.

Suddenly it was all so clear.

Like a vision, even.

As Big Gus was rescuing and returning her safely to Daddy, evidently Joaquin was turning his surveillance over to the law. If she ever needed proof that Joaquin had out-foxed and played her from the beginning, now she had it. The damn dirty hound.

So, they'd been business partners of sorts for a long time. Years. The Princess just hadn't known it. Well, she knew it now. And it bugged her. Big time.

'I want you to wear these.' Martha gave Sharon some of her least sexy silk underthings. 'I'm tossing away the old cotton granny panties and nightshirts you've been wearing. Sharon, you deserve something soft and pretty. Something that will remind you that you're an attractive female, not a damn beast of heavy burden.'

Sharon had never owned anything silk. It'd been years since she'd owned anything feminine like a dress, let alone anything pretty. The hand-me-down gift moved her to noiseless tears.

It was while comforting those tears that Martha first kissed her. A slow sensitive caring kiss. A slightly open-mouthed kiss. Tender. Sweet. Seductive.

Bewildered, Sharon hadn't responded or commented, so Martha handled the whole sensual kiss as if it were the most innocent of affectionate gestures. Something natural that happened between loving sister-wives all the time. But that simple kiss changed everything. The very next day Sharon began working less than five hours a day outdoors, and within a week it had gone down to less than three hours.

Soon, Sharon only went out when absolutely necessary.

The sister-wives were now lovers and constant companions.

After a late lunch they'd ridden double on the old mule over to the watering hole for a leisurely swim and a bath. Feeling easy with one another, the sister-wives washed each other's hair and scrubbed each other's back. Martha had started it, by touching Sharon's breasts, and she encouraged her sister-wife by bringing Sharon's hand between her legs. Sharon didn't need much more encouragement, and she was soon on her knees licking away at Martha. It felt so good to have someone else handle her, and Martha pulled on Sharon's hair as she felt herself start to come. She returned the favour afterwards, fingering Sharon to a climax, then thought about the fun they could have back at the ranch. They were a long way from town. Anything could happen.

'Why did you marry Bradford?'

More out of boredom than curiosity, Martha endeavoured to encourage and improve Sharon's meagre conversational range.

Lying relaxed, sated, and naked now on the ranch house's crude excuse for a veranda, both women sipped the iced water Martha served in old Mason jelly jars. Sharon nibbled on a fresh peach.

It took several attempts before Sharon finally managed a complete answer. 'I don't remember having a choice.'

'Well, that's for shit.' Resting her head on her elbow, Martha arched her back and studied her sister-wife's solemn expression. 'The nineteenth amendment says a women is entitled to pick who she fucks.' Sharon always flinched whenever Martha used inappropriate language. But recently it often made her smile too. Smiling good. Very nice. So Martha let her Princess of the Faithful façade slip and talked trash. Today it made Sharon smile.

The ever-extending sky grew rapidly darker as enormous sinister clouds formed, gathered, spun, and expanded. Watching the summer lightning storms high over the red desert floor proved a major source of entertainment for the two secluded lovers. The exciting odour of the gathering electrical energy filled the arid air. Martha could taste it in her mouth, feel it on her skin and through her hair. Swallowing and licking her lips, she felt restless and reckless from the energy.

'Why did you marry Bradford?' Wow. Sharon actually managed a question to contribute to the conversation.

Martha smiled with approval. 'I didn't. Not really. Legally I'm Mrs Joaquin Xavier Lee. Actually, our first anniversary is coming up real soon.' Because they shared so much, she shared another truth with Sharon. 'I miss him.'

And she did.

Concerned, as if some undeniable threat had suddenly appeared, Sharon reached forwards to touch Martha's cheek tenderly with her fingertips. In response, Martha smiled sweetly and playfully danced her fingers along Sharon's shoulders, arms, and hands, tickling her sister-wife just enough to make her squirm and smile again.

Sharon was jealous. Poor baby.

She had a right to be. Martha felt something for her wounded Warrior. It broke all her personal Princess mottos of royal life but she did.

'Joaquin Lee? Is he Mexican or Chinese?' Wow. More

questions. Gee, big verbal happening between the sister-wives. They were having a real conversation this afternoon.

Giggling, Martha enjoyed the success and smiled thinking of Joaquin. 'I haven't got a clue. We didn't exactly discuss detailed genealogy. Who cares, anyway? His bloodline didn't matter.'

Frustrated and almost uncontrollably jealous, Sharon turned her attention to the gathering storm. The poor creature was so emotionally and mentally fragile. So delicate. So lost. Martha experienced a rush of tenderness and something else. Something that might be close to ... responsibility. Woo. No. Wait. She'd seduced Sharon. She didn't want to hurt her. They were sister-wives.

Sexual intimacy mixed with what? Responsibility? Tough concept for a Princess. Cruel reality.

A warm rush of something washed over her, forcing her to reach out, hug, and soothe Sharon's lean body. Tenderness. She understood tenderness and didn't want to move, didn't want to break the physical or emotional connection Sharon shared with her at that moment. Unlike affairs with straight or among gay men, most female affairs, lesbian or not, are most often based on intimacy issues, not sexual ones. This was a crisis.

Talking aloud about Joaquin with her lover Sharon was perhaps the most intimate thing Martha had ever done with another human being – more intimate than almost all the sexual encounters of her life. She felt vulnerable. Exposed. And emotional. She felt closer to Sharon than to anyone since her mother's death.

'I only knew Joaquin for a few hours before we eloped to Las Vegas, and during that time we didn't waste much of it talking.' Martha sighed. 'You should have seen him. He had a body of a Warrior god. He was absolutely gorgeous. Muscular. Macho. A true primo fuck. I mean the best. And I should know.'

Lightning. Boom. The never-ending sky brewed bruised storm clouds. Heatwaves rolled across the red dirt to prickle their naked skin. While Martha shuddered, Sharon fingered the All-Seeing gently, and unsuccessfully tried to keep jealousy out of her tone. 'You've known many men?'

'Many men and then some.' Nodding cheerfully Martha took a bite out of Sharon's peach. It was good. Juicy. She ate half of it while playfully smacking away Sharon's exploring hands. 'And I've know a few women too. How about you? Anyone before Bradford and me?'

Sharon shook her head in the negative.

Lightning again. Wow. Big boom. The earth rumbled and the sky rolled. Lightning crackle. Electrical energy teased the tiny hairs of their bodies.

Amazed at the sensation, Martha was filled with excitement. The land rumbled around them. The wind raced into heated action, whirling her hair. Bolt. Blast. Blazing white light followed by an almost immediate sonic boom.

Wow. Big bang. Genesis.

Martha was a huge fan. She sat in the lotus position to admire the natural opera phenomenon before her. Great stuff, this awesome natural energy happening. Now this was a rush. A thrill. She kissed Sharon.

And something inside Sharon snapped. 'Your husband was beating you. I've seen the pictures. And the videos.' Sharon cuddled her body against the Princess. 'Now he's plotting in the divorce courts to seize your family's great fortune. Bradford can't stop him. The Faithful have proof that it was his mistress who sent the assassin to the Whitmore. Those people died protecting you. Your husband wants your money and his mistress wants you dead.'

Lightning bolt. Pause. Wind. Boom.

Taken back slightly by Sharon's sincerity the Princess pondered her unexpected revelation. How much of what Sharon said was true?

How much could she trust?

Trust.

'Trust me.' His voice boomed in her head as the crackling sensations rushed through her body.

Vibrating from the electrical energy waves Martha wrapped her arms tightly around her sweet, sensitive sister-wife. Together they surfed the heatwaves charging their bodies. What an incredible sensation. Talk about being the meek in an electric tornado. Bada bing. Drum roll please. Oh, a deity existed all right, and today was getting ass in the desert.

It was exciting.

It was inspiring.

It made her wet.

And in that sensual wet moment she saw the truth.

As she looked into Sharon's frightened blue eyes her thoughts returned to her sister-wife's comments about Joaquin, and she knew what she had to say. 'You show me one picture and I'll give you ten thousand words. It's weird, but right now, for the first time in my whole life, I'm absolutely sure of what I want. And I want Joaquin. He's wonderful for me in a way I can't explain.'

Flash.

Sonic pop.

Woo. Wow.

Sharon screamed. Martha's eardrums hurt. Her teeth

hurt. She gasped for air. Oh, what a thrill! Alive. Even her clit was tingling. Excited. Wet. Her god was alive. And his name was Joaquin.

The naked, trembling Sharon clung to Martha with an emotional desperation – a desperation that the Princess not only recognized but understood. The Dante *Inferno* thing was happening in her sister-wife's blue eyes. To comfort her, Martha maintained the physical contact and continued to share her secret truth. 'From the moment I met Joaquin, my life got better. He gave me direction. I feel him watching over me. It's like a blessing. You believe in blessings? I do. I was raised on them.'

The air stream, fuelled by the explosive electrical currents, swabbed the desert floor. Unexplainable pleasure drowned her body. Talk about a natural rush. According to mythology ancient prophets found the Lord in desert storms. No doubt about it. Even a confirmed atheist could find a supernatural being today. Tingling happening.

And that natural magnificence and supremacy brought the Princess tears of pleasure. Her ears crackled and echoed with an electric charge. No wonder the Apaches had bled to the last man for this land. It was hallowed. It was exciting. Gorgeous. Alive. Like an excellent lover. Breathtakingly powerful and massively beautiful.

The oddly emotional Princess blessed her sister-wife now with her full attention, and continued her holy confession. Stroking the shaky Sharon, she laughed in solemn glee.

'Joaquin tied me to a bed and did things to me that only a god should do. Have you experienced true bliss? I have. And his name was Joaquin. Did you look closely at those photographs of him? He had the body and spirit of a true Warrior. Beat me? He made me come like a freight train. He made me beg. Made me...' Sighing, she lost the words for a moment. 'And in return, Joaquin gave me a new beginning as Mrs Lee. He's the real reason I'm here. We're gathering and selling information. I think the law is looking for some fugitives, but I don't really know anything, nor do I care. We're partners. Private dicks.'

'No!' Sharon screamed in horror, revulsion and shock. 'No. You are of the wheat! It can't be true.' Sharon's strong fingers dug into Martha's flesh in despair.

Wheat! Blood Atonement. Now Sharon knew the truth, she must tell Bradford or suffer alongside Martha if she was discovered. 'We must run away.'

The Princess now acknowledged accountability for sharing the truth. Funny feeling too. Odd. Frightening.

Anxious, she wanted Joaquin. She longed for him to rescue them both. To take her away. But the truth appeared to her in the desert storm. Joaquin wasn't coming. Even if he tried, he'd never find her in this desert.

The cavalry wasn't coming.

Suddenly Martha couldn't wait to escape, and nor could she allow Sharon to remain behind. The responsible, mature thing to do was to take her sister-wife with her, even though the action marked Sharon for death.

Yup. The Faithful would call for Blood Atonement.

Flashes of bright light. Dark clouds rolled. Boom.

Big boom.

This whole stupid life-threatening crisis came from sharing the truth. Damn truth. Good for the soul, huh?

Martha always knew there was a reason she preferred being a hopeless liar – knew there was a reason life was better when relationships were kept to casual sex with strangers and con marks.

'You got the keys to the truck?' Martha tried to sound calm and reassuring. Yeah, she was going to move on down the yellow brick road. And she was taking Sharon with her. No reason to leave her behind for the Blood Atonement ceremony. Only Sharon knew the road out of the desert and the way to civilization.

Besides, every Thelma needs a Louise.

14 **The Heart Wants What the Heart Wants**

Removing her designer sunglasses, she pounded hard with a closed fist on the front door and gave him her best Ricky Ricardo imitation, calling out loud enough for all the neighbours to hear, 'Honey, I'm home.'

He didn't answer, but her instincts told her he was inside; startled by her unexpected arrival, he was playing possum. Again, Martha pounded on the door before hitting him with another Cuban Ricardo routine. Placing both hands on her hips, she pouted and delivered in her hottest Latin tone: 'Joaquin, you have some *splainin'* to do.'

The Princess almost giggled. She'd spent way too much time watching TV lately. The damn courts had kept her under wraps in Salt Lake City with nothing to do but dance, ride bikes, and watch old reruns on cable, until all the stupid criminal cases had come to a successful conclusion. The boring legal crap took forever. It was now late September, almost October.

September was always the hottest month in the Valley.

However, now all the legal junk was finished. Of course, the men with the badges and the men dressed in black robes with gavels had won. The religious freaks and the fugitives lost. Big whoopee. They had been doing OK, too, until the Internal Revenue Service showed up.

Then it was all over but the jail time.

The cult and the fugitives should have taken a Soprano lesson from Capone. Never fuck with the IRS. Not in America. It's called the Alcatraz view.

And yoo-hoo! Every polygamist since the Kennedy days understands a man may legally claim all his children, but only one wife as tax deductions.

What do they say? Pay taxes and die.

Speaking of dying, the inheritance legal crap with Margaret was finished too. Martha had passed all the silly little tests while she'd arranged for Sharon to receive help at a private hospital in Washington State, far away from Bradford and the Faithful. The Princess had set her sister-wife up with a trust fund all her own.

Yes. Now the Princess was beautiful and sitting prettier than ever. Amen. Hallelujah. The family jewels and her millions were safely tucked away in the traditional banks. Taxes paid. Legal. Clean. It was good to be tax-free, beautiful, and rich in America again.

Hot damn. The Princess was really loaded, in that for-generations-to-come-I-will-never-have-to-work-for-anything-ever-again kind of way. Margaret had made them both richer than their Daddy could have imagined. Damn straight. In only one year Margaret, her good respectable sister, had turned their honest inheritance into a freaking fortune.

'I'll never be hungry again.' Martha did a damn good Scarlet O'Hara impression when her sister had shown her the numbers. It was wasted. Margaret had no sense of humour.

But Martha forgave Margaret that. Having no sense of humour was most likely her only flaw. Everybody's a critic. Cheers to the well-educated, well-disciplined, and generous big sisters everywhere. Rah! In the end,

Margaret had done right by Martha. But the sister-bitch wasn't back on Martha's love list. Not yet. There remained the Joaquin business between them.

Business that brought Martha back to the damn Valley.

The shade from the camphor trees and extended front porch made the summer morning almost cool. The heat wouldn't strike its devilish assault for a few hours yet.

Martha hated the heat. She'd driven her freshly purchased classic 1967 Stingray Corvette all night long across the sweaty dirt deserts of four western states without stopping in order to avoid the intense summer daylight desert heat; that, and to ambush Joaquin first thing in the morning.

'Back in the sweltering Valley rancho,' she muttered in amusement at her fate. 'Come on, Joaquin, let me in, baby,' she called sweetly.

Inside this small white wooden and stucco house with its knee-high, white picket fence, Joaquin was hiding from her. Well, not exactly hiding. Not precisely. OK. So her partner-hubby was still playing stubborn, refusing to see her or even accept her phone calls. Joaquin Xavier Lee had left her no choice.

The Princess was attacking. Invading his castle. Bombshell, baby.

The Princess wife was moving in. Woo-haw.

'Joaquin, please open the door.' She knocked again and waited. Nothing. 'Don't be this way. Don't treat me mean, baby,' she pleaded in her best little sticky-sweet let-me-fuck-you voice.

No answer. He was ignoring her.

Damn. That man had real control issues.

Well, the poor guy would just have to adjust.

Oh sure, he'd signed the divorce papers before the

conclusion of the Utah trials; before their agreed year was even over. Forfeiting his share of the fortune. Demanding nothing. Wanting nothing – only his freedom, and to be left alone.

Well, maybe he'd signed the divorce papers and moved on, but guess what, darling? The Princess had other plans. She liked being Mrs Lee. Having a partner brought focus and purpose to her life. So there it was, no divorce. And poor Joaquin – he'd have to accept the fact that he had a rich, beautiful, white Princess for a partner.

Not exactly a fate worse than death here.

They were partners. He'd proposed it first. Wanted it. Wanted her. Now, she wanted him. It was good for a Princess to know exactly what she wanted in life. God damn it. He wasn't dumping her. Sure, maybe she was a total bitch Princess and he was nothing but a working dick from the Valley, but they were partners. And partners didn't walk out on one another. That was the whole concept behind having an until-death-do-us-part partner.

'Joaquin?' Martha mumbled in frustration, and rested her forehead against the clean white frame of the door of his house. 'Don't treat me bad, baby. I deserve better.'

Turning to admire the undersized, smart front yard, Martha ever so gently clicked the tip of her sunglasses against her front teeth in thought. His gardener had come early to clean, trim, and water. She could smell the damp earth of the front yellow and white flowerbeds.

'Welcome to suburbia.' She laughed aloud. Martha so hated the nine to five, three kids, barbeque-in-the-backyard, middle-class American urban lifestyle. And this neighbourhood reeked of exactly that. But here she was, within walking distance from beautiful down-town Burbank, in the heart of the freakin' San Fernando Valley again.

'Oh, gag me with a spoon.'

The picturesque homes on both sides of Catalina Street were absolutely blue-collar cloud nine, with gigantic gorgeous camphor trees lining both sides of the Brady Bunch Boulevard, their uppermost branches arching across to embrace over the centre of the dark road. The early morning sunlight was just beginning to filter down through countless fluttering leaves.

The entire scene was so last century. *Leave It To Beaver.* Traditional and extremely tight. Serene and tasteful. A true Norman Rockwell happening. Probably had a Danny Partridge hiding in every garage shagging Keith's leftovers.

Most of the tasteful homes had been built back when the internationally significant local aviation industry was setting the world on fire. Some went way back to when the last land of the great Spanish ranchos was sold to Warner Brothers Studios. The nearby Hollywood Hills and the historical crumbling rancho abodes had served as backdrops for western B-movies. No wonder Gene Autry put his museum down the road in the pass. This was old Spanish California. Actually Joaquin's place wasn't far from the major Valley studios. Warner Brothers. Universal. Disney. Not far from the St Joseph Hospital.

Not far from where she'd started, a little over a year ago.

Wondering if she could hear the bells of St Charles this far east of Lankersheim Boulevard, Martha paused and listened. Nope. Only the fluttering leaves and the distant traffic of Hollywood Way. No bells. Bad luck.

Too bad. She could use a little luck.

Well, she'd come this far to do combat with Joaquin and she wasn't going to let his whole juvenile-behind-a-locked-door-in-suburbia routine stop her now, or even slow her down. Oh no. Prepared with a whole new understanding of his reality, the Princess had a plan.

Even a possum had to move sometime. She could wait. Oh yes, she'd learned patience. Patience, from the moment of the killings at the Whitmore Mansion. Patience, with Mr Bradford Henry and his wives. Patience, through the stupid legal crap. Patience, until this moment. Yup, with patience, she'd thought about nothing but Joaquin Xavier Lee for a whole year.

He was a tricky guy, that partner of hers.

Good thing Princess Patience had taken the year to plan.

A year. Wow.

The first year of her life that hadn't been all about herself and cheap thrills. That's what Margaret had said. Big sisters were very big on truths.

And the truth now was that Joaquin was in for a rude awakening.

The first thing the Princess did was to open the unlocked driveway's high-backed wooden gate, and then open both doors of the double-car garage. Oh darn, no David Cassidy. But she did discover Big Gus's old Caddy inside. It was a good sign. She warmed at the very sight of it. Big Gus hadn't survived that tricky heart surgery last summer. Margaret had finally told her the truth about his death during one of their screaming battles.

Memories of Big Gus tugged at her heart.

The Caddy was clean and polished. Actually Joaquin's garage was a lot cleaner than most of the motels she'd fucked in as a teenager. The parking stall alongside the classic Caddy was empty. So the Princess introduced one classic to another, unloaded her bags, and closed the garage doors before locking the back gate.

The Princess was capturing the castle, and without any resistance from Joaquin, it seemed. Interesting. His black jeep was absent. But that didn't mean anything. She'd never known if the jeep had even belonged to him at all.

In fact, after a little over a year, Martha still didn't know much about her partner and husband Joaquin Xavier Lee. They'd only been together that short time in Vegas, and thanks to his pills she'd been feeling no pain. Then he was that bloody pulp in an ICU bed. She hadn't seen him since. He'd sent one letter. Made one call. Then all communication with him had ended when she was taken away by Bradford Henry.

However, once she was stashed away in the Unitah Mountains during the legal trials, law enforcement people who'd known Joaquin or worked with him in the past shared information and personal opinions about him readily enough. Everyone respected him, even including her big sister Margaret, who'd ordered Martha to sign the divorce papers.

'Leave the poor guy alone. Don't make trouble for him, Marty. Do the right thing. Sign the papers. Let it go.'

Oh, fer shure. Fer shure.

Martha wasn't conned by the information fed to her. She believed less than half of what other people told her about Joaquin. And that included the stupid story the now dead *vaquero* Harvey had laid on her.

Yeah. All the Utah State and federal badges, men in black robes with gavels, and *Jaws* lawyer types, all of them respected and admired the hell out of Joaquin, calling him honest and smart. Margaret openly adored him.

Yes indeed, another little hot spot for Martha. Evidently Margaret and Joaquin had become great pals. One night, during a heated sisterly discussion, Margaret had confessed to visiting her hospitalized brother-in-law only hours after Martha had last seen him.

But of course, responsible bitch that she was, Margaret had taken charge of Joaquin's extensive medical care. Sent for all the best doctors. Picked up all the medical expenses along the way. Her trusted and loyal sister had spent days at poor Joaquin's bedside. More time than Martha ever had.

And for some reason this really ticked the Princess off.

The enclosed yard behind the small house was breathtaking. The orange and lemon trees were loaded with ripening fruit, as were the grapevines. Blooming jasmine climbed everywhere, filling the air with perfume.

The gardener had also been here, and everything was wet and clean and beautiful. Cool. Fresh. A mixture of shade and lovely morning sunlight. Ignoring the house totally, the Princess explored the garden by following the overhead grape vines through a maze of wonderfully fragrant greenery. The red tiled stepping-stones and overhead grape trellis led her to three separate and totally secluded patio areas. Each was surrounded with lots and lots of sweet-scented flowers mixed with the aroma of recently turned wet rich rancho dirt.

The property went way back sixty to seventy-five feet to a hot tub by a twelve-foot-high brick wall. The wall contained the fire-ready access-required gate that led in turn into an alley behind; it was padlocked. Even if the tiny house turned out to be a dump inside, the Princess loved the new castle garden. Smiling, she began marking her territory.

First, she started the hot tub and removed the cover from it. While the water whirled and heated, she grabbed her dirty laundry from her bags and adjourned to the screened summer porch at the back of the double garage, which housed the bright and shiny washer and dryer. She found big white fluffy bath towels in the dryer. Chuckling to herself, she folded his towels and started a load of her delicates in his washer. Laundry. Penance. 'I know I'm doing penance for being cruel to a laundress in a past life,' she joked to herself.

Martha stripped and, taking one of his big luscious bath towels, tiptoed back along the cool damp stones through the greenery maze to the warming hot tub.

Ah. Garden life was absolutely astonishing.

The rising sun reflected off the swirling bubbles in the circular redwood tub. Yes, the Princess had truly captured a little bit of paradise. She checked the water temperature and decided to let things warm up a little. Besides, Joaquin was a real curious guy. Unless he still had her necklace working or there was hidden property surveillance equipment, Martha figured he'd be making an appearance real soon.

He'd be curious.

The Princess prepared herself. Moving the extended canvas lounge chair into the sunlight, she covered it with the white bath towel and stretched out. Even after all her time outdoors in Utah, her skin remained pasty white. A Princess couldn't live in California without a tan. She was on it.

Wearing only her sunglasses, the All-Seeing eye and a sly smile she carefully arranged her new and greatly improved body into one of her best don't-you-want-to-fuck-me poses. Relaxing, she sighed, closed her eyes and waited, tanning.

It'd been a long drive across the desert alone.

The sun warmed the sensitive skin of her gorgeous tits. Oh yeah, baby, she felt hot. She was so ready for this guy. And he didn't keep his Princess waiting long.

'You've decided against being a blonde?'

Her pussy warmed in response to his deep tenor tones. All right. Tingling titillation happening. Good. Good. Good.

'This is my natural colour.' Removing her dark glasses she flirted with him, flashing her best Princess smile. 'Don't you like it?' Sticking out her lower lip into her favourite young Traci Lords pout, she awaited his response.

Unfortunately she couldn't really see him all that well. Between the bright sunlight and the lush greenery he appeared only as a shadowy silhouette in among the deep shades of green. A true snake in the garden.

Patience. Patience was a virtue. One the Princess had mastered in the last year. Or at least she thought she had until she'd heard his sexy voice. What she most wanted now was to leap from the lounger, throw him down, and fuck him until his narrow green eyes rolled back into his head.

But patience. Patience. A virtue. Right?

Damn virtues were always so contrary to her true nature.

Not wanting to frighten her possum, Martha struggled to push her intense physical urges aside. She hid behind her dark glasses, relaxed her new luscious locks against the back of the lounge chair, sighed deeply in satisfaction and proceeded to mind-fuck him.

And it was good too. Oh yes.

Between the sighing and the mind-fucking she gave him her best tit action. She was very excited.

Joaquin finally spoke, but still didn't move into the light. 'You appear so different. Beautiful, as always. But changed. Your white skin, blue eyes, and then that shock of almost black hair, reminds me of a porcelain doll my grandmother owned. Long curls and everything. The new look is good. I admit I never would have recognized you, Princess.'

Good. Compliments. Nice.

Flushed and totally pink from the attention he was paying her, she continued to smile in honest delight. Then, wiggling her shoulders ever so slightly, she jiggled her great tits again in the warming summer sunlight. She felt hot. Rita Haywood *Gilda* hot.

Unfortunately, she found it difficult just to flirt. Come to Mama, baby boy. She wanted him. Her body wanted his. Unsure exactly how to move her plan into play, she hesitated. They'd been apart so damn long.

The man in the shadows was a stranger. But basically Joaquin had always been a stranger – a fantasy figure. This guy was reality. Except for his voice. The tenor was the same.

As was her physical response to his magic tones.

Damn sexy tenor tones. Damn sexy responses.

'Margaret believes that it's brunettes who have more fun. And having recently discovered how truly brilliant my big sister can be, I decided to let myself go *a la* Ashley Judd.' She fluffed her shoulder-length dark curls. The new dippy-do was working for him. The bouncy hair moves created a little more tit action.

That too worked for him.

Good. He was appreciative. Living clean, eating healthy, and exercising for an entire year had actually done her body good. Done her body great. She'd never been this healthy or this beautiful or more alive. Plus, she'd maxed-out her Princess Perfect beauty with days spent at the most exclusive spa in Snow Bird before hitting the highway last night. Yes, the pretty Princess was pampered and polished and puffed and perfumed.

'If you don't like the colour, maybe I'll change it. Cut it. Bleach it. How do you think I'd look as a redhead?'

That did it. He moved a few slow shuffling steps forwards.

She held her breath.

He stopped.

'No. I like it this way. I think.' Still basically in the shadows and slightly unsteady on his feet, he shoved both his hands deep into his Levi's pockets.

'You're absolutely stunning,' he added with sincere warmth. 'But then, you've always been beautiful. And sexy.'

Ah, baby. More compliments. She strangled the urge to rush into his arms and smother his face with wet kisses. But no. Stupid patience. Shouldn't rush a timid possum.

Therefore, instead of jumping his bones, she twisted her wedding ring, and flashed her honest smile as she whispered in her most sincere voice, 'I've missed you, Joaquin.'

He shifted his weight anxiously from one foot to the other, obviously most uncomfortable on his feet.

'Missed me?' His warm tenor hardened. 'Hell, you don't even know me. What do you want here, Princess?'

Ouch. Mean. Brittle, even. He'd suddenly turned from pretty compliments to nasty. It was so Joaquin.

Licking her lips as sensually as possible, the Princess slowly rose to her pampered, polished feet. Wearing only the All-Seeing she stood before him, shaking out her curls in the sunlight while observing his body language carefully. He'd frozen. When she took a few steps forwards to check the water temperature he appeared to be upset, forcing him into abrupt action.

Taking his hands from his pockets, he moved too quickly. Off balance, he grabbed the frame of the grape trellis above his head to steady himself. Not wanting to contribute to his distress, she pretended to ignore his struggle to stand unassisted. Although he remained mostly hidden from close examination by the shady shadows of the garden, she'd gotten her first semi-good look at Joaquin Xavier Lee.

Poor baby. He was thinner. A lot thinner. His long dark luscious wavy hair was cropped now close to his head. Without shoes he wore only faded Levi's covering his legs, and a clean, freshly pressed, long-sleeved, formal white shirt to hide his arms and chest.

How thin was he? And how disfigured?

According to Margaret the keloid scars were bad. Very bad. The overgrowth of scar tissue left poor Joaquin readily available for work without make-up in a Hollywood horror flick.

Martha didn't care.

She didn't care if he was a fucking monster.

It didn't matter. Not one bit. Not to her.

Wiggling her cute ass, the Princess carefully reached forwards to test the water with her hand, flashing him her pussy.

He shuffled and groaned slightly behind her. Pain. She recognized it.

Concerned, and unable to remain casually composed, Martha kept her pussy facing him as she spoke quietly and calmly, as if comforting a frightened child.

'Sit down, Joaquin, before you fall. We need to talk.'

'Talk? Us? About what?' he shouted.

Yeah. The water temperature was ideal. The sunlight

in the fantastic garden was superb. Princess Perfect was beautiful – in fact, she was fucking gorgeous. Why was he being so mean? He wanted her. She could smell it. And the scent of his lust did it for her. Something deep inside snapped and all her so-called virtues were forgotten.

She was hungry for him. Starving. Some twisted appetite inside erupted into something close to physical agony. Lifting her arms, she executed her best sex-kitten stretch and purr before gradually turning to confront him. 'Are you finished playing mercenary?'

'Mercenary? Who, me?'

Silent for only a moment he glared at her, evidently appalled by the gulping sound she made when he unexpectedly stepped from the shade into the bright morning sunlight. But Martha stared right back, straight past the hideous ugliness of his new face and into his almond-shaped green eyes, unable to do anything more than relish the tremendous sexual energy rising within her.

'Joaquin, be nice to me.' It was more a plea than a scream. 'Treat me right.'

'Right? Did I take anything from you?' he demanded. 'Jewels? Money? No.'

She couldn't speak.

He laughed deep in his throat. 'You're a beautiful and rich Princess now. Go play with the other shallow royals.'

And that was the final blow. Attack. Before he could stop her, she rushed him, throwing her arms around his neck and forcing her naked body against him.

Startled, he gripped her arms and attempted to retreat. But she wasn't having any of it. Not this time.

This time the Princess was taking no prisoners.

This time the Princess ruled.

This time he was her captive.

Crushing her great tits against his chest, moulding her hands along the back of his neck and head, standing on pretty painted tiptoe, and slamming her pelvis against his, she attacked his mouth with repeated open-mouthed kisses.

'Stop. No,' he groaned. 'No. I don't need a pity fuck or revenge fuck or whatever this is.'

Struggling, he managed to withdraw, but not before she felt the beginnings of his erection. Sorry – no retreating. Stepping forcefully forwards into him, she knocked him slightly off balance. In order to right himself and remain on his feet he clutched at her.

'Joaquin, I will feel you deep inside me again.'

Cruel tenor laugh. 'Not going to happen, Princess. Leave me alone.' But even as he roared his commands his hands palmed her great ass. And then, kneading her flesh tenderly, he moaned in frustration. 'This is crazy, Princess. Absolutely crazy.'

'Kiss me, Joaquin,' she begged sweetly. 'Kiss me. Please.' He smelled so good. Smelled so sexy. So Joaquin.

Seeking a firmer stance, Joaquin retreated a few more steps. She let him go, never allowing her body to break contact with his. Without warning he collapsed against her. Struggling desperately together, they managed to stumble towards the lounge chair before he collapsed in self-conscious pain.

So he was having some trouble standing on his own two feet, huh? Well, Margaret had said that he'd taken one too many blows to the head that had unfortunately left some serious inner-ear balancing problems. 'I need my cane. Inside the door. Fetch it for me.' As soon as he was safely seated in the lounger, he shoved her away hard, hanging his head like a hound dog.

Oh, he was a dirty dog, all right. A damn dirty dog.

The Princess didn't take orders from dogs.

'No,' she said flatly. 'You don't need a cane or any other help. You have me.'

Damn. He smelled so macho.

The Princess had no intention of letting her prisoner escape. No way. Prowling like only a good sex kitten knows how, she almost danced around the back of the lounger, so that he had to jerk his head to watch her pace.

'What do you want from me, Princess?'

Oh yes – she liked the way he said 'Princess.' Woo! Naughty vibes happening. Her entire body radiated with passionate heat, erupting and flaring whenever he spoke. After circling the lounger several times she finally came to stand directly behind him.

After only a brief pausing, she attacked by reaching over his shoulder.

Joaquin took in a deep breath as, with the lightest of touches, she traced the deep scar exposed above his collar, along his neck to the buttons of his shirt.

'Don't play with me.' He smacked at her hands.

Didn't stop her assault. Nope.

But it did quicken her pulse into an erratic rhythm. She unbuttoned his white starched shirt. Then, with his pulse leaping beneath her fingertips, she touched her nose to his neck and inhaled. Oh, yum, yum. Her favourite. Joaquin.

Oh, she was going to eat him up.

Handsome. Hideous. Gorgeous. Blemished. God. Monster. It didn't matter. Not one damn bit. It was all the same to her. It was Joaquin. She wanted Joaquin. A Princess always gets what she wants, to live happily ever after. It's a rule in part of the Princess code. And she wanted him deep inside her. Now. She was wet with need and panting with urgency.

Ah, but patience was virtuous. Well, fuck virtue.

With the conclusion of the button business, she gently glided her fingertips across the thick scars of his collar-bone to his still strong, broad shoulders and down his surprisingly muscular arms, to remove the entire garment from his body. Oh, he was thinner, lighter, less agile than before, but he still reeked of primeval power. Still had great abs and strong muscles.

God, he was wonderful. Compelling.

'Please don't do this.' His warm breath moaned across her neck as she absorbed the shivers of his flesh beneath her touch. 'Don't, Princess. Don't play with me. Stop it.'

Stop it? Not likely. This Princess was warm and wet and wanting him. There was no stopping. Not now. Not after all the intense cravings of the months pining for the primo. Not after a year of penance. Now she stood before him exposed and shaking with only a semi-controlled passion. Hanging his hound-dog head, he remained seated on the lounger. Martha lowered her open lips to brush her tongue across the top of his ear.

Yahoo.

His entire body tensed in reply.

'Princess?' Without looking up at her, he curved one hand around her ribcage, drawing her nakedness in closer to his face. Was he surrendering?

Maybe. She held her breath.

It could be a trap. One of his clandestine ploys to manoeuvre her into another of his deceptions. Martha reminded herself to proceed cautiously. A monster must be handled with caution. But all her good intentions were challenged when his other hand started lightly massaging her ass.

Following moments of anxious silence his fingers inched along her ribs one slow movement at a time, one rib at a time, creating one glorious sensation at a time, time after time, forcing her into a ragged breathing pattern. Closing her eyes, Martha swallowed hard, fighting to maintain physical control. She wanted to devour him and be devoured by him.

Her sexual appetite detonated.

She was ravenous. Suffering.

Mumbling something soft and wonderfully needy, he pressed a tender kiss into the flat of her stomach.

Ah, shivers and lust. Blood pumping. Heat rising.

Restraining from pouncing and yet very appreciative of his moves, she let a whimper of pure pleasure escape her when he cupped one of her breasts. Ah yes, commence with the kissing and the massaging, big boy. Excellent beginning. The Princess relaxed, lowering her guard, filled with high expectations.

Proceeding slowly, so as not to frighten him away, she lowered her nose to his short curly locks, inhaled deeply, and strangled the mounting compulsion to smack him back and take his dick in her mouth and suck. Ruthlessly.

Test. Trial.

Just when she'd restrained her more violent sensual urges, he pinched her nipple hard, forcing her to squeal in wanton approval and desire. Oh, fuck patience. Eyelids fluttering open and closed, she arched her back towards him.

Little by little, torturously lingering, his fingers slid from her nipple, lower, lower.

Ah, his touch. Instant recall. Yes, a familiar touch that successfully ignited old sensations. Thrills. Hot damn. Ah yes, her body remembered this pleasuring touch and reacted. Instantly. Obediently her female juices readied her body for the Warrior's invasion.

Slowly, almost in a leisurely way, his two fingers slid into her lower dampness and touched her clit. Bombs-bursting-in-air excitement happening; her entire body shuddered with want.

'Oh, Princess, do me right,' he begged in a whisper. 'Take pity. One last time, Princess. Do me good.'

One last time? Not one time. Not last time. Not likely.

The poor guy had no idea.

Controlling herself, the Princess didn't laugh aloud; lots of time to burst his control bubble later. Much later.

At present, she moaned sensually to encourage his exploring fingers. This wasn't their last time. And this was no pity fuck or mercy fuck or revenge fuck. This was something else. Something . . .

Right now, with her body willingly and unwillingly responding to his rich voice and tender touch, the Princess decided it was probably not wise to mention the new plan.

She was into playing the good wife and steady sex partner.

Partners. They were partners. To remind him she opened her thighs wider and rocked hard against his hand, her hips swaying forward and back with rising need.

Hard. Soft. He worked her clit. Slow. Fast. Pinching. Flicking. Caressing. Ah.

Oh yes, he remembered how to work it. Good. Ah.

Cradling his hanging head in both her hands, she lifted his face and, leaning forwards, kissed him. A great kiss, too. One that screamed, 'I'm going to fuck you long and hard, until we're both sweaty, sated, and senseless.' Oh yes. A wicked kiss that allowed her to taste every bit of his lips, tongue and mouth. And he was mighty tasty too. Warm. Willing. Wanton.

The Princess melted. The intoxicating thrusting of his tongue and the pressure along her clit intensified, producing and trapping extreme body heat between them – uncontrollable heat that burst into flames.

Within seconds she was lying flat on her back across the flat, cool stepping-stones surrounding the whirling water. Her knees were up and open, his lips and tongue sucking and circling her clit.

All right. Oh yeah. Oh, baby. Ah. Ah. Ah.

'Joaquin,' she screamed in rising urgency.

Using his pearly whites to nibble expertly along her clit ever so gently, he gripped her hips and then suddenly slid his tongue inside her while his lips and mouth continued to suck. She gasped.

Shivers. Tingling. Melting. Tensing.

Climax happening. Wow. Bursting-in-air.

'Joaquin.' The primeval scream tore from deep within her.

Yes. Yes. Oh glory. Oh hot damn. This was heaven.

Weaving her fingers through his luscious locks, Martha managed to slow her panting as she moaned his name again and again in satisfaction. He was so good. Excellent. And this was only the beginning of something primo happening between them again. The Princess was eager to continue the feast. It'd been forever between erotic banquets.

Unfortunately, with the completion of the first satisfaction, Martha suddenly remembered her game plan. It took her a great effort to pull away. Pause. Think. This was not going exactly to plan. Out of his reach she hugged her knees tightly to her chest, unable to explain. She was way too turned on. But she had to stick to the plan.

His green eyes, startled and confused by her sudden withdrawal, now studied her carefully.

Made her weak.

But he was the one who'd taught her this part of the game, right? Shying away, she struggled sweetly, saying, 'Keep it hard for me, Joaquin. I'll be back in a minute.' Somehow she managed to escape long enough to breathe deeply again. The Princess was resolved in her plan. And this was not it.

'Where are you going?' Puzzled and stretched out on the stones, Joaquin rolled over to watch her unexpected behaviour with his hungry eyes.

'I'll be right back. That was good. I owe you one.' She skipped around him lying almost helpless on the stones and, lifting some of her bigger bags, headed towards the house before her willpower dissolved. 'I'll be back to pay my debt.'

'No. Wait a minute. What are you doing?' he roared after her. 'Don't go in there.'

But she did. She captured his castle.

Even with the back extension, the palace was tiny, maybe seven hundred square feet. Maybe. The entire rear of the house must once have been an extended summer porch. Now, enclosed totally in glass, the highly polished light oak floor contained gym equipment. Exercise bike. Treadmill. Martial arts crap. Weights and dumb-bells. A rugged guy's guy stench. She spotted a heavy cane perched against a wheelchair, not far from the sliding-door entrance. The mirrored three walls of the gym area reflected the garden, bringing it inside. The room contained a breakfast nook and an open-plan kitchen.

The nook was very 1950s *Happy Days*, with red and

white plastic cushioned seats and silver chrome legs around the circular Malt Shoppe table. Very red. Very art deco in contrast to the posh oak floors, cupboards, and traditional lines of the rest of the house. The spotless kitchen counters extended and divided the nook from the cooking appliances and sink area. Martha paused to eyeball the scene more carefully. No woman had designed this house or this kitchen.

'Only a guy would remodel a house so his kitchen and gym could share space,' she lamented, shaking her head in amused disbelief. Guys. Most of them haven't got a clue.

But it was OK. Joaquin could keep his gym in the kitchen if it made him happy. The Princess held control of the garden.

With a strong effort she ignored Joaquin's calls from the back, as he demanded his cane. She explored to discover who, if anyone besides him, occupied her partner's palace, or in this case, cottage, or even more appropriately, freaky 50s love shack. Real 'I like Ike' era stuff.

Once she was in the hallway, she found the bedroom immediately on the right. Pale sky-blue walls. Sterile. No artwork or photographs. Next to no closet. Not large enough for a queen-size bed, only a double. If the back of the room hadn't been expanded there would have been absolutely no space. Daddy's family palace had closets bigger than this room. Hell, she'd fucked in trucks with bigger beds.

One thing was clear. She'd ambushed him all right. The cotton bed sheets remained warm and ruffled.

Dropping her bags, she collapsed on the stripped white and blue sheets and inhaled deeply. Joaquin smells. No sex smells. No female perfume. Good. She lifted the sheets and, once again, only Joaquin smells.

Excellent. Just as she was beginning to feel confident, she spotted the earrings.

Shit!

On the far nightstand, next to the opened French doors, lay an exquisite pair of emerald and diamond earrings. Without hesitation Martha coveted the jewellery.

Good stones. Expensive setting. Someone had taste.

Nice booty. Quickly the Princess made an exchange. Now her golden loops lay next to her partner's bed and the gems adorned her lovely ears.

With women, it's all about marking territory and seizing booty. Fluffing her curls, the Princess admired her reflection in the oval mirror above his dresser. Outside, Joaquin continued to raise a racket about his cane. She had to do something or no doubt a concerned neighbour would show up on the doorstep.

And she didn't want any visitors.

Exploring the enclosed small garden outside the French doors of the bedroom, she cheerfully called out, loud enough for all the neighbours to hear, 'I'm coming, darling.'

On tiptoe she danced back through the house, out of the sliding door of the gym-cook-and-dine, and with her best Shirley Temple smile approached the fuming Joaquin. Before he could complain, she knelt before him on the stones and pleasantly suggested, while watching his nervous hands, 'Remove your Levi's.'

Off with all fig leaves.

'No.'

Woo. Bad attitude. Serious rejection.

She spoke melodiously. 'I want to make it right.'

'No.' He spoke spitefully. 'I've decided to pass.'

245

Ignoring his nasty tone, she sighed sweetly, giving him a little tit action before striking again. Flat on his back on the stones, his scarred face and chest now bathed in sunlight, Joaquin didn't move, or complain, or respond when she cautiously, slowly covered his shirtless body with her nakedness. She tenderly kissed his marked cheek.

He didn't react. Playing tough guy.

'Does this hurt?' she asked considerately.

As an answer his hands accepted her, clutching her back muscles, making her smile sincerely sexy.

He didn't speak, so she kissed him again. It was almost chaste. A little-girl, sweet-Princess kiss – one whispering of compassionate affection more than mature lust.

His hands, then his arms, and finally his entire body caressed hers. Anaconda cuddling. Warm blood. Ah, good snake.

With the rising sun and his enthusiastic embrace fuelling her passion, Martha kissed him again, another affectionate more than lustful lip action. And again he responded. Then he spoke.

'Keep it hard? I'll be right back? Your new con? With all your faults, you've never been a tease. Why now, Princess?' His voice was less hostile than defensive. 'Why me?'

Relishing his anaconda caress and rich voice while he continued to stroke her ass, back, and shoulders the Princess couldn't help frowning as she answered him truthfully. 'Teasing takes time. I never wanted to waste the time.'

'And now?'

Kissing his cheek, chin, throat, and ear while his hands increased their pressure, she considered her answer. 'Now, there's time.'

His hands stopped, releasing pressure.

'How do you figure?'

Resting on her elbows, she gazed adoringly down into his almond-shaped eyes and thrust her pelvic bone into his soft dick. No reaction. Hip pressure. Slow circles. Pressure. Release. Tension. Release. Pressure and gyrate. Release.

His hands tensed. He was frightened. Overwrought. To help relax him, she dry fucked him.

Pressure. Swivel. Release.

His anxious hands resumed caressing her ass, back, and shoulders, but his erection didn't happen.

She kissed him, an affectionate but also hungry one.

He kissed her back, hungry too. But not necessarily affectionate. And no erection. What the hell? It shouldn't bother her, but it did. Wasn't this the guy who'd praised her? Written her a damn love letter telling her she'd been an ideal wife? Expressing how proud he was to call her his partner?

No.

No. This was the other guy. The one who'd slapped around a Princess in meltdown, used her body and talents, and then walked away without so much as a goodbye-I'm-dumping-you polite pity fuck. This was the partner who'd manipulated and used her. Toyed with her affections, made her vulnerable, then discarded her, like used tissue the morning after. This was the jerk that ignored her calls. Refused to open his door.

This was the guy who said it was over.

And this was the Princess who wasn't having any of it.

Quickly escaping his arms, she rolled away from temptation. He made her feel weak. Soft. Weakness was part of the plan.

Shielding his eyes from the bright sun with his hand, he struggled to sit and watched her in silence.

'Do you need help getting up?' She made it sound suggestive. Playfully nasty.

'Why?'

Woo. Defensive. Mean. He'd forgotten they were partners.

'Because I'm here to help.'

As if to prove his own masculinity, he frowned at her. Shifting all his weight to one hip, he bent his knee to place one foot flat on the stones before pushing with his hands and legs. Joaquin was almost up and standing when she rushed forwards to help him balance.

After a proud struggle, he was standing and aggressively embracing her. He was sweating. Hungry. And in pain. 'What are you doing here, Princess? Slumming? What do you want from me?'

Wiggling, she teased him with some of the Last Vegas Ballet moves. 'What do you think?'

Shaking his head, he appeared briefly lost in some secret fantasy briefly. Then he kissed her. And it was a come-fuck-me-now hot one. Scorching. Serious. Hard. Cruel. Heaving with lustful sting.

Somehow it pleased her that she wasn't particularly impressed. Made it easier to take the next step in the plan.

'Nope.' She did her great *Gilda* moves. Eyes. Hair. Lips. Hips. 'That wasn't it.'

'Wasn't? What?' Confused, he released her, managing to stay on his feet without her help.

The Princess backed away respectfully.

'Believe it or not, the primo fucking isn't why I'm here. Not that I don't want it. We both know I do. And you *will* perform your husbandly duties, and perform them well. Encore style! Again and again. Trust me.'

Joaquin appeared totally stunned, almost trauma-tized. Swaying her cute little ass around him, she once again danced on tiptoe over to collect the last of her bags, and then Last Vegas Ballet waltzed it into the house, through his gym, and into the boudoir to unload. Capturing the castle was much easier than she'd imagined.

With all her booty bags in a neat row it took only minutes to unpack. Making room for her new silky wardrobe in his dresser drawers and already packed closet took much longer. While she was establishing space for her washing stuff in the micro-mini bath-room, Joaquin appeared in the wheelchair, framed in the doorway.

'What are you doing?' Concern echoed in his deep tones.

'Putting my tampons under the sink.'

The poor guy looked liked she'd slapped him.

'Clearly a girl didn't design this bathroom. No tub? What's that all about?' Amused by his sincere alarm, she laughed aloud before explaining, as if to comfort a frightened child. 'Relax. Trust me. Princesses don't pee when marking their territory. We accessorize.'

'Accessorise? What con are you running here?'

Ouch. Demanding. Annoyed. She paused, noting how, although his bare arms and shoulders were much smaller than before, he still appeared muscular and utterly fierce as he sat in his invalid chair. Perhaps he wasn't as dominant as before, but he was still truly powerful enough to be totally sexy and threatening. The vicious scars from the slashing of the knife attack only enhanced his already dangerous aura. He was one sexy dog, even in a wheelchair. And he belonged to her. He was her treasure.

The Princess wanted what belonged to her.

Demanded it. That's why she was here. To rescue her lost great treasure. She'd killed to be here, and now the war was over. Victory won. Joaquin was more than just another primo fuck; he was her partner.

She didn't understand it all exactly, yet.

She only knew that it was something primal.

Admiring his fierce physique and fighting off a full on mind-fuck, she turned around. 'Good news, darling, I'm all unpacked.' She wiggled the few steps from the bathroom to what appeared to be an electronic heaven. 'Is this the office? Show me how you record from the All-Seeing. When does our next adventure begin?'

Frowning, he didn't answer at first. Then he told her, 'No more adventures together, Princess. We're divorced. You're free.'

Oh yeah? Maybe she was. Why didn't she feel it?

Ignoring his lie, she forgave him and explained. 'My family lawyer, my good sister Margaret, and your lawyer Stan all endeavoured to remove both the All-Seeing from around my neck and the wedding ring from my finger. As you can plainly see, it didn't happen. And it's not going to.'

He studied her in disbelief.

'Halt. Kirk to Enterprise.' She gave a long and sexy whistle. From floor to ceiling his office was packed with all kinds of intimidating computer and techno equipment. Enough for a satellite link-up with NASA or the international space station.

'Beam me up, Scotty.'

The Princess opened what was clearly once a bedroom closet door, only to discover an enormous, antique, standing iron safe on wheels. Playfully, she spun the combination dial.

Big surprise. Didn't open. Forbidden fruit.

'Ill-gotten gains inside? Maybe your family jewels?'

He answered too quickly. 'Guns.' Either to avoid her or draw her out of the office, he wheeled the chair into the grand room of the tiny cottage.

Interested, she followed to explore the grand room.

'What kind of guns?'

He frowned. 'Big ones.' Woo. Nukes, huh? Sweet.

Be bad, baby boy. Martha kept her voice cheerful. 'Do you usually lock and load before Emily arrives?' Emily wasn't arriving. Ding dong, the witch was dead. Only he didn't know that. No one did. Not yet. It was all part of the plan.

Joaquin acted annoyed, but she could tell it was only a façade. He wasn't annoyed. Nope, he was concerned. Vexed, even. Excellent. Petrified, maybe.

Good. Now this was going more according to the plan.

A little torment happening here. A little torture.

Grand room, huh? Not much. Highly polished bare oak floor. Great marble and mirror fireplace. Pristine rows of windows framing the front flowers outside. The L-shaped room contained only one massive black leather throne and another full wall of entertainment equipment. Media central control. The so-called grand room wrapped around through an empty dining area to the open kitchen-diner-gym. Small loop.

'Would you please put on some clothes. This is Burbank. The neighbours will be phoning the police to complain.'

'Tell them your wife is a nudist. Oh my gosh, it's *so* California.' She kept her voice saccharine.

'Wife? You're not my wife,' he grumbled, and then barked at her. 'Get out of my house.' Woof. Woof dog nasty.

The Princess totally ignored his yowl, and moved over to check out all the kitchen cupboards. Yuck.

Brown bread. Oh, more yucky. Brown rice. Send it back to the swamp. She'd have to adjust the plan to include her taking over the kitchen and baking cookies. 'This isn't entirely your house, darling.' She added real punch to the *darling*. 'I've paid off the mortgage. The title is in the mail. We're married. Filed a joint tax return last year and everything. Besides, California is a community property state. So this is our house, darling.'

Oh, he hated the punched-up *darling*.

She could live with that.

'Princess, you can't stay here. I mean it.'

The protective force behind his words won a giggle from her. The poor guy had no clue. Good. His refrigerator, however, forced a scowl. Healthy food central. Puking. Gaseous storm brewing. Full of fresh fruit, vegetables, white cheese, lean meats, and only good-for-you crap. Gagging here. No. No. No.

Horrors! Not even one cold beer. Major problem. Crisis developing. No fall-back, either. No liquor. No wine. Catastrophe. Today's weather forecast said triple digit heat in the Valley and he didn't have even one cold beer.

Lord, help her. She'd married an idiot.

Aggravated, she cut to the next assault and rolled his chair back into the gym before twirling it around to look him in the eye. 'Are you expecting Emily to make an appearance today, darling?'

He freaked. 'Emily?' His voice cracked. Scary witch.

Damn it. He did think she was some stupid Princess bitch.

'Yes. Oh, darling, you remember Emily. Once upon a time she broke your heart. Remember? It happened one night in a Vegas dump. You were working. Undercover.' Teasing him about the absent Emily worked for her. Made him sweat. Made him tense. Gave her pleasure.

'Do you think I've got time for a beer run before she arrives to torture you? I wouldn't want to miss any of the action.'

Too stunned to respond, Joaquin allowed Martha to set the brakes on his chair. Then she sat in his lap, facing him, and wrapped her legs around his forearms and the back of the chair. Slamming her pussy hard into his groin, she made him wince.

She didn't care.

She didn't care if he hurt. Not one bit.

Pain was part of the plan.

She intended to make it hurt *good*.

Pain and pleasure.

He'd taught her the technique well. Command. Completion. Reward. Now the Princess was playing the master Warrior herself. Using her new, more powerful leg and arm muscles, she hauled him into her, tight. He didn't squirm. But he did gasp. She inhaled the scent of her earlier climax on his chin, lips, and hot breath. Sexy. Growling. Wicked thoughts happening.

'What do you think you're doing?'

Snarling, she wiggled her pussy. 'Marking my territory.'

Joaquin closed his eyes. 'Princess, this situation is complicated. You don't understand.'

'Don't understand?' Ever so gently she nipped at his earlobe; the taste of him forced her to suck and chew the soft part of his ears for a moment. He shook a little but didn't respond. So she gave him a little innocent Shirley Temple giggle before returning to the snarling bitch. 'Oh, I admit, I walked into you blinded by meltdown. But even a spoiled Princess without ethics or job skills figured it out.'

Using her tongue, she traced the thick ugly scar from a nasty knife slash across his lower throat.

He groaned in pain.

She paused in her pleasure. 'I only wanted a job. You made us partners.'

No response.

'I knew nothing about being a partner. Or having a partner. Another half.' She licked again, this time the slash trail following along his jaw line to his temple. Pausing again only for effect, she told him the truth. 'I discovered I enjoyed it. A lot.'

His green almond-shaped eyes never blinked.

One hard rock slam from her hips forced a semi-pained gasp from his lips. His green little eyes beamed anguish into hers.

'You made me your partner in hope of winning a fortune. Or was it something else? Care to share?'

'Martha –' was all he managed before she hushed him with a gentle little-Mama kiss, her lips lingering over his. For only the third time ever he'd called her Martha.

With an unanticipated powerful move, his arms rocked. His body weight beneath her shifted. Suddenly his hands were all over her.

She quaked in jubilant emotional satisfaction.

His chest flexed against her hardening tits, their temperatures rising. His hands gripped into her back, her ass, her shoulders. With her fingers woven through his hair she pressed harder, in rocking encouragement.

Muffled moans of sexual agony escaped his throat. He was in pain. Lovely pain. Tortured, he could only pray to obtain any pleasure. He hurt for her. His moans pleaded for release. For pleasure. His tongue prodded against her lips.

She opened to the hot taste of him. Oh yes.

The past and present pain and pleasure escalated. Communion. Vision. Woo. Macho flavouring. Ah. Ah.

As his tongue aggressively explored her mouth, his hardening erection pulsed beneath her ass. His glorious hands on her bare flesh. Hungry. Explosive. Desperate.

Mounting desperation. Harder, hotter, more demanding.

Wrapping her arms around his head she tore her lips from his, leaving them both panting. Hot breath into hot breath. Hungry eye into hungry eye. Pleasure into pain.

'This isn't a good idea,' he moaned in a whisper.

'Too late. I'm into the happily ever after mode.'

He couldn't answer.

So she teased him a little. Because she could. And because it was all part of that pain thing happening before the intense pleasure. 'What's wrong, darling? Afraid Emily might see us and have another temper-tantrum? Hurt you bad again? Trap you? Torture you? Don't tell me a big tough *hombre* like yourself is worried about that dumb wicked witch?' As much as she tried, she couldn't smother her rising sense of amusement. With sexual tension and pleasure she laughed aloud at her own little joke, right into his face, which was riddled with agonising pain. He hurt. He hated hurting. Too bad. Teasing and pain were all part of the plan.

'Don't worry, baby. Your Princess is here to protect you from the wicked witch. Trust me. I'm your partner.'

'You're a bitch,' he whispered in pure tormented agony.

'Duh. Ya think?' She giggled in gratification.

It was like an explosion. With incredible strength he jerked her body from his and literally tossed her off his lap. She landed flat on her back on the oak floor, with one foot near his groin and the other on the arm of the wheelchair. Unfortunately she couldn't hide her sudden fright or tremendous desire.

'Bitch, huh?' Her voice cracked as she controlled a rising shriek. 'Bitch? Oh yes, total bitch. A royal rich, wonder-bread Princess ho bitch. But bite this, bad boy. This bitch wears your collar. Yours. You made it so.'

'I don't want you.' His intense fury forced his blemished muscles to bulge and flex aggressively in unusual patterns. Hot damn. He was one nasty angry frustrated monster.

Her monster. Hers. Oh, and she wanted to keep him.

'You don't want me? Too bad. Get over it, we're partners. And surprise, surprise, turns out that being your partner is the best part of my life. Go figure.' Using her pretty polished toes the Princess taunted his cock by applying and releasing pressure. 'Besides, you love me, Joaquin. You want me. So treat me nice.'

'Love? You don't love me. So don't even pretend.'

Dismissing his anger, she laughed lightly. 'Excuse me? Did I say I loved you? No. No. No. Everyone, including all the shrinks through history, would testify under oath, and I think we'd both agree, that I'm probably not capable of love. True love. Not as other people love. After all, this Princess bitch isn't anything more than a good time. Cheap thrill. Nevertheless, you love me, Joaquin. Admit it.'

Actually there was a slim chance that she might actually love him, if that was truly possible. Months ago she'd realized she actually felt something real and honest for him. But love? It remained a tough call. With so little experience in emotion, honest emotion, how would she know? But, love aside, he was her partner. That's all that mattered. All that was necessary for her to live happily ever after was to fuck him.

Clenching his jaw shut he played the gruff bully as

he removed her feet, released the brakes from the chair, and attempted to roll away, but she flopped around and blocked his retreat by hanging on to the chair. OK so he wasn't into admitting he loved her. Not yet, anyway. So she took another, more comfortable approach.

'Our partnership never had anything to do with love, Joaquin. Remember?'

Flustered, he paused, looking down at her. 'Get out.' It was a command. He hurt inside and out. She could see it. Feel it. Pain.

'No.' Hot tears appeared from somewhere. Her tears. She felt the wetness on her face. Damn it. Tears were not part of the Princess plan. 'Cruel until the bitter end, huh? Mercenary, huh? Is this how you treat all your bitches, or only your wives?'

'Only the Princesses,' he growled fiercely. Callously even. Ouch. Growl. 'Now stay away from me. Get out. I don't want you. I never wanted you. You were only a job. And now my career is over, so take your trash back to the streets. Back where you belong. Find some other poor guy to use in one of your sick little cons.'

On some stupid impulse, maybe sparked by his harsh rejection, or maybe brought on from her lack of sleep or the long drive, or maybe from sexual disappointment and frustration, Martha started crying. She couldn't stop herself. Dumb. She hadn't cried in a long time. Now they flowed uncontrollably. Damn it. Crying made her pretty face puffy. A Princess needed to be beautiful in order to win a Warrior. Tame a beast. Ugly tears weren't a part of her carefully plotted plan.

Stupid tears.

'I understand, Joaquin.' Trembling both from disgust with her own tears and his stubborn bullying posturing, she now, in true Princess style, rose from the floor, flipped her lovely curls away from her pretty face then wiped her nose with the back of her delicate manicured hand. Lifting her chin in proud defiance, she slowly strolled towards him. 'Treat me mean. Go ahead. Torment me. Whip me. Beat me. If that's what turns you on and makes you happy, do it. Enjoy. But, baby, this bitch isn't going anywhere. So adjust.'

From his slouching position in the chair, Joaquin suddenly appeared dazed and confused. 'Adjust?'

She hurt for him. Her body ached for him. Her tears weren't the only wet happening. Ignoring her sobbing she told him the truth. 'You're my partner, Joaquin. Partners rescue one another. They do. It's part of the partner code. A year ago, you rescued me. And now it's my turn.'

'You're here to rescue me?' His voice went flat as he folded his shaking hands and studied her with those hard little green eyes. 'From what?' Woo, nasty. He didn't wait for her to answer. 'Princess, you're crazy.'

'Crazy? You have no concept.' She nodded in agreement, which only appeared to fluster him more. 'Not exactly a hot newsflash. You've always known that I was crazy. But not dumb. Not stupid. It's amazing how all those little mysteries of life become clear when a Princess gets clean and sober. It took time, but even *this* Princess figured it out. All of it.'

Joaquin puffed up like a rooster. Or more like a pit bull.

It didn't matter. She wanted the cock. She'd take it dirty-dog style. And what's more, she knew he could smell desire on her. But playing the tough Warrior, he pretended he didn't want her. 'What do you think you know, Princess?'

'Why you're always in mercenary mode.'

He clearly didn't believe her.

Oh no? Crazy, but not dumb.

Ignoring her carefully conceived plan, she laid out a few truths between them. 'You? Always a vicious dog protecting me. The Princess bitch. And the whole mercenary mode is for Emily's benefit. Not yours. Not mine. Not even for business. Too little. Too late.' Suddenly picturing Emily's fate, she found herself trembling and, not wanting to reveal the secret, she paused to lick her lips. It took her a minute to compose herself. Ugly stupid tears. The plan required the Princess to be beautiful.

When she spoke again, her voice echoed with true Ice Princess status. 'Hell, you probably don't even like it rough. That's OK. Faking is legal in a dogfight. Emily took you down in Vegas. Down hard. Down for the count. And then went after me. So then my down and dirty dog with the dick worked terms of surrender. Princess? Left with the Faithful. Witchy bitch? Takes home the prize mutt from the pound. A fairy tale?'

Now he laughed. 'You don't understand.'

'I understand Emily can't hurt you if she's dead.' The Princess sighed deeply and shared another truth. 'And you can trust me. We're partners.'

15 Just Call Me Angel of the Morning

Her first awareness was of his fingertips removing strands of hair from across her face. Wonderful. Already sated and exhausted, she almost slipped back into comfortable REM mode. The sex-soaked damp sheets reeked.

She felt his warm breath first on her neck, then on her cheek, then in her hair. The warmth and the delicious aroma stirred her sexual juices. With her inner moistness awakening she began to stir, but sleep still held her. She floated on the edge of REM.

Heat flowing from his very aura ignited a deep hunger she'd never known before. Primeval heat. Animal. The Princess tried to ignore it.

'My precious Princess.' Affectionate mumblings. Terms of endearment. Sexy. Loving.

Tingling.

'Never more beautiful than when plotting a murder.'
Huh?

He was thinking aloud. Only thoughts. Thoughts barely whispered. Not for her. He thought her in a deep sleep.

She was.

Sleeping. Yes. Almost.

But her primal instincts couldn't ignore the tenor. His deep voice commanded, and some animal mating urge awoke within her. His breath in her ear made her sexual heat glow like embers, or quivers in teeny internal sparks. Warmth. Expanding warmth.

Feather strokes along her skin. Snug. Sated. Princess going down into comfortable REM. But there was no going back. She felt his heat in her hair. His rich whisper smelled of shared fiery passions. An intoxicating urge ignited primal passions within her. The intimacy of his aura demanded her sexual attention and obedience, in an animal way she'd never felt before.

Macho. Yum. Hunger.

Her mate brushed her forehead with his lips, and her entire body whimpered with pleasure. Was he touching her now? His heat was teasing her. Desire roused her from sleepiness. Her hunger swelled. The nagging, anguished hankering for him flared. With a tiny baby sigh, she instinctively lifted her lips.

He kissed her. A tiny fairy kiss, so as not to awaken a sleeping Princess, only to satisfy the Warrior.

Too late. Kissing enthusiasm floating to the surface.

Sleeping Princess rising to kiss. But there was no kiss.

His affectionate tenor whispered something instead, but she didn't hear it.

The stirring Princess breathed deeper, inhaling the hot perfume of an aroused Warrior prince. Oh yeah. Appetite. She licked her lips. Moisture happening. Hungry.

With a mere whisper of a caress, his warm breath floated along her belly and down her thighs, teasing her. Dreamily aroused by the new tingling sensation, she purred. Pulse flittering. Rising. Hot breathe on her nipples. Along her belly. Between her legs.

'Aah.' The purr of pleasure escaped her lips.

So light was his caress, and so intense his heat, that

her naked flesh responded in tingling, prickly pin-points. She shuddered with excitement, her hips rolling.

He stopped, and whispered in a warm reverberant tone, 'Shhh, sleep, Princess. Sleep.'

As much as she wanted to fall back into slumber, anticipation loomed. With her body shuddering and tingling and awake beneath his touch, she moaned faintly, expressing need.

His tongue tasted her feverish lips. Sleep evaporated. Heatwave. Blistering. Sweltering.

Sighing, swimming with excitement, and drowning in her own senses, she opened her eyes to discover Joaquin gazing down at her, devouring her with his hungry green eyes.

'Don't look at me. Close your eyes, Princess.'

She did.

'Don't move.'

Feathery sensations along her breast. Unable to stop herself, she reached for his thick erection.

He hissed softly. 'No. No. Sleep. Relax. Don't move. Sleep, my Princess, sleep, my beauty.'

Some delicate and feminine muscles tugged inside her.

Heat fanned up from her pussy, warming her entire body. Every stroke of his fingers violated her slumber. As always, Joaquin, attuned to her body, manipulated every minute quake and quiver. He eased between her legs and lifted her pussy to his mouth. She flinched slightly as a sudden stab of pleasure almost lifted her off the bed.

Oh yes. Now, this was the royal treatment.

His tongue caressed her clit. Sweet suction. His wild tongue delved into her pussy. Sucking. Licking. Thrusting. Sharp nibbles. Starry pinpricks of light beneath her eyelids.

Oh, baby. Oh, baby.

'Please, Joaquin. Please.'

His body arched over her. Bracing himself with his hands, his mouth feathered hers with a kiss. Then with one great stab he was in her.

She gasped in both surprise and pleasure. 'Oh, baby, yes.'

He froze. 'Shhh, don't move, Princess. God. Don't move.'

Pressure. Intensifying. Her inner muscles tightened against his hard cock. Bliss. She wanted to move, but didn't.

He hurt. He hurt good. Patience. Patience was a virtue.

Eyes now closed in utter frustration, she licked her lips and gasped slightly for air. He was playing dirty. Nasty. Don't move. Right.

He lifted himself and moved slightly, locking himself into the position he desired before slowly applying pressure to her throbbing clit and centre. His lips barely touched hers.

Then he rammed his big thick dick hard, deep inside her.

A cry of surrender escaped her lips.

'Princess.' His voice was low and gruff. 'My Princess.' He plunged again. Her hips shoved back, slamming his hard cock against her G-spot. A wedge of heat. Solid muscle pulsing and thrusting deeper, harder. Oh, yeah.

Her thighs hugged his hips. Her hands flung around his shoulders, clutching his weight down, solid against her.

'Oh wait. Stop,' he panted. He froze again, catching

hold of her wrists. 'Don't move. Please. Wait.' He was in pain.

But she was wild for release, and her hips rose and fell in violent shuddering strokes. He felt thick, massive. Full of him, she trembled with life, gloriously hot. Her inner muscles gripped him with tiny intimate tugs and hugs.

'Princess, don't move!' It was more of a bellowing plea for mercy this time than a command, and Martha ceased to move. Mercy granted. She wanted to move, but didn't. She just panted.

Without warning he rolled their bodies over. Now with him flat on his back, she sat upright, straddling him. His rigid cock smashed solid against her G-spot. Oh this was good. Very.

Catching her beneath her arms, he lifted her entire body up, and paused before slamming her down again with great force, impaling her onto him. Again and again. Harder and harder. Demanding and more demanding. Grunting. Growling. Snarling. Almost there.

Frenzy.

Lost in powerful sensations, the Princess rode her mighty Warrior hard, shuddering with orgasm after orgasm until she finally felt his body buck, convulse, and jack-knife into hers.

The echoing screams of his climax smothered hers.

Magnificent. It was wonderful. She almost fainted, it was so damn glorious. It was so primo. So Joaquin.

Withdrawing from her, he lifted her face to his and kissed her, a fiery, intense kiss. 'We've got to get up, and out of here. You don't know Emily. We must go. Now.'

Oh no, not Emily again. This was not fun. But this time he'd said *we* must go? No more *she* had to get out? No. Good. It was incomprehensible at first, but the Princess finally realized he'd surrendered. Joaquin was hers. He wasn't throwing her out, or divorcing her, or abandoning her to cruel fortune's fate.

The intense, raw, untamed passion they felt for one another lashed them together in some kind of desperate way. Made them good for one another. Made them perfect partners.

'Emily again?' Sighing, the Princess yawned. 'I told you before, Emily can't hurt anyone if she's dead.'

'Princess, I'm no killer.' Shaking his head, he used that kind, gentle, explaining-it-to-a-child voice. 'And bad girl that you think you are, neither are you.'

Oh yeah? The poor innocent had no idea. He'd surrendered now, and so she considered confessing more of the ugly truth. But how? Instead, the smiling Princess teased him. 'And Emily is the killing kind?'

'You've no concept.' He was firm in his warning.

'Oh, I think I do.'

He dismissed her like she was clueless, and she slipped into laughter. She couldn't help it.

Encircling him in her arms, Martha took pity on him and finally hinted at the happy ending. 'Let me tell you a story.'

Joaquin frowned and tensed. 'What kind of story?'

Oh, he really did think she was stupid. Breaking it gently to him, she kissed his forehead as if he were a child. 'Let Mama tell her baby boy a little Princess bedtime story. Once upon a time there was a handsome Warrior named Joaquin Xavier Lee, who made quite a respected reputation for himself as a super private dick. Oh yes, a true hero who played by all the rules, including contacting the local law when in town jousting with the villains. Now our hero's major task was protecting a wayward Princess for her rich Daddy. Unfortunately the naughty Princess ran with some pretty shady characters, not the sort her Daddy wanted left running free when she skipped town. Therefore, before returning Daddy's wayward treasure, the Warrior never failed to give the law all the dirt gathered on the Princess's associates. Our hero collected rewards from both private and public sources whenever possible.'

'So I got paid for working. This has nothing to do with us now.' He remained in her arms but dismissed her. He was thinking about something else. Someone else. Emily. Not good.

Using her best bedtime story voice, Martha continued. 'The hero enjoyed busting the vile associates of the Princess for two reasons. One, to make friends and influence people. And two, to protect his meal ticket, the wayward Princess, from violent or unpleasant retaliation.'

He grunted and faked a chuckle. 'Your Daddy never believed in taking prisoners. He removed obstacles.' Poor baby had broken into a sweaty chill. She hugged him closer, tenderly kissing his hair, then his forehead. He pulled back. His upper lip curled into a sneer. He hurt. She understood.

'Can't fault Daddy. Retaliation. Revenge. Blackmail. Daddy's big corporate private security bucks kept the entire agency alive for decades. Protecting his Princess might have been a very small part of the big-buck picture, but nevertheless a crucial part, a treasure of sorts. After all, if the agency couldn't protect Daddy's wayward Princess, then how could they protect his more important business interests? Hence, the standing order was to bust my associates as soon as I pawned the family jewels. It was all so very routine. Big Gus would take me down the back stairs and you'd bring the law up the front. Except for that last time in Miami.'

Slightly more agitated now, he casually removed her arms from around him. A nasty dark gleam appeared in his green eyes.

'I don't want to talk about Miami,' he growled.

Yawning and stretching, she purred as only a good little sex kitten knows how. To hold his attention, the Princess tormented him a little by dragging out the Gothic details. 'It was a mistake leaving the Cuban free in Miami after you'd documented the dirt. This time in Miami the only evidence that'd win a conviction would also unfortunately place the Princess in the cellblock. The wicked witch Emily wanted the Princess removed to jail. She wanted to marry the handsome Warrior and live the fairy-tale ending. It was the perfect time for a new beginning, for everyone. Daddy had died. After a quarrel with Emily, good sister Margaret cancelled all the agency's services, including her wayward little sister's watchdog. No more big money. No wonder Big Gus had a heart attack. That summer was hell. For everyone. But Emily figured she was at least suffering in hell with a loyal, loving and trusted partner, Joaquin Xavier Lee.'

Oh yes. It'd been that Dante *Inferno* thing happening; she remembered it all so well. She'd been broke, sick, and alone. Feeling the heat. Feeling the panic and fear. But ever the protector, the handsome Joaquin set the Miami villain free. Unbeknown to Emily, he then used the last of the agency's big cash to rescue the family jewels and then go back to North Hollywood, hiding but not destroying the evidence. Hiding it in an old piano stored in the back of the antique Ford, perhaps thinking he might use it one rainy day. However Joaquin proved himself a true hero, no blackmailer. No villain. Protecting the wayward Princess was his only bad habit. Only grave sin.

'I never touched Emily. I never loved her. I never lied to her about that. I'll never marry her. I've told her so. Besides, this is all ancient history.' Clearly he didn't like her bedtime story.

'A year ago? Ancient history?'

Well, maybe, but it was their history. And history was recently her favourite study. Martha stretched her gorgeous naked body in the gathering shadows. The sun would be setting soon. They'd been in bed since way before noon. Soon the Valley heat would dissipate, leaving an entire night for them to enjoy the pleasures of the garden. The whirling waves of the redwood tube would be heaven beneath the stars. She'd phone and have food delivered. And cold beer. Maybe some wine too. They'd eat in the garden.

New thought. Maybe she'd plant some heathen devil weed.

Almost lost in the fantasy, she sighed again and whispered to the night ahead, 'Why did he rescue me that morning?' She imagined it was because he hadn't been able to watch her walk away forever. Because he loved her? Because she was a nasty habit? An obsession? It didn't matter. Not any more.

The only important part was, he hadn't abandoned her.

The rest was history. 'Emily loved you. She trusted you. And you used her. Betrayed her trust. And when she discovered the truth, that you'd eloped with a Princess in Vegas for the big bucks, she attacked. And then it was all over for the hero but the crying.'

Looking like a puppy with a puddle on a clean floor, Joaquin hung his head and remained respectfully silent. Glowing with victorious contentment, she explained it gently to the little bad boy. 'Hell hath no fury like a woman –'

'She never loved me. She doesn't understand love.'

Whoa. Defensive.

'What's to understand? The heart wants what the heart wants. And a broken heart, plus betrayed trust, plus jealousy fuelled with suffering and stirred by revenge, could turn even a true Princess Perfect into a real rabid bitch.' Using her most comforting voice, she continued. 'Maybe you did something to deserve what she did to you. Maybe. Having only recently discovered my green-eyed monster, I won't ever judge Emily.'

That pissed him off. Suggesting he might have been in any way responsible for his own current suffering didn't please him. Not one bit. Ouch. He puffed up and curled his lip. His narrow green eyes grew cold. Oh, he was one unhappy monster.

Too bad. The Princess wanted him to think about the truth. All women were crazy when it came to matters of the heart. Perhaps he should consider the consequences of this truth. Maybe Martha was another Emily waiting to snap. Another Carrie. *Misery*. Only worse than Bates. *Play Misty For Me*. Yeah. She could see herself cutting off his dick in the sexually charged fury of passionate revenge. Only if ever she were angry enough to take him down, they'd never find the pieces. Wheat! *Texas Chain Saw Massacre* time.

'Emily will do worse than kill us both when she finds you here,' he warned her, looking for his pants. 'We'll take Gus's Caddy for luck.' He was seriously frightened. Running scared. Panicked. And in pain. Poor baby was having difficulty moving with precision. Nerve damage and physical fatigue from all the sex weakened his balance. The Princess had planned to tell him this much and no more. The plan was for the two of them to run away together, escape to someplace isolated and romantic where she could hold him a helpless captive.

The plan required him to believe they were protecting each other from Emily. Rescuing each other. Escaping. Suddenly she didn't want to bother. He'd already surrendered, and in truth she wasn't much interested in jetting off anywhere other than the back garden. He was in pain; he needed to rest and heal, to recover. So she shared another truth.

'Her biggest obstacle at first was that she didn't actually have the evidence. She thought Margaret did. She didn't. But sometime around Easter she bluffed and managed to blackmail you into surrender, threatening to give the evidence to the District Attorney's office if you didn't divorce me. Threatening to murder Margaret if you touched my money. Demanding what she always demanded. The fairy-tale ending. By then, I was physically vulnerable, alone in the desert with only Sharon to serve as witness to my murder. You had no one to turn to for help. Frank dead. Big Gus dead. Harvey butchered in your failed attempt to rescue me.'

'Who told you all this?' He was surprised. Why?

'Emily wasn't very bright.' The Princess smiled in sweet victory. 'Big surprise, by the way – the law wasn't particularly interested in putting the star witness needed to confirm all the evidence gathered from the All-Seeing transmissions into a cell. Imagine Emily's rage when the law actually suggested that the Princess and the Warrior had been a successful working undercover team long before as well as during Miami.'

Fear and horror darkened his face. Dropping his clothes he collapsed on the bed, staring up at the ceiling. 'Emily gave the evidence to the law?'

'Oh yes.' She didn't tell him she'd snatched it back.

Serious pain.

'Trust me?' Running her fingers through her long dark locks, the Princess smiled at Joaquin reassuringly. 'I trusted you. Emily wanted you, hurt you, and trapped you. But you're mine. And nobody ever takes anything from me that I don't choose to give. So I made a phone call.'

Certainly Martha wasn't the first Princess to arrange a murder to protect what was hers. Joaquin belonged to her. And he was the only monster with a garden worth keeping.

'She's dead?' He didn't believe her.

It didn't matter. It was true. Kneeling on the bed next to her sexy monster, Martha stroked his knees, thighs, and soft cock. 'And the evidence inexplicably lost.' Actually, she'd destroyed it herself.

Something in his eyes told her he wanted to believe her, but couldn't quite do it. It didn't matter. Not one bit. Because it was true.

Turns out that some truths are reality after all.

In order to protect himself, the Cuban had taken Emily. No doubt someone someday might discover and identify her body parts floating in the Great Salt Lake. Until then, the Princess didn't want to think about it.

Instead she took his trembling hand in both of hers, using his fingertips to tickle her own cheek lightly. Emily wasn't going to hurt her baby Joaquin ever again. Never again.

The Princess had rescued him.

'Joaquin, you married me for the money. It's yours. More than you could ever spend. Amuse yourself. Once you told me you could really do something with that kind of cash. Blaze of glory and all that crap. Do it. Do something good. This time you've won the treasure and the Princess and the happily-ever-after thing.'

But they both knew theirs wasn't a fairy tale.

It didn't matter. Because it was as close as it got for people like them.

The sound floated in through the open French doors on the eastern wind. Church bells ringing clear and sharp, filling the early evening sky. Hot damn. Bells.

'You hear that, Joaquin?'

'What?'

Rushing naked through the doors, Martha stepped into the cool air of the garden. 'Can you hear the bells?'

Lingering behind her, gripping the wall to help keep his balance, Joaquin listened. 'Oh yeah. Burbank has a church on every other corner. You can hear lots of them in the garden.'

It was a sign. Good luck. Damn good luck.

Gallantly pulling himself up proud and stepping forwards, he wrapped his arms possessively around her. As if he could protect her from danger. Hell, he couldn't even stand alone yet. But it didn't matter. Not one bit. Not when his deep rich voice massaged her flesh. With his mind still adjusting to the truth about happy endings, he was weak. Poor baby. He was plagued with doubting, and still in massive pain.

But that was ending. For both of them. Oh, this Princess liked it a little rough, particularly first thing in the morning. But the intense misery and pain of her royal life was over. Only pleasure lay ahead.

The bells grew silent, lingering and resonating simply in Martha's mind. Filled with inspiration, she made one final confession. 'Turns out I *am* my Daddy's little Princess. A daughter tutored in the wisdom of removing all dangerous obstacles.'

Enough truths spoken aloud. Ah, truth. Reality.

Strange concepts to grasp, sometimes. To her amazement Joaquin appeared to be stifling tears. Appeared to be realizing what had actally happened.

Yup. The All-Seeing recorded the storm that dropped the house on the wicked witch. She'd negotiate with the law from a power position if it came to that. In Utah the condemned may chose between the firing squad and hanging. But they had nothing to fear from the Cuban. No need for anxiety. Or fear. Or pain.

The enduring echo of bells hung in the Valley as the sun was setting.

In the last of the day's heat, shaking with truth and emotion, he tenderly kissed her.

And that was the moment. The kiss.

The happily-ever-after, once-upon-a-time thing.

All right. The Princess had found paradise.

Behind a white picket fence in the freakin' Valley.

Go figure.

LOOK OUT FOR THE ALL-NEW BLACK LACE BOOKS – AVAILABLE NOW!

All books priced £6.99 in the UK. Please note publication dates apply to the UK only. For other territories, please contact your retailer.

COUNTRY PLEASURES
Primula Bond
ISBN O 352 33810 5

Janie and Sally escape to the countryside hoping to get some sun and relaxation. When the weather turns nasty, the two women find themselves confined to their remote cottage with little to do except eat, drink and talk about men. They soon become the focus of attention for the lusty farmers in the area who are well built, down-to-earth and very different from the boys they have been dating in town. **Lust-filled pursuits in the English countryside.**

ARIA APPASSIONATA
Juliet Hastings
ISBN O 352 33056 2

Tess Challoner has made it. She is going to play Carmen in a new production of the opera that promises to be as raunchy and explicit as it is intelligent. But Tess needs to learn a lot about passion and desire before the opening night. Tony Varguez, the handsome but jealous Spanish tenor, takes on the task of her education. When Tess finds herself drawn to a desirable new member of the cast, she knows she's playing with fire. **Life imitating art – with dramatically sexual consequences.**

Coming in August

WILD IN THE COUNTRY
Monica Belle
ISBN O 352 33824 5

When Juliet Eden is sacked for having sex with a sous-chef, she leaves the prestigious London kitchen where she's been working and heads for the country. Alone in her inherited cottage, boredom soon sets in – until she discovers the rural delights of poaching, and of the muscular young gamekeeper who works the estate. When the local landowner falls for her, things are looking better still, but threaten to turn sour when her ex-boss, Gabriel, makes an unexpected appearance. **City vs country in Monica Belle's latest story of rustic retreats and sumptuous feasts!**

THE TUTOR
Portia Da Costa
ISBN O 352 32946 7

When Rosalind Howard becomes Julian Hadey's private librarian, she soon finds herself attracted by his persuasive charms and distinguished appearance. He is an unashamed sensualist who, together with his wife, Celeste, has hatched an intriguing challenge for their new employee. As well as cataloguing their collection of erotica, Rosie is expected to educate Celeste's young and beautiful cousin David in the arts of erotic love. **A long-overdue reprint of this arousing tale of erotic initiation written by a pioneer of women's sex fiction.**

Coming in September

SEXUAL STRATEGY
Felice de Vere
ISBN O 352 33843 1

Heleyna is incredibly successful. She has everything a girl could possibly want – a career, independence, and a very sexy partner who keeps her well and truly occupied. Accepting an invitation from her very naughty ex-boss to a frustratingly secretive club, she begins a journey of discovery that both teases and taunts her. Before too long she realises she is not the only person in the world feigning a respectable existence. **Sexual experimentation at its naughtiest!**

ARTISTIC LICENCE
Vivienne La Fay
ISBN O 352 33210 7

In Renaissance Italy, Carla is determined to find a new life for herself where she can put her artistic talents to good use. Dressed as boy – albeit a very pretty one – she travels to Florence and finds work as an apprentice to a master craftsman. All goes well until she is expected to perform licentious favours for her employer. In an atmosphere of repressed passion, it is only a matter of time before her secret is revealed. **Historical, gender-bending fun in this delightful romp.**

Black Lace Booklist

Information is correct at time of printing. To avoid disappointment check availability before ordering. Go to www.blacklace-books.co.uk. All books are priced £6.99 unless another price is given.

BLACK LACE BOOKS WITH A CONTEMPORARY SETTING

To find out the latest information about Black Lace titles, check out the website: www.blacklace-books.co.uk or send for a booklist with complete synopses by writing to:

Black Lace Booklist, Virgin Books Ltd
Thames Wharf Studios
Rainville Road
London W6 9HA

Please include an SAE of decent size. Please note only British stamps are valid.

Our privacy policy
We will not disclose information you supply us to any other parties. We will not disclose any information which identifies you personally to any person without your express consent.

From time to time we may send out information about Black Lace books and special offers. Please tick here if you do not wish to receive Black Lace information.   ❏

Please send me the books I have ticked above.

Name ....

Address ....

....

....

....

Post Code ....

Send to: Cash Sales, Black Lace Books, Thames Wharf Studios, Rainville Road, London W6 9HA.

US customers: for prices and details of how to order books for delivery by mail, call 1-800-343-4499.

Please enclose a cheque or postal order, made payable to Virgin Books Ltd, to the value of the books you have ordered plus postage and packing costs as follows:

UK and BFPO – £1.00 for the first book, 50p for each subsequent book.

Overseas (including Republic of Ireland) – £2.00 for the first book, £1.00 for each subsequent book.

If you would prefer to pay by VISA, ACCESS/MASTERCARD, DINERS CLUB, AMEX or SWITCH, please write your card number and expiry date here:

....

Signature ....

Please allow up to 28 days for delivery.